D1706797

Murder By Natural Causes

A Novel by Craig Changfoot

Printed in USA & Canada
First Printing, 2021
Craig Changfoot
craigchangfootwrites@gmail.com

Disclaimer

**All Characters appearing in this work are fictitious. Any resemblance
to real persons, living or dead, is purely coincidental.**

Cover created by: iqra_ansari98 at fiverr

Contents

Chapter 1

The old man grabbed the wall with one hand – his other hand grabbed his chest. He staggered into the kitchen; bumped into the hutch and knocked idyllically displayed tchotchkes loose; commemorative plates crashed and became uncommemorative; and he shifted the heavy dining table to the side – chairs went askew. The pain in his chest was excruciating. His head spun and he sweated profusely as his hand wished it could stop the agony – to no avail. He groaned and yelled for crying out loud, "No! Not-this." No one heard or no one cared.

He worked hard to provide for his family, and his children raised their own families – it was the circle of life, now at an end. This was not the way it was supposed to be after retirement – not this soon anyway.

He lost his balance and crashed with a thud onto the floor in a heap, and the images that he could make out were haloed and bright. He managed to muster what little strength he had left and turned on his back and watched the ceiling fan spin in a dizzying spiral.

He then saw the ominous cloaked hood of the figure as it waited for him to pass on. He breathed heavy and tears dribbled from the corners of his eyes – it was here for him.

His head turned to the side and he saw his wife of fifty years lying on the floor across from him. Her dead eyes stared at nothing. He felt the breath leave his body for the last time in a moan of grief for the very last time. "Ugh..."

The hooded figure stood up and surveyed the kitchen. He adjusted his facemask and gloves and went to work rearranging the bodies and furniture just so. It had to be that way and no other way. This was not his first kill, and it would not be his last. It paid too well, and he got a kick out of it because he was just that type of guy.

He stood back and surveyed the position of everything, so it looked just right and did not look like a crime had happened, but an accident – a terrible and unfortunate accident. He then went over to the range and worked the propane line until there was a small enough tear that he could now hear gas seep into the open kitchen. It had to look like wear, and not a tear.

He stepped back and looked at the two bodies and nodded that he was satisfied. It would all play out just as he had envisioned in his head – his assignment completed. His eyes went to the pack of cough drops on the counter. He hemmed-and-hawed and thought, 'They won't need them anymore.' He sneered deliciously at his callous handiwork.

He picked it up and marvelled at the full pack of Halls cough drops – bonus. He growled with delight, "Cherry. I like cherry."

He pulled one out of the pack and put the wrapper in his pocket and his ordered mind thought, 'Can't leave a wrapper in here with no package of cough drops around.' It was all in the details.

He pulled down his balaclava and popped the drop in his pie-hole and played with it in his mouth. It was sickly sweet and delicious. Just what he needed to wet his whistle.

He also thanked his good fortune to have a couple that lived in butt-fuck nowhere. Neighbours were scarce so no one would check on them for days or longer. All that was left was for him to make an undetected exit and disappear – until the next unfortunate accident.

Scotland Yarde was happy, but by no means go-lucky. She cued up her favorite song when she was driving top-down on the highway – Peter Hernandez's Born to Be Alive started with the synthesizer beat and drums, then the cymbal rhythm. She smiled as her Bentley Continental GT Convertible – the one with the W12 engine, of course – effortlessly propelled itself down Highway 10 towards downtown Los Angeles. It was a gorgeous early evening for the top-down experience, and she wanted to get there with plenty of time. Traffic heading this way was light as opposed to the opposite side which was bumper-to-bumper. It was this stress-free way she did things that kept her mind orderly. Her mind wandered at the evening's events yet to come. 'Have to grab a coffee and some cake.'

Everything she did involved planning and careful thinking. Her penchant was to ensure her own financial well-being and independence and to make her parents proud – both of which she achieved at the ripe old age of twenty-eight – which would be in one week. Never mind the private schooling, her parents' love and doting, the Ivy-league colleges – yes both – that prepared to propel her for greatness. Her parents never let her get too big for her britches and she was appreciative of the leg up in life that many would kill-for given the opportunity.

After her forays at the colleges – was that mentioned? – her graduate degree, her Masters degree and her PhD plus a co-op stint with her daddy's Manhattan law firm, she decided to move from the Empire State to the Golden State with her meagre designer belongings and her dynastic eight-figure trust fund. She decided on Los Angeles to develop roots and in two short years she parlayed her knowledge, experience, and tenacity – to not accept no for an answer – to within a hair's width of a tenured position at UCLA, a lucrative portfolio of erotic romance e-books, a weekly podcast called 'Writely So' and to teach evening writing classes at a local community college once a week.

Scotland Yarde was lovely for heaven's sake and had a body and a smile that would melt hearts, make women wet, and erect male members. She strongly felt that strangers were just friends she had not met yet. Her look reminded people and anyone who happened to meet her of Kristen Stewart – but more approachable and more smiley. She dressed well, kept herself in excellent physical condition, and lived rent-free with her doting aunt and uncle in a custom-built pool house on their sprawling property in Beverly Hills. She did not have to dip into her trust fund for any of this because her mommy, daddy, aunt, and uncle ensured that if she was going to set herself up in Los Angeles, she needed to do it right – and right they did.

The road hummed in tune with her Bentley Convertible, and the GPS bleeped the directions in the pre-set British accent, "In five hundred meters, take the exit to one-ten south." Scotland always used metric because why not? She flicked her turn signal – checked her mirrors and blindspot monitor as she piloted the car towards her destination.

She went over her course material in her head once more and breathed a sigh of relief that she was prepared as always and let her mind wander for just a bit more. 'Fortune favors the bold...and the prepared.'

It did not take long for her to arrive at Aspen Hall Community College and she easily found an available parking spot because it was, after all, a night course. She felt safe because there was always a guard patrolling the parking areas and if she had to use her wits and physicality, the boxing classes, her third-degree black belt in Brazilian Jujitsu, and her Krav Maga lessons came in handy. 'Bring it, fuckers.'

The walk to the commons was quick and she still had ample time to grab a snack and perhaps add some flourishing touches to her most recent erotic romance novel, 'Strangers in Heat.' A wry smile curled over her kissable lips as she let her sultry senses get away from herself for her latest novel. She would get wet writing some of the love scenes which went from PG-13 straight to triple-X without warning. It was sure to be another hit for her. 'Fuck, I'm good.'

The janitor stopped and smiled brilliantly at her. "Scotland..." He leaned in for a fist-bump and felt the reciprocated return. "How are you this evening?"

Scotland flashed her perfect porcelain veneers and her indulgent, slight overbite. "Joe." She let out a customary giggle to lighten the mood. "So nice to see you this evening. How're the family?"

Joe perked up. He always loved the small talk with the generous and gorgeous woman. "They're both doing really well, thanks, Scotland..." He beamed with pride. "Thank you for asking."

Scotland continued to smile and headtossed at him. "You take care, Joe."

"Thanks, Scotland." He waved a reassured hand of confidence at her. "You have an excellent class tonight."

"Will do, Joe." She could smell the delicious aroma of coffee and light snacks calling to her from the cafeteria. "I'm just going to fuel up on some coffee and some of Ida's coffee cake."

Joe smacked his lips. One of the joys of working here at Aspen, besides the generous staff and students, was Ida's coffee cake. "Enjoy it..." He licked his lips and wondered if he should attempt another slice. "Ida just made a batch for the night classes."

Scotland felt her mouth drool at the edges at the thought of a slice or two of Ida's cinnamon coffee cake with that delicious pecan crumble on top – warm out of the oven. She smacked her lips with purpose. With a supplementary cup of coffee, it was a worthy reward to an excellent and productive week. "Mmm, Joe. I can hardly wait."

Joe simply giggled and watched the classy lady dreamily saunter away. 'Such a nice young lady.' He returned to his duties and could not wait to get home.

Scotland multi-tasked as she walked into her classroom with her hands full and her mouth clutching the bag with her cinnamon cake tucked inside. She placed her charcoal Smythson of Bond Street monogrammed satchel on the desk, and her large Americano just so it was out of the way of anything to accidentally topple it over. She looked around at the cleanliness. Joe had prepped the room for her and arranged the chairs just how she liked – in a comfort circle so everyone could participate and be seen. She murmured in approval, "What a great guy."

She deliciously opened the bag and took a heady whiff of the aroma that wafted up and stoked her senses. She inched it up carefully, so no crumble escaped the opening, and she took a mouthy bite. "Mmm..." She let her other senses doing the talking as she filled her mouth with the delicious cakey and nutty goodness – allowing it to soften and melt with the addition of some coffee goodness. She groaned with satisfaction, "Fffuughk...that's delicious..." Chew after chew led her to Nirvana. "Mmm."

It took very little effort and time for her to devour the entire piece Ida specially cut for her – the center of course and a little larger than the typical slices. Scotland ensured that every crumb made it into her mouth. She tilted her head back like a Pez dispenser and tapped the bag to coax the remnants out. She licked her lips for good measure and took a sip of coffee to wet her whistle.

She placed her handouts evenly on the desk and waited until class started which was a mere forty-five minutes away. Scotland shrugged her shoulders and pulled out her computer and thought that she would at least get a few pages in on her novel. 'Idle hands...'

She lost herself in her typing when the first student arrived followed by a few more until the class was full.

Scotland checked her word count and was surprised that when she was in the zone, she really went for it. She checked the clock and forty minutes had flown by and she had completed twenty pages of writing – first draft writing of course.

The class went off without a hitch and she could not help but notice Emilio Vasquez was distracted for most of the lesson – which was odd since he was the most attentive in her class. Tonight, was different and she could not figure out what was wrong. The two hours, with break, zipped by without a hitch and she did not want to miss her opportunity to talk with Emilio. One-by-one they filtered out saying their adieus until the next class.

Scotland moved quick and stopped him in his tracks. "Hi, Emilio..." She smiled invitingly at him but saw only sadness. "Can you stay for a few minutes?"

Emilio simply nodded and grunted. He moved to the closest seat and got comfortable.

Scotland watched the last student exit and she sidled up to Emilio and took a seat. "Hey..." She peered into his eyes. "Why so sad?"

Emilio sniffed and shook his head. "It's nothing." He looked at her with his watery eyes.

She shook her head. She knew when someone was somber and said there was nothing wrong it meant that there was something wrong. "C'mon..." She cleared her throat and took a breath. "Something's bugging you. I can see it and you were distracted all class. Is there something I can help you with?"

Emilio swallowed the knot in his throat and took a breath. "It's my grandfather..." He sighed as he exhaled. "He passed away yesterday."

Scotland was shocked. She wanted to know why he was here at all. "Oh my god..." She shook her head sympathetically. "I'm so sorry, Emilio."

Emilio forced a smile. "It's okay, Scotland..." He pursed his lips. "He went peacefully if you don't count him falling out of the bed and cracking his head on the nightstand."

Scotland's shock turned to horror. 'That's not peaceful!' She was at a loss for words. "You should've stayed home."

Emilio shook his head and smiled for real this time. "This class is the highlight of my week..." He scoffed. "Are you kidding?"

Scotland laughed. "Is your grandma okay?" She knew just enough about all her students to make herself dangerous.

Emilio simply nodded and bit his bottom lip. "She's in a bit of a funk but that's understandable."

"Hmm..." Scotland nodded her head. "Well...give her my sympathies."

"Will do, Scotland..." Emilio felt a hundred times better now. "Thanks for asking and thanks for caring."

She reached over to hug him and felt him return the favor. "Hey..." She looked over at the desk. "Give me a few minutes to pack up and I'll give you a ride home."

Emilio perked up. "Are you sure it's not out of your way?"

Scotland was already up and quickly organized the remains of her handouts and assignments. "No trouble at all." She snapped her satchel closed with purpose and took a last look around. "I'm set."

The ride to Wellington Heights was uneventful and they bantered mainly about movies and television shows that they both enjoyed. Emilio was a recent high school graduate and worked full time to help the family which consisted of himself, his grandmother – and before his untimely passing – his grandfather. Scotland found out more about Emilio's small family in that fifteen-minute ride. It was both enlightening and a bonding experience for them both.

She pulled her car up to the house on North Gage Avenue and shut the Bentley down.

Emilio was amazed at the Bentley. "This car is so quiet..." He admired everything about it. "I've never been in a Bentley before."

Scotland smiled in appreciation. She had to order it and waited a good two months for it to arrive. Her reflex-silver beast was just what she wanted. Her smirk said it all. "Silent but deadly." She chuckled.

Emilio laughed at the double-entendre and picked up his backpack. He paused and looked at the Kristen Stewart lookalike only a lot more comedic and approachable. "Would you like to come in and say hi to my grandma?"

Scotland nodded and thought it was the decent and polite thing to do when someone lost a family member. "Of course..." She hesitated for effect. "If I'm not intruding."

Emilio shook his head. "Of course not. The amount of stuff I've told them about you..." He shrugged and smiled. "You're almost family."

Scotland laughed at that and the figure rushing out of Emilio's house caught her attention, but she assumed it was someone who offered their condolences. However, it piqued her interest as he or she looked like they did not want to be noticed as they exited and scurried off. She shook it off.

Emilio opened the door and held it for Scotland to enter. He bellowed out to his grandmother, "I'm home, Grandma..." He postured for Scotland to come inside. "Make yourself at home."

Scotland simply smiled appreciatively and nodded.

Emilio's grandma came around the corner and she looked agitated. She was breathing heavy like she was having an anxiety attack.

Emilio dropped his bag, and his eyes registered the kind of concern where deep in his gut he knew something was awry. "Grandma...what's wrong?"

Emilio's grandma did not even take notice of the woman that stood in her foyer. She simply blurted out, "Emilio..." She was ashen with fright. "Papa was murdered."

Chapter 2

"Grandma..." Emilio had a wide-eyed look of concern peppered on his face. "What makes you think Papa was murdered?"

Mrs. Vasquez had a wild-eyed look on her face but there was an air of awareness, too. "I know it sounds crazy..." She shook her head like she could not believe what the man told her. "But I could feel it in my bones."

Scotland studied Mrs. Vasquez intently. She used her powers of observation and her minor in psychology to see what was going on behind those eyes. There was an unmistakable belief that what she was saying was true. "Mrs. Vasquez..." She placed her hand on the old lady's. "What makes you think that Mr. Vasquez was murdered?"

The old lady snapped out of her stupor and turned her attention to the Kristen Stewart lookalike but much prettier and warmer. Her eyes narrowed, and she pulled her arm away. "Who-the-hell-are-you?"

Emilio groaned under his breath, "Fucksake..." He pursed his lips and took a breath. "Grandma..." He held up his hand and presented his friend – again. "This is Scotland...Scotland Yarde" He tilted his head toward the very attractive woman and widened his eyes to show to his grandmother that she was friendly. "The lady I was telling you about for the last few months...the English writing teacher."

Mrs. Vasquez's eyes lit up and her mouth opened like she had just been told a top-secret secret, but she paused, and she looked at Scotland, and then turned back to Emilio with a quizzical look. "No..." She shook her head quizzically. "I thought Scotland Yard are the British police."

Scotland curled her mouth up to stop herself from laughing. A smirk took its place as she looked at Emilio. He only stared back at her with an apologetic look. She pursed her lips and shook her head. "It's okay. I get it all the time."

Emilio rolled his eyes comically and grumbled under his breath, "Well..." He dropped his shoulders in defeat. "I've got to live with her." He felt a whack across his arm and yelped, "Ow." He blinked at his grandma and did not know what else to say.

"How about I give you another fresh one, Emilio Vasquez..." Mrs. Vasquez cocked her hand. "I'm old..." Her stare drilled into her grandson. "Not deaf."

"Sorry, Grandma..." He forced a smile and he blushed with embarrassment. "Her name is Scotland Yarde...with an 'e'."

Mrs. Vasquez looked at him like she was lost. "There's no 'e' in Scotland."

Emilio groaned under his breath. "I know, Grandma...the 'e' is in Yarde."

Mrs. Vasquez again looked at him like he had two-heads. "There's-no..."

Emilio cut her off. "Never-mind-Grandma..." He let out an imperceptible sigh. "She's my English writing teacher."

Scotland smiled and popped up her perfectly groomed eyebrows. "It's nice to meet you, Mrs. Vasquez." She held out her hand for a handshake and felt a soft hand lock into hers like a glove.

Mrs. Vasquez smiled and liked the young lady's warm and inviting touch. She turned to Emilio and she burbled in a hushed tone, "She doesn't sound English, Emilio." Her look turned quizzical at her grandson and wondered what he was talking about. All she saw was his head drop and his body registered a dejected state.

Emilio moaned out, "Dear-god..." He shook his head at the floor. "Kill-me-now." All he heard was Scotland giggling softly at his condition.

"More tea, dear?" Mrs. Vasquez held the pot ready to refill Scotland's cup.

"Yes please, Mrs. Vasquez." She held her dainty cup up and watched the delicious liquor spill into it. "I definitely need a refill so I can have some more delicious flan." She smacked her lips at another sweet choice to go with her second cup of tea.

Emilio rolled his eyes at Scotland. "Please..." He waved his hand over the endless sea of flans. "Feel free to take one or two of them home with you."

Mrs. Vasquez shot her grandson a perturbed glare and simply huffed as she sat back down.

Emilio randomly chose a flan pan and cut a slice for Scotland. He tilted his head and flashed a sarcastic smile. "It's like playing Mexican Roulette..." He snorted a chuckle. "Not sure if this one is savoury or sweet." He slid the plate in front of Scotland like he had been trained at Food and Hospitality School – now redundant since the coronavirus obliterated the industry.

"Thanks, Emilio." Scotland raised her fork and carved off a small chunk from the tip of the firm triangular slice and slipped it in her mouth. She chewed and let the explosion of flavors cascade over her senses. "Mmm..." She took a sip of tea. "Definitely sweet."

Emilio giggled as he sat down and gave her a thumbs-up.

Scotland turned back to Mrs. Vasquez and wanted to continue their conversation. "So..." She licked the caramelly-goodness from her lips and took a breath. "Out of nowhere this man showed up at your door and told you this story that Mr. Vasquez may've been murdered?"

Mrs. Vasquez registered a look of shock reserved only for those who believe in one path but have been forced onto a new one. "No!" She shook her head and noticed she had shocked her two guests. She toned it down just a tad but wanted to make sure they knew she was not lying. "He's positive my Juan was murdered."

Scotland looked at Emilio and only saw him purse his lips to go with the worried look on his face. She turned back to Mrs. Vasquez with a more curious tone in her voice. "Okay..." She took a sip of tea and leaned forward and politely rested her forearms on the table. "What makes him so sure Mr. Vasquez was murdered?"

Mrs. Vasquez looked at them both. "Ever since Juan retired and got sick, he'd been receiving these calls and letters from his pension..." She shook her head in dismay. "He never let me know what the calls or letters were about."

Scotland went into full curiosity-killed-the-cat mode but made sure her tone was as polite as possible. "Did Mr. Vasquez ever let you know about the calls or letters?"

Mrs. Vasquez shook her head. "He would burn the letters, but the calls would always make Juan quiet afterwards."

"Unfortunately, Mrs. Vasquez..." Scotland took a breath. "Letters and calls don't amount to murder. What makes this man seem to think it does? And come to think of it..." She had a quizzical look on her face. "Just who is he?"

"Because he said it's not the first time this has happened." Mrs. Vasquez nodded like she had just struck oil. "He said that this has happened to a number of other retired people." She reached into her apron pocket and pulled out a stickie-note. "He gave me his name and email address."

The look of surprise drained out of Scotland's face. "Uh, Mrs. Vasquez..." She blankly, blinked a couple of times. "You didn't give this guy any money..." She watched Mrs. Vasquez nervously fidget as she took the stickie-note from her. "Did you?" She cocked an eyebrow knowing full well how unscrupulous people can take advantage of grieving people in their time of need.

Emilio only groaned with contempt as he toyed with his half-eaten flan.

"He said he needed some money to get home..." Mrs. Vasquez cleared her throat. "It was only thirty dollars."

Scotland did not want to judge her. She looked at the stickie-note – 'Richard Moranis; moranis@gmail.com'. She could not believe the audacity of this guy. "Not even a phone number? Just an email address?" She pursed her lips and let her mind wander for just a bit. 'And on a stickie-note, to boot. Classy guy.'

"Do you mind if I take a picture of this? I'll email him to see what he's up to." Scotland was slowly going for her iPhone but wanted to make sure it was okay to insinuate herself in their business.

Mrs. Vasquez beamed at her savior. "Thank you, Scotland. That would be very helpful." It was as if a weight had been lifted off her shoulders. "Would you like some more tea?" She looked at the table. "Or more flan?"

Scotland held her belly. "Oh..." She smiled and shook her head. "I've had so much already, Mrs. Vasquez. Thank you, no."

Emilio piped up as he tapped his plate. "Are you sure?" He cocked a sarcastic eyebrow at her. "We've got lots." His head tilted back at the field of flan on the counter.

Mrs. Vasquez wanted to slap him again. "My grandson..." She shook her head in mock contempt for her only living member now. "So sarcastic...just like his mother."

Emilio could only smirk and acknowledged his departed mother and father.

Scotland smiled at them both and finished the last sip of her delicious tea. She licked her lips and was curious. "Mrs. Vasquez. You said Mr. Vasquez retired and then he got sick?"

She nodded her head and wondered if she should tell her about what they did. "Umm..." She took a breath and decided to take the plunge. "Juan worked for the city for forty-five years. He was an excellent worker. Never missed a day." Mrs. Vasquez teared up a little but stood strong and took a deep breath. "Six months after he retired..." She went silent for a bit and had that look old people get when their life with someone flashed before their eyes. "His diabetes got worse...much worse."

Scotland reached over and touched her hand. It was the least she could do. "Mrs. Vasquez..." She looked into her teary eyes. "If it's too difficult to tell, we can call it a night."

Mrs. Vasquez wiped her eyes. All her life she had struggled so telling a story of her life should be the least of her worries. "No..." She patted Scotland's hand. "It's okay..." She looked up at the ceiling. "Now...where was I? Oh yes. Juan's diabetes got worse, and we could not afford the insurance so..." She hesitated. "Umm...I was still working at the walk-in clinic and I had one of the doctors fill out a prescription for insulin in my name and we used my insurance to pay for it. That was eight months ago."

Emilio knew all too well that you had to do what you had to do. He looked at Scotland but did not see any judgement in her face.

14

Scotland knew how expensive medication was when someone just retired, and they got sick and had no insurance. "Umm..." Her brain churned all the information that was being dropped in the hopper. "May I ask how Mr. Vasquez died?"

Mrs. Vasquez went silent, and her hand clenched the pretty young woman's soft hand.

Emilio could see it was difficult for her to say it, so he interjected, "Papa fell last week and had to go to the hospital. He broke his leg. The doctor said that a clot from his broken leg caused a pulmonary embolism."

Scotland nodded and now had some more information. She looked at Mrs. Vasquez because she was putting the jigsaw puzzle together one piece at a time and the picture was kind of clear for an accidental death, but it was nowhere near murder. "So, this Richard Moranis told you it was murder?" She looked quizzically at Mrs. Vasquez. "And he said this has happened before? What proof did he provide?"

Mrs. Vasquez shook her head. "Something spooked him, and he said he would be in touch later this week." She pursed her lips. "He asked for the money and when I gave it to him, he thanked me and rushed out the door."

"Thank you for your hospitality, Mrs. Vasquez." Scotland leaned in and hugged her tight.

She looked at the attractive young woman and had a perplexed look on her face. "Scotland..." She pondered for a second and her thoughts stewed in her head. "Has anyone told you that you look exactly like that actress from that movie?"

Emilio could feel his face flush. "Uh...Grandma..." He cleared his throat. "I don't think that's the right thing to say..." He dropped his head and mumbled something to her, "Especially when I was the one that told you."

Scotland giggled at the two of them and decided to play along. "Which movie..." She played dumb just to see how red Emilio could get. "Twilight?"

Mrs. Vasquez paused, and then shook her head. "No..." She took a breath and looked at Emilio. "Emilio, you told me that Scotland looked like that girl from that movie..." She stroked her chin. "You know that Marvel movie."

Emilio side-eyed her. "Kristen Stewart was not in a Marvel movie, Grandma."

Mrs. Vasquez took a breath and her mouth opened like she was going to say something but paused. "Um, no..." She had a quizzical look on her face. "Is she the one with the twin sisters?"

Emilio just shook his head. "I'll show Scotland out, Grandma."

Mrs. Vasquez went back to saran-wrapping the flans and cleared the table.

Emilio walked Scotland to the front door and thumbed back at the kitchen. He shrugged half-heartedly and mumbled comedically, "Old-people-right?" He rolled his eyes and shook his head.

Scotland chortled at him. She reached into her pocket and counted out thirty dollars. She forced it into the young man's hand and leaned into him and made sure Mrs. Vasquez did not hear her. "Put this money back in your grandma's purse."

Emilio protested in a hushed tone. "This isn't your problem, Scotland."

Scotland looked into Emilio's eyes to make sure he understood her. She could physically strong arm him if it came to that. "Don't argue with me..." She balled a fist and held it in front of his face. She pursed her lips like she meant business – but in a playful way because she was not going to take no for an answer. "I'm making it my problem."

Emilio nodded and knew it was not worth arguing with her. "I'm only taking this because of all of your Twilight money." He giggled at the look on her face.

"You're very funny..." She tapped his shoulder. "You should write comedy."

Emilio pursed his lips and nodded in agreement. "I might just do that."

"Have a great evening and take care of you grandma."

Emilio nodded and watched her get into her car and drive away. He waved once more and noticed the black sedan a few houses away. Ordinarily, he would not think anything of it, but this sedan had two people inside sitting in the dark. 'That's so odd.'

He shook his head and made sure the front door and all the doors and windows were securely locked.

Emilio then went into the kitchen to help his grandma tidy up.

Chapter 3

"So…" Carter Deklava gave a sideways smile and popped up her perfectly groomed Dua Lipa eyebrows at Scotland. "What do you think of this?" She lifted the top over her perfectly toned torso and made sure it frosted itself over of the reliefs of her perfectly augmented breasts and toned abdominals. She used her other hand to smooth it down so Scotland could give her an opinion she was aching for. "Huh…don't you think it looks good on me?"

Scotland eyed her pretentious, best friend and took a sarcastic breath and her eyes yelled volumes. She knew what her vacuous friend needed to hear, and she stated it as robotically as she humanly could. "Oh-god. You-look-great-with-it-on…" She rolled her eyes. "Please-show-me-more." She felt like a Kardashian-sycophant and it made her nauseous.

Carter pulled her augmented lips to the side and cocked an unassuming eyebrow at her. "You know, Scotty…" She added the top to her burgeoning pile that the helpful and commissioned saleslady was more than happy to help her with. "Why do you come with if you're going to be snarky? Huh?" She placed her hands on her perfectly formed Peloton hips.

Scotland balled her fists and narrowed her judgemental eyes at her. "Because you forced me to use my Saturday morning to go shopping with you on Rodeo Drive…" She flicked a finger at Carter's shoulder. "That's why. All I wanted was for you to help me locate someone."

Carter playfully scoffed and flung her frosted, blond extensions back in the air. She knew she was hot, and she knew everyone knew she was hot – even if they did not know it yet. There was no denying it. On the hotness Richter scale, she was tectonic plate shifting that no seismic restraint could hold. Carter glared at her friend that she knew since she could remember, and gave her the most common retort of retorts, "Pppffht." And stuck her tongue out at her. "Well…" She smacked her lips at her. "You've got a lot of nerve since I did buy breakfast for you."

Scotland leaned into her space and came small-breasts-to-augmented-breasts with her oldest and bestest friend. Up close she reminded her of Bella Hadid – and she smelt fantastic like warm caramel or fresh cotton candy. She clenched her jaw and showed her perfect overbite. Her deep blue eyes drilled into her. "I-paid-for-breakfast."

Carter pish-poshed her friend's generosity. "You've paid…" She playfully used her hands like she was conducting an orchestra. "I've paid." She gave a playful shrug to discount their many efforts over the years. "It all evens out in the end. Tomato-potato. It's all water in the desert." She loved messing up all the similes which she knew well, but in doing so she prodded at her friend and loved the internal growl.

Scotland wondered if Carter would feel anything if she clocked her in the side of the head. She always had an affinity for her but some days she really pushed her buttons. The one thing that Carter always did well was fall ass-backwards into money. Regardless of her trust fund that eclipsed many dynastic families, she always managed to use her entrepreneurial streak to make more money for herself. This really irritated Scotland.

"How much clothes do you need?" Scotland scoffed at her. "Huh?"

Carter had a shocked look on her face like her friend just put ketchup on caviar. There was scorn in her tone. "Scotty, I'm going to make like I didn't hear that." Her look of haughty derision could have lasered her dear friend where she stood. "Anyways..." She shot a look at her friend's expression when she purposely fucked around with the English language, and she smiled inside knowing she got one on her. "What good is money if you can't spend it on nice clothes?" She again waved her hands in the air. "Case in point..." She screwed her mouth up like she got a whiff of something unsavory. "Didn't I see you in that gauche ensemble last week?" Her head bobbed up and down as she scanned her friend's bourgeois-style. "Did Neiman Marcus have a blowout sale?" She snorted a giggle, but stopped and gasped. "Oh-my-god!" Her eyes were as wide as saucers. "Are-you-poor-now?" There was a genuine look of concern on her face. "Do-you-need-money?"

Scotland narrowed her eyes at her gorgeous friend who seemed to make it a career out of pushing her buttons. "Listen-bitch..." She clenched her jaw. "Just because we're Kappas..." And, poked her in her augmented boob. "Doesn't mean I won't beat the Kappa out of you."

Carter blinked at her friend's furrowed brow. She had a glare about her that could cook an egg and she knew just when to pull back – she knew her that well. A content smirk curled over her kissable mouth. "Calm down, crazy-lady..." She tick-tocked her head from side-to-side and giggled. "Or you're going to have to Botox the fuck out of that brow-furrow you got going on there."

Scotland pursed her lips and let out an abused sigh to control her emotions. 'Breathe, Scotland...just breathe...'

Carter reached under her best friend's arm and walked with her to the cash register. "C'mon...cheer-up..." She giggled cutely. "You know I'm only fucking with you..." She chortled a laugh. "Because you love it when I fuck with you." She could hear Scotland growl under her breath but simply let her lead the way.

Heads behind displays popped up like whack-a-moles.

Carter stared them down with an impassioned contempt.

The saleslady smiled as she rang in all of Carter's purchases. Carter Deklava was her best customer, and she would surely make the employee-of-the-month once again with her commissioned sales. All she had to do was text Carter and her bevy of friends of the new arrivals and they would come a running to buy, buy, buy.

Scotland looked at the total as it started to grow exponentially. She shot a look at Carter and only saw her flash her trademark grin back – her aquamarine eyes twinkled like disco balls. Her American Express Black Card gently tap-tap-tapped on the glass like Morse code.

Carter winked and popped up her eyebrows just for effect. "Are you sure you don't want anything, Scotty?" Carter flicked her head back at the displays behind them. "I'm-a-buying." She smacked her lips.

Scotland shook her head with impertinence and a little disgusted at her friend's lack of financial sense. "I'm-good..." She snarled her lip. "Thanks."

Carter took a deep breath and gave up trying. "Suit yourself, Scotty."

Scotland pulled out her iPhone and got the information she wanted Carter to find for her. Apart from her many social websites where she was an influencer, she had contacts of a nefarious nature that could, when the need arose, hack into computers at dubious locations to extract important information – and to get out undetected. "I need you to get me some information on this guy."

Carter side-eyed the name and information and then proceeded to roll her beautiful, aquamarine eyes all the way around. "Fine...but only for my bestest friend..." She paused as she tapped on her iPhone. "Wait..." She snorted a laugh. "This guy's name is Richard Moranis?" She cocked an eyebrow at her.

Scotland narrowed her eyes to go with her blank face. She knew Carter had an infantile sense of humor and it was easier to just let her get it out of her system. "Yes, Carter..." She pursed her lips for what was about to come. "His name is Dick Moranis."

Carter could not help but let out a muffled guffaw at that because it really made her morning – well, that and bugging Scotland to no end. "Dick Moranis?" She pulled her cute mouth to the side. "What is he? A gay pornstar?" Her head tilted back like a Pez dispenser and she cackled out loud like Norma Desmond.

Scotland shook her head and looked down in defeat. "No..." She pursed her lips. "That's what I'm hoping you can find out for me."

Carter's head popped back like a startled ostrich. She screwed her beautiful face up quizzically. "If he's a gay pornstar?" She blinked at Scotland with a child-like innocence.

Scotland mumbled an expletive or something under her breath but recomposed herself. "No, what this guy does."

"Well..." Carter rolled her eyes once again as she continued to tap the iPhone. "With a name like that I'm sure he's not a rocket scientist."

She stopped mid-tap and looked into her friend's eyes. "Wait...you're not stalking this guy..." She narrowed her suspicious eyes at her. "Are you?" Carter tilted her head interrogatively. "So, you can become Mrs. Dick Moranis?"

Scotland blankly glared at her. She knew the only way to shut her up was with one of Carter Deklava's own trademark retorts. "Puhleeze..." She screwed her mouth to the side with contempt and shook her head with derision. "Do I look like I need to do the stalking?"

Carter blinked and her mouth dropped open just a bit to study her friend – then she continued. "Fair-enough."

She stopped mid-type and there was a mischievous smirk on her face as she stared at her with an arched eyebrow. "How long have we known each other, babe?"

Scotland glared at her with an impatient impertinence. She grumbled at her matter-of-factly, "Too long."

Carter casually discounted that comment but thought about it for half-a-heartbeat. "Hmm, perhaps..." She shook her head because she had a killer joke. "No. There's one thing I know you need and that's more dick and more anus." She bent over and laughed her pert ass off but stood up straight. "No wait. That's two things." She continued to chuckle.

Scotland glared at Carter as she giggled uncontrollably. "Carter, I love you and it would break my heart if I had to fucking kill you, but needs must when the Devil drives." She clenched her jaw, and her fists.

Carter poo-pooed her and finished tapping the information and sent it. "Done..." She looked at her friend longingly. "Happy now?"

Scotland relaxed and smiled from ear-to-ear. "Ecstatic..." She hugged her friend. "Thank you."

Carter returned the hug and let her best friend coil around her – and always loved the way she felt. "You're welcome, Scotty."

Scotland lost herself in the feel of her friend.

Carter shook her head with a little contempt. "That guy should've changed his name or killed himself."

Scotland's jaw dropped. "My god..." She shook her head in disbelief. "That's such a mean thing to suggest. He can't help it if his parents were oblivious to the suggestive name."

Carter pursed her lips and narrowed her eyes at her friend. "You're right. My apologies..." She handed her credit card to the sales lady. "It's a pain to change your name."

Scotland just went back to rolling her eyes at Carter.

Scotland knew the information would take some time for Carter's little spiders to garner – no questions asked, of course.

They walked out of the store with the saleslady in tow as she carried all the well-gotten gains. Outside, Carter's driver, Mason, hopped out and power-lifted the trunk of her Bentley Flying Spur to swallow all the bags in one fell swoop.

Carter headtossed and smiled at him and she popped her designer sunglasses on. Paparazzi came out of the shadows and started snapping pictures of her and her gorgeous friend. The digital cameras clicked expectedly so their treasure could be uploaded to many social sites for cash as soon as possible. Videographers joined the fray and shouted question-after-question at them both.

"Carter, what did you get?"

"Carter, who's your friend?"

"Carter, how's your new clothing line doing?"

"Carter, does your scented candle really smell like your vagina?"

"I didn't know you knew Kristen Stewart, Carter."

"Carter, who was that guy you were with at Spago's last night?"

And on-and-on it went.

She just smiled politely and answered what she wanted to answer and discounted any question she did not want to answer with a polite wave. Unlike other celebrities who discounted the paparazzi or ignored them, Carter Deklava was a consummate communicator having been press secretary for four years for a certain well-liked President who was easily on his second term – until she found a more lucrative career as a social influencer. Her connections were far-reaching in those that basked in the light and those that preferred to remain in the dark.

They decided to walk down Rodeo Drive to The Peninsula Hotel – with the adoring paparazzi in tow. Carter's driver would meet them there, but first afternoon tea was on the agenda.

Scotland filled her friend's cup again as she watched her nibble away at one of the most delicious scones fully topped with every accoutrement laid out for them. They lounged and enjoyed their early afternoon repast in the most delightful and luxurious of hotels in Beverly Hills. Of course, they always got the best seat in the house – and why would they not? Beauty such as theirs was meant to be showcased – like a valet making sure the nicest cars were out front and the pedestrian ones were tucked away out of sight.

Carter reclined back and chewed her delicious scone, complemented with a dainty sip her delicious tea. She murmured to her friend who also took a relaxed position on the sumptuous couch. "Fffuughk..." She shifted like a cat trying to find the best position. "I'm stuffed."

Scotland took a labored breath and shook her head. "Why do we do this to ourselves every time we come here?" She side-eyed her friend. She knew the answer – because they could.

Carter shrugged politely and breathed in the luxurious smells. "Because we're gluttons..." She sipped her tea and resumed her train of thought. "For punishment." A smirk curled over her mouth and saw her friend giggle.

She felt her iPhone vibrate and she drew it in one motion like a seasoned professional. Her eyes lit up and her face acknowledged the good work her many spiders had done. She looked at Scotland who was curious. "Here's your info on your next victim, Scotty."

Scotland narrowed her eyes at her. Her mouth straight-lined with contempt. "You're starting again."

Carter playfully shrugged. "You know very well that when I'm full, I'm in a playful mood." She stuck her tongue out at her. "What can I say?"

Scotland felt her iPhone vibrate and she too drew it in one motion to review the information Carter forwarded to her on one Richard Moranis. Her brow frowned at the limited information. "That's it?" She pulled her mouth to the side. "No address?" Her eyes scanned down the information. "No phone number?"

Carter shrugged. "That just makes it easier for you to make him disappear..." She snorted a giggle. "After you have your way with him, of course..." She sarcastically eyed Scotland's iPhone. "And judging by his picture, no one is going to miss that fugly..." She looked at her friend with a playful concern. "You've chosen well for your first serial kill, Scotty." There was a twinkle in her devious eyes as she took a sip.

Scotland slowly peered up at her friend with an aggressive scowl. She took another labored breath. "I'm not trying to do anything with him or to him for that matter. I'm looking into him for a friend of a friend." She pursed her lips and narrowed her eyes.

Carter played along and forced a wink. "Oh..." She bobbed her head up-and-down comically and scanned the area to ensure the coast was clear. "Sure..." She again forced a sarcastic wink at her. "Your friend Dr. Lecter. Got it." She giggled cutely.

Scotland rolled her eyes at her. "What makes you think I mean to do this guy harm? Huh?"

Carter leaned forward because she had something witty to say. "Babe..." She smacked her lips. "There're only three reasons someone looks for someone. To-fight-them, fuck-them or kill-them." She presented her iPhone up for Scotland to see the screen with Richard Moranis' picture, and used her fingers to increase the size of Exhibit A. "I've seen you fight, so that's one option gone." She took a look at the picture again and made a gag-face. "The only way someone is going to fuck this guy is if money's exchanged." She looked intently at Scotland who had a curious look plastered on her face which wanted to know what silly conclusion she would draw. "A-shit-ton-of-fucking-money."

Scotland shook her head disagreeably. "That's-so-mean-to-say."

Carter scoffed at her. "Oh really?" Her eyebrows popped-up with curiosity as she shoved her iPhone screen in Scotland's face. "Would you fuck him?"

Scotland felt the bile bubble up in her throat at the less than stellar suggestion. Her screwed up face said it all. "Hmm."

Carter smiled and sat back with a content look on her face. "Your Honor, I rest my case..." She sipped her tea and sighed with satisfaction. "Which leaves option three..." Her eyebrow playfully arched like she had just solved the crime of the century. "You want to kill him."

Scotland took a final gulp of her tea and smacked her lips as she daintily placed the cup and saucer on the table. She looked up at Carter and took a breath. "You've forgotten option four, Mr. Holmes." She too playfully arched her eyebrow.

Carter turned her head and waited for the rebuttal. She had a playful look of intrigue. "And that would be, Dr. Watson?"

Scotland leaned forward. "You're full of shit."

Carter was shocked at her friend's response. "That's rather harsh..." She tick-tocked her head from side-to-side. "And only partially true."

Scotland held her iPhone up. "And the information was pretty damn sparse. I had a feeling he was a reporter, but he tried to take advantage of a friend of mine, and I don't like that."

Carter shrugged her shoulders. "Sorry, Scotty. If my spiders only found this..." She tilted her head towards the iPhone. "Then that's all they can find on the guy. I do have..." She leaned forward and made sure no one was listening in on them this time. She murmured in a hushed tone, "A small group of well-muscled, nicely tanned and perfectly circumcised Israeli commandos I can recommend looking for your Richard." She forced a playful wink.

Scotland did not know what to say but the what-the-fuck look painted on her gorgeous face said it all. "What?" Her eyes narrowed. "I'm looking for one disgraced reporter with no known address. Not launch Operation Entebbe." She shook her head with derision.

Carter tick-tocked her head. "Suit yourself. The offer still stands." She took a breath and looked at her iWatch. She swished her mouth from side-to-side and looked at her gorgeous friend. "Ready to go? Mason has the Bentley out front."

Scotland nodded. She had hoped that finding Richard and interrogating him for taking advantage of Mrs. Vasquez who just lost someone would have been easier. Now all she knew was his past occupation and a few other useless tidbits. 'Argh!'

Carter nudged her friend as the paparazzi descended on them again but had to stand on Santa Monica Boulevard and not on private property. "Cheer up, Scotty..." She scanned the faces and all the equipment getting prepped for some additional shots of the two gorgeous ladies before they got whisked away in the Bentley. "If anyone can find this guy, it's you."

Scotland swished her mouth from side-to-side. "I only wish I had more to go on. Trying to find this guy in a city with over twelve million people is going to be like looking for a needle in a haystack."

Carter popped on her sunglasses and smiled and waved at her adoring paparazzi stalkers. She took a deep breath and looked at the gorgeous property.

Scotland shook her head. "If only I had his address..." Her head dropped in dismay. She had failed her friend's grandma. "I could ask him some questions."

Carter nudged her once again. "So..." She stopped dead in her tracks and felt Scotland tug at her before stopping too. "Why don't you ask him?" She looked at her.

Scotland looked at Carter like she had two-heads. "Ask who what?" She scoffed at her obviously ridiculous, out-of-thin-air suggestion.

Carter had a blank stare. "The needle..." She smacked her lips. "Just ask him."

Scotland tilted her head to the side, rolled her gorgeous blue eyes all the way around and sighed loudly at her friend. "That's what I'm trying to do, but I can't ask him if I can't find him."

Carter headtossed toward Santa Monica Boulevard. "He's-standing-right-over-there." She took to pointing right at him this time.

Scotland snapped her head to the driveway entrance and zeroed in on who Carter pointed out. There in the sea of paparazzi stood Richard Moranis – the needle in her haystack trying to look inconspicuous. He was in the same outfit she saw him in last night, only this time it was daytime, and he was trying to hide with the nameless paparazzi and behind one of the ferns – unsuccessfully of course. She blurted out the deus ex machina stroke of luck that stared right back at her in the face. "What-the-fuck?"

Chapter 4

"Hey, Moranis!" Scotland sprinted towards the shocked man. He froze where he stood. "Dick Moranis! I want to talk with you!"

The paparazzi roared out with laughter and cackled. They looked amongst themselves at who would be called that.

Richard's mind raced at what he should do next – never mind the assholes laughing at his name. He wanted to watch the woman he saw at Mrs. Vasquez's house as he tried to sneak away last night. He caught sight of her and the small listening device he planted in her kitchen allowed him to clandestinely listen in on their conversation. He did not know which way to run. Either way only led into another open area.

Carter saw Scotland's speed fling her across the driveway towards her target, but she knew he could and definitely would bolt. His look was at first fright, but now it was beginning to look like fight or flight. He did not have the posture or build for fight, so he looked like he was prepared to make a run for it. She then took the opportunity to use her ace up her sleeve. She yelled at the top of her lungs, "Guys..." She pointed to the one that stuck out from the rest of them. "The guy with no camera! Grab-him!"

The paparazzi turned their attention to the suspicious man and swarmed him like a bunch of blood thirsty sharks that just had chum thrown into the water.

Richard looked at all quarters and immediately found himself surrounded with no escape. He let out a pained scream, "Argh!" And he just froze where he stood as their hands grabbed onto him and held him.

Scotland reached them in record time, but even she knew without the paparazzi's help Richard could have escaped or made her chance of catching him a little more difficult – but not by much.

She held up her hands and looked at the terrified man. Her look tried to console him but with so many others that surrounded him she knew he did not know what to expect. "Hey, Richard...Richard Moranis..." She looked at the paparazzi holding him for her, and she smiled at them all. "Thanks, guys. I'll take it from here."

She looked over at Richard. "Hey..." She took a breath but was hardly out of it. "I just want to talk with you."

Carter sauntered up and posed as the paparazzi resumed their picture-taking and question asking. One would think she was the center of attention in apprehending the suspicious guy. "Thanks for helping out, guys..." She smiled and glad-handled the loving crowd. "Why don't you have something to eat and drink at the hotel's restaurant? I'll arrange it."

Scotland and Richard simply stood and watched as she worked her magic.

The paparazzi thanked her and finished off their snaps until all of them had disappeared into the hotel for a free meal and drink.

Carter took to her iPhone and arranged everything. Satisfied with her Good Samaritan work she turned her attention to the two people as they watched her finish off.

Scotland scoffed at her. "It must be tough being you, huh?"

Carter smirked and shrugged playfully. "It's tough..." She beamed at them both as she popped her sunglasses back on. "But I manage."

Richard looked at Scotland and was curious. "What do you want to talk about?"

Scotland looked at him and scanned him from head to toe. It looked like he had lived in his clothes and was in desperate need of a shower since both she and Carter were standing downwind from him. She tried to breathe through her mouth, but she was sure she could also taste it. "Mrs. Vasquez..." She shifted to another part of the sidewalk and watched Carter do the same thing. "Why are you telling her that her husband was murdered?" She glared at him and waited for a plausible answer.

Richard shuffled where he stood. "Because it's true. Juan Vasquez was murdered..." He pulled out a crumpled paper that looked like it was used to wrap stuff in. "Same thing happened to two dozen other people..."He looked at them anxiously. "And that's just the tip of the iceberg."

Scotland took the paper and looked at the names on the list. It looked like any list anyone could easily make up and print out. She looked up at Richard and pursed her lips not convinced at all. "This proves nothing."

Carter looked at it and shot a sarcastic look at Scotland. "Are you kidding? Of course, it's real..." She took the sheet and held it up. "It was printed on a dot matrix printer. That proves everything." She snorted a giggle.

Richard snatched it from the sarcastic woman. "If you bitches aren't going believe me, then..." He had an agitated shake that angry people get when they cannot conjure up a more convincing argument and everyone is shitting on their idea. "Fuck-you-both!"

Scotland and Carter were shocked at Richard's outburst. Their jaws dropped at his impertinence. They stared at each other and could not believe he had the audacity to yell at them. They then turned and glared at him.

Scotland was incensed and her tone and body language spoke volumes. "Why you cheeky, motherfucker." She clenched her jaw and took an offensive step towards him and watched him take a defensive step back.

Richard clutched the piece of paper close to his chest like it was going to stop the pending assault. A whimper squeaked from deep inside him and his head volleyed from one woman to the other.

Carter was a little perturbed but let Scotland do the talking and fighting for her.

"I paid Mrs. Vasquez the thirty dollars you took from her and I'm going to take every penny out of your ass, Moranis." Scotland poked him in the chest. "How do I know you didn't just look through the obituaries so you could prey on their families?" She poked him again. "Huh?"

Richard gulped. "Be...because it's true." He was nervous. Before the incident he was a ruthless, go-getter reporter who stopped at nothing to expose the truth. Now he was a broken man being accosted by Bella Hadid and Kristen Stewart. His wife left him. He lost his house, his car, and worst of all his reputation because someone had it in for him for some unknown reason.

Scotland snarled her lip and nodded sarcastically. "Oh...and we're supposed to just take your word for it?" She narrowed her eyes. "Like that time you wrote about that guy that did that thing in the place that you got wrong?"

Richard stiffened his spine for the first time in a long time and he had it with people bringing that thing up again. He clenched his jaw. "Listen here, lady..." He advanced in her direction one step just to make his point. "That story about that guy doing that thing in that place was kosher. I got fucked when the other guy that knew about the thing because he swore he was at that place at that time just happened to change his tune and I couldn't prove anything because the first guy and the second guy said those things just to discredit me for some unknown reason."

Carter and Scotland both had a confused look on their confused faces as they stared at him.

"What?" Scotland furrowed her brow.

"What?" Carter had a confused look on her face.

Richard shook the paper in their collective faces once again. "This..." He pointed to the evidence with his free hand like Atticus Finch. "This is my proof. You're just going to have to take my word for it."

Scotland pursed her lips and narrowed her eyes at him. "Well, then..." She shook her head wanting to know what she should do. She needed him to prove his conviction to his story and her PhD thesis professor always told her that as long as you believe it, you should prove it. "You're going to have to do a little bit better than just a printed-out piece of paper to convince me."

Richard stared at her blankly. "Why?"

Scotland looked at him and then looked at Carter who was just as confused and then back to Richard. "Why-what?"

Richard narrowed his suspicious eyes at his interrogator. He scoffed and bellowed at her with divine impertinence, "Why the fuck do I have to convince you? Who the fuck do you think you are? Kristen Stewart?" He scoffed again. "I hated Twilight – the books and the movies." His face soured.

Scotland had an expression of bewilderment and scorn on her face at his outburst and she aloofly turned to look at Carter. "Did this And-Justice-For-All-Al-Pacino-little-motherfucker just ask me that?"

Carter nodded her head because it was not going to end well for Dick Moranis. Her finger followed an imaginary ball in the air as she replied, "He did, and he did."

Scotland turned to look at Moranis. "Because you've been following me just by the fact that you're here." She shook her head. "I don't know how you knew about me." Her face lit up as the wheels in her head churned the moment she caught sight of him. "I can only guess that you bugged Mrs. Vasquez's house and you overheard our entire conversation last night." She saw him gulp and there were beads of sweat on his forehead. A smile curled over her lips because she knew her deduction was spot on. 'I knew it!'

Richard thought as quick as he could, but he had not had a decent meal in a while and his brain was not functioning too well without sustenance. He scoffed off her deduction to double-down. "Phhhfft..." He shook his head to disagree with her. "You don't know what you're talking about."

Scotland poked him in the chest. "Well..." She narrowed her eyes at Moranis because he threw the gauntlet down. "My friend and I are going to go to Mrs. Vasquez's house and find that listening device that you put somewhere..." She thought for a moment. "Probably in her kitchen, and then..." A devious smile curled over her lips and she did not finish but cackled with glee.

Richard swallowed hard and he could not control his anxiety. "And-then-what?"

Scotland flashed a satisfied, smug smile at him. "And then you're fucked just like Richard Nixon, motherfucker. Only, you're not going to get impeached and then take a helicopter ride into the sunset. No..." She shook her head because he was trying her patience. "You're going to ass-raping prison."

Carter glared at him with animosity. "I hope you like looking at headboards, Dick…" She smirked uncontrollably. "Because that's the way you're going to be facing for a very long time when you're getting ass-fucked. They're going to be able to runs trains through your anus, because all your big dick swinging buddies are going to want more of your anus, Moranis."

Richard swallowed hard. He laughed nervously. "Hey…" He cleared his throat and looked at the two women who had him dead-to-rights. "C'mon…" He forced a nervous laugh and looked at them both like he had just come up with a great idea. "W-why don't I take you…" His hand trembled as he nervously folded the paper and put it back in his pocket. "Both of you, to prove that there's some sort of conspiracy, and these people were really murdered."

Carter and Scotland nodded and looked at each other, and then at Moranis.

"Yeah…" Scotland looked at Moranis. "Why don't we do just that?"

Carter dropped her shoulders. "Ugh…" She looked at Scotland and then at Moranis. "Are you going to need a ride?"

Richard looked at her and blinked. "Well…yeah. I had to take three buses to get here." He nodded matter-of-factly.

Carter turned to Scotland and only saw her comically raise her hands and shrug at her. She groaned with dissatisfaction, "Ugh. Fffuughk me. Mason just had the Bentley detailed."

Chapter 5

Scotland looked over at Carter and sandwiched in-between them was Richard Moranis.

Even though he was in the middle with nowhere he could go, he still felt uncomfortable as the two gorgeous ladies glared at him inside the elegant sedan. He swallowed hard and he cleared his throat. "You know..." He bit his bottom lip gingerly. "For two very beautiful women you sure can make a guy feel uncomfortable."

Scotland pursed her lips and looked at Carter and saw her shake her head. She turned back to Richard. "We just don't like being jerked around."

Richard shook his head with conviction. "Swear to god..." His head volleyed between the two of them while the driver simply kept his eyes forward and on the road ahead. "The info I've got on this will floor you. It's big. It'll be Pulitzer Prize winning."

Scotland pursed her lips at the man. "Calm down there Woodward-and-Bernstein. All you've got is a lot of conjecture."

Carter side-eyed him as he sat nervously and spun his conspiracy theory. "And what would be the end game of murdering these people?" She cocked an eyebrow. "What ties them all together? Huh?"

Richard swallowed hard and once again volleyed his head from side-to-side. "Well..." He licked his lips nervously. "I don't know just yet."

Scotland groaned an exasperated sigh. "You're wasting our time, Richard."

Richard shook his head. "No, no..." He held his hands up. "I thought so too until my friend told me about these deaths that seemed a little like murders."

Scotland cocked an eyebrow. "A little?" She scoffed at him. "Your friend?" She saw him nod his head. "The coroner?"

Richard shook his head at her. "No. Not the coroner." He started to get nervous. "He works in the coroner's office."

Scotland side-eyed him. "That's not what you told us earlier. Carter and I had the impression that your friend was the coroner."

Carter narrowed her eyes at him because she sensed he was not telling them everything. "What exactly does your friend do in the coroner's office, then?"

Richard swallowed hard this time and pressed his back against the cushy seat. "Umm..." His head volleyed once again. "He's the janitor."

Scotland clenched her jaw and groaned out loud. She glared at him violently with her eyes. "I think you're wasting our time, Dick."

Carter rested her head against the headrest and closed her eyes. She only let out an exasperated sigh.

Richard shook his head. "No way. You'll see when we get there. He'll tell you why he believes there is a conspiracy."

Scotland eyed him interrogatively. "And he only mentioned this supposed conspiracy in what?" She hemmed-and-hawed. "Passing? Seems like you're peddling hearsay, Richard."

Richard shook his head vehemently. "This guy is solid. Before he retired he used to work at the LAPD, and he used to feed me information..." He cocked an eyebrow at both ladies. "Solid information and he never let me down before."

Scotland looked over at Carter and then turned her attention back to Richard. "And what exactly did Deep Throat do at the LAPD?"

Richard swallowed hard once again. "Umm, he was the janitor."

Scotland stared at Richard blankly. She did not want to discount the reporter and his confidential informant, but it could very well be the ramblings of a couple of lunatics. "Okay, Richard..." She pursed her lips and took a deep breath. "It's a beautiful LA Saturday, and my friend and I are full and shopped out..." She shrugged her shoulders and held up her hands as she watched Carter roll her gorgeous eyes all the way around. "What the hell else do we have to do but entertain you and your friend Deep Throat? Right, Carter?"

Carter shot her a look but backed down because Scotland always had a way with her eyes. She stared into her soul when she wanted her to help her out with something. Far be it from her to question or leave her best friend hanging. She simply screwed her mouth to the side, smiled at a smiling Richard Moranis and sat back into her cushy seat. She groaned a little because she could be out shopping some more or doing something more fun. "Sure, Scotland. What else could we be doing?"

Scotland looked at Richard. "But if you're hustling us..." She pointed at Carter. "My friend over there has a Taser with your name on it."

Richard swallowed nervously and forced a smile. He could tell they were only placating him for this short period of time. No matter, they would see it when he talked to his friend. He never led him astray before and if he said there was a conspiracy of some kind, then he believed him. After all, he was the one who led him to Mrs. Vasquez's husband. It was a way for him to redeem himself. A conspiracy so large it involved money – lots of it, power, and assassins.

Mason pulled the gorgeous Bentley into an available parking spot in the parking lot of 1104 North Mission Road – the LA Medical Examiner's office.

They got out of the Bentley, and surreptitiously made their way inside to find Richard's informant so he could convince Carter and Scotland that he was being serious and not paranoid.

They all marched into the lobby and Scotland noticed the rather librarian-looking receptionist whose face brightened up as she saw them coming toward her desk.

Joanne Middleton recognized Richard immediately and beamed a mega-kilowatt smile at him. "Hi, Richard. So nice to see you. Isn't it terrible?" She gingerly bit her bottom lip and her eyes darted around the foyer. She pushed up her spectacles.

The smile on Richard's face disappeared. "What's terrible, Joanne?" He looked at the receptionist quizzically.

"Ron…" She looked at him startled. "Didn't you hear?"

Richard shook his head and he started to get nervous.

Joanne looked at the two gorgeous ladies and wondered what they were doing with Richard. "Ron died this morning." She looked at him with sad eyes. "Heart attack."

The blood in Richard's face drained and he had to put his hand on the desk to steady himself. He mumbled to himself, "Jesus Christ."

Joanne smiled at the two women and then looked at Ron with sad eyes. "So sad…" She shook her head to lament at the news. "First his wife and now Ron…" She pursed her lips. "All in a matter of six months. Looks like when your spouse dies before you, you just lose the will to carry on." She eyeballed Richard and bit her lip gingerly, and she murmured in a low tone, "Too bad I'll never experience that."

Scotland smiled at Joanne and introduced herself. "I'm Scotland and this is my friend Carter. We're friends of Richard's."

Carter looked at Scotland with an impertinent glare but decided to remain quiet. Her thoughts clouded. 'Friends is pushing it.'

Joanne smiled and tapped her nametag. "I'm Joanne Middleton…" She could not help but notice how beautiful they both were. "Nice to meet you both." The bespectacled receptionist basked in their gorgeousness.

Richard was not paying attention at their salutations and then turned to look at Scotland and Carter. "You see. They did this to shut him up."

Joanne looked at them quizzically. "They did what to whom, Richard?"

Scotland smiled at Joanne and held her hand up to quell her growing anxiety. "Nothing. Richard's just having a bad day and he's making things up…" She rolled her eyes comically and screwed up her mouth to discount the man. "Reporters, right?" She gave a playful shrug, pointed at him, and snorted a giggle.

Carter and Scotland grabbed him under each arm and forcibly marched him to the side, out of earshot of Joanne – and sat him down on one of the benches.

Scotland felt sorry for him and looked at him. "I'm sorry about your friend, Richard..." She looked back at Joanne who still had a confused and worried look on her brow and smiled. She turned back to Richard and growled through her teeth, "But you can't go saying shit like that without proof, or you'll be strapped to a hospital bed somewhere with a Thorazine drip stuck in your arm – okay?"

Carter also kind of felt sorry for the man. She reached into her Hermes fanny-pack, rummaged past her Taser and her wallet, and pulled out something he needed right now. "Hey, knucklehead..." She handed it to him. "Looks like you could use one of these." She popped up her eyebrows and smirked.

Scotland looked at her perplexed. "How's that going to help, Carter? He just lost his friend and his only lead."

Carter looked at her wild-eyed and matter-of-factly. "I know he lost his friend..." She pointed to him and watched as he opened the snack and partook. "It's a full-sized Snickers. No one says no to a Snickers..." She shook her head derisively at her friend. "Especially a full-sized one."

Scotland let out a sigh. She turned back to Richard. "Ron obviously had some medical issues, and he had a bad heart."

Richard looked up at the two heavenly faces and shook his head. "Ron ran ten miles every morning. He didn't drink or smoke..." He munched on the bar and did not want to let any go to waste as he savoured its deliciousness. "How'd someone like that have a heart attack? Huh?" His head volleyed between the two women once again because he wanted answers. He was so close to the truth but now all he had were more questions.

Scotland looked at him. "Life's funny that way. Maybe he was heartbroken his wife died."

Carter nodded her head and she looked at Richard. "It happens, Richard."

Richard finished the last morsel and pulled his mouth to the side and cleaned his teeth with his tongue. He thought of Ron's wife and what she went through when she got sick and passed away a year after she retired. "I know it happens but it's just so sad when you work all your life and hope that you would be able to spend some quality time with one another in retirement and then this happens."

Carter pursed her lips and nodded. She looked over at Joanne who was now busy with another guest at reception. "Tell you what, though..." She surreptitiously pointed to Joanne for Richard to see. "If look past her Ross Dress for Less ensemble, stringy wig, and pasty features, I think Joanne Middleton has the love-jones for you, mon ami."

Richard peeked between the two ladies and looked at Joanne. He murmured to them as he eyeballed Joanne, "Really?"

Scotland feigned disbelief. "Are you kidding, Richard..." She scoffed. "You couldn't sense it?" She snorted a giggle. "There was some definite sexual tension there."

Carter shot her a look like a startled ostrich. "Whoa..." She held her hand out to slow Scotland's roll. "I would say there was some very friendly coffee tension there, okay?" She shook her head derisively at her. "Let's see if a date is manageable first and then decide if sex is involved – six months to a year later. How 'bout that?"

It was highschool all over again for him. Richard blinked at both of them. "You think so?"

Scotland looked at Carter blankly and turned back to Richard who had that innocent boy look about him. "Think so what?" She pursed her lips at him. "The date?" Her eyebrows postured at him.

Richard shook his head. It may have been his proximity to Carter and Scotland in the car, but it made him horny – and the Snickers did not help. "The sex." His eyes opened wide with desire.

Carter scoffed and blinked blankly at him. "You better slow your roll there, Dexter..." She now shook her head at him derisively. "Good girls like Joanne marry guys like you after they get to know them better. They don't think of fucking them before a first date unless you're Bezos-rich or look like Boris Kodjoe..." She shook him by his shoulders. "And you are light-years from either, got it?"

Richard looked a little put off but he hemmed-and-hawed and knew there was some validity to that comment. He tick-tocked his head and screwed his mouth up pensively.

Scotland narrowed her eyes at Carter's mean streak but there was some truth to that, she had to admit. She turned back to Richard. "C'mon. We should go..." She took a deep breath. "This is a dead end."

They started to walk past the reception desk, and they waved at Joanne.

Joanne smiled and then she yelled out to Richard, "Oh, Richard..." She dug deep in her folder and pulled out an envelope. She ran around the desk and met up with him. "There's this letter addressed to you." She giggled cutely at him and played with her hair. "I almost forgot."

Scotland and Carter could not deny she had the love-jones for Richard, and they could not understand why. Different strokes for different folks apparently.

"Thanks, Joanne." He rolled the sealed envelope in his hands and noticed no return address or sender, but it had his name perfectly typed on the front. He smiled at her awkwardly.

Joanne smiled cutely and held her hands across her chest. "Yes. Funniest thing. I saw it on my desk yesterday morning and placed it in the folder. Not sure how it got here."

Richard noticed how thick it was so there was something of substance inside and he acknowledged her courtesy with a wave and a smile. "Thanks, Joanne. I appreciate you holding it for me."

Joanne giggled and tapped him gently on the shoulder. "It's nothing at all…." She narrowed her eyes and beamed at him. "It was my pleasure."

Carter and Scotland looked at the pair flirting with one another and were perplexed to say the least.

They left, after Richard waved repeatedly to Joanne, and made their way down the steps as Richard tore at the envelope to coax its treasures to him.

Scotland murmured to Carter, "Apparently you can have no money like Bezos or look like Boris and…" She emphasized the perplexing social interaction they both just witnessed. "There's at least one woman who would still fuck you."

Carter shook her head in disbelief. She shrugged comically at her best friend and wondered the same thing. "Perhaps we should set the two horndogs up on a date."

Scotland and Carter followed Richard as he plowed through the information in the letter.

Scotland nodded at Carter. "I think it's the least we can do for him…" She tick-tocked her head and the scenarios started to flash in her mind about the two of them going at it like rabbits. She groaned and she shook that image out of her mind for good. "Seeing how you were so mean to him."

Carter looked at her derisively. "Fuck off."

Scotland shot her a shocked look. "Now you're mean to me." She pulled a pout and a sad face to show her tears-of-a-clown.

Carter did not get sucked into her madness. "That's why I bought you that vibrator for your birthday."

Scotland wrapped her arm under Carter's. "And I almost think of you every time I use it." She giggled sweetly at her best friend.

Carter pursed her lips and side-eyed her friend. "Good to know."

Richard stopped and was shocked at what he read. He stood straight up and turned to look at both gorgeous ladies. There was an astonished look on his face as he showed them the papers he was holding. "It's from Ron..." He giggled with glee at the information he was given by his dead friend. "He's given me proof there is some sort of conspiracy going on." He laughed and convulsed at his good fortune that the trail was still hot.

Scotland and Carter just looked at Richard and then at the papers clutched in his hands.

Chapter 6

Scotland scanned through the letter that Ron Little left for Richard. She still seemed skeptical but gave him the benefit of the doubt and continued to scan through the pages. She then re-read something just to understand what Ron was getting at. The veracity of Ron Little's claims of a conspiracy to murder read like it was grounded in someone's fiction – his. She was incredulous at his conclusions, and the list of names almost seemed to be pulled from an obituary column when cross-referenced with a browser search.

She handed them off to Carter to review further and she pursed her lips and shook her head as if to mirror Scotland's, but she drew her own conclusions.

They sat inside Philippe The Original and chewed through the information, as Richard chewed through his French Dip sandwich – wet, of course – with the same amount of gusto. He enjoyed his sandwich more than the ladies enjoyed the letter, unfortunately.

Scotland put the papers down and took a deep breath to enjoy the delicious meaty smells permeating throughout the deli. She chewed her thoughts and looked at Richard who was mid-scarf on a rather hunky bite he took out of the sandwich. She pulled her mouth to the side and semi-scoffed at the contents she was digesting in her miraculous head. "This is bound by fiction, and statements are set-up to look factual, Richard."

Carter could not agree more. She had seen things like this before when she was White House Press Secretary and she had to stretch the truth a little – well, a lot. She could only nod and agree with Scotland.

Richard chewed through his bite as he chewed through the scenery. He had nothing except for the information Ron surreptitiously gave him and now he was dead. He washed down the remnants with some coffee and politely cleared his throat. "This can't be a coincidence..." His hand waved at the papers and he stared at both of them. First Ron tells me about this and then he's dead?" He looked at them both incredulously. "They did it to his wife as well."

Scotland narrowed her eyes because she was processing the information. She took a deep breath and licked her lips trying to size Richard up. "So..." She side-eyed him suspiciously. "You're saying this pension fund management company is killing off pension holders?"

Richard nodded. "That's what Ron believed, and I believe Ron." He held his hands up incredulously. "Why else would he get a job with the Medical Examiner unless it was to build his case?"

Carter chimed in and she wanted to believe the story but was having a hard time with the conspiracy theory. "Richard, Ron could've just been lonely and needed the work to keep him busy or…" She shrugged. "He needed the extra money."

Scotland processed the information and punched some of the information into her iPhone and waited for the results. "Hmm…" Her head tick-tocked as she scanned the information closely. "California Public Employees Fund is run by said management company…" She scanned some more. "Over Four-hundred-twenty billion dollars under management."

Carter took a breath and then shook her head. "It would look very suspicious if their pension holders started to get murdered…" She popped up her eyebrows and added, "Well, the ones that've retired already."

Scotland looked at Carter and Richard and narrowed her eyes as the tipping point for her to get suspicious just occurred. "Not if it looked like natural causes."

Carter took a breath and narrowed her eyes at her friend. She had never crossed or doubted her since they were small children, and she had no reason to disbelieve her now. Scotland had always been level-headed, and Carter trusted her implicitly. "You mean and then keep all of the money under management?" Her eyes met Scotland's and all of a sudden, they were on the same train of thought. She saw her nod gently.

Scotland scanned the papers on the Formica table, and she had considered all of the options and played devil's advocate and promoter of the cause. She simply nodded as the jigsaw started to come together in her head. She looked at the standard policy and chewed through her thoughts on the main highlights. "If one spouse dies, the other gets the remaining balance. But if both die then the remaining pensionable money reverts back to the fund."

Carter smirked and took a breath. Her face scanned the faces of both of her table companions. "That's quite a tall tale to prove, though…" She had a pensive look on her brow. "And just who the hell would you get to carry all of this out? Jason Bourne?" She snorted a laugh.

Scotland opened her eyes wide and almost nodded at the prospect of the conspiracy of this magnitude. "Yeah…" She pursed her lips at the level of commitment to carry out something like this. "I think you're right, Carter. Hire someone to make the murders look like an accident or natural causes. The police and medical examiner would deem it as such, and case closed."

Richard smiled and finished off the last morsel of his delicious sandwich that Scotland bought for him, while she and Carter opted for a juice. He washed it down with some of the remaining coffee, and then cleansed his palate with some water. It was the best meal he had in over two days. "So…" He nodded appreciably for the sustenance and now wondered how he would be able to rebuild his reputation. "How do we prove it?" He was shocked to see the confused looks on both of their gorgeous faces.

Scotland's face soured. "Prove it? We?" She shook her head with indignation. "We're not private investigators or detectives." She shot a glance at Carter and she agreed with her with just a look. "We've got to be careful with this information or SoCal Management Company Incorporated is going to sue you, Carter and me for defamation until we're eating in soup kitchens and busking for loose change." She looked at him, so he understood. "We can't accuse a management company with uncorroborated and suspect information no matter how convincing it looks."

Richard looked at them in silence and wondered what he and they needed to do. That was all he had and even going to the police with this information would be circumstantial at best. Coincidental, yes. But the proof was not rockhard. His shoulders dropped in defeat.

Carter looked at Scotland and she smirked. "We could always just ask them outright?"

Scotland looked at her with a perplexed look on her face. Her tone and body language said it all. "Carter, in the history of all of your ridiculous ideas, that's the most ridiculous."

Carter shrugged her shoulders and grinned. "Well…" She pursed her lips and tick-tocked her head from side-to-side. "Then I've got nothing."

Scotland shook her head at her brilliant friend. "Thanks for contributing…" She narrowed her eyes sarcastically. "Excellent blue-skying there, Carter."

Carter simply shrugged her well-toned shoulders at her friend.

Richard looked at her and moved his mouth from side-to-side like he chewed a thought. "We could break into SoCal Management and steal the information." His eyes glistened like it was a good idea.

Scotland looked at him like he just ripped a fart in front of the Queen. She slowly turned and looked at Carter – blankly. "Remember when I said your idea was ridiculous?" She saw her nod her head and rolled her eyes at what was about to come next. She pointed at Richard. "That one just topped it…" She turned to Richard. "And it sucks balls…" She looked at him like he was touched. "Are you out of your fucking mind?" Her derisive look topped that sundae like a one-hundred-pound cherry.

Richard blushed and took another sip of water. He just shut up for now.

Scotland knew she could get an audience with the CEO, Dirk Stafford, of SoCal Management. They had been trying for years to land Yarde Pharmaceuticals as a client. That crown jewel always rested with Deklava Management. She knew it would be prudent to get as much information as she could but that would be a tall ask and she put it out of her head.

Scotland shrugged her shoulders and looked at Richard. "I'm afraid there's nothing left to do. If you go down this path, we can't help you..." She looked at him apologetically. "Our hands are tied, Richard..." Her eyes twinkled a bit like the light at the end of the tunnel. "Although, Carter and I can set you up on a date with Joanne." She popped up her eyebrows at the consolation prize no person in their right mind would refuse.

Richard scoffed. "She'd go out with a guy with no job, no prospects and no car?"

Scotland brightened up a bit at his slightly positive uptake on that idea. "Sure. I'm sure you'll bounce back and I'm sure Carter and I'll be happy to lend you some money to see you through until the end of the month."

Carter snapped her head like a startled ostrich at her too-generous friend. "Say-what-now?" Her look soured at having been voluntold.

Scotland glared at her and there were daggers flying out of her eyes.

Carter instinctively knew not to pursue this with Scotland and shirked back. She turned to Richard. "Sure..." She pointed at Scotland. "What she said."

Richard smiled at them both. It had been a while since he was on a date especially after his wife took what little he had and kicked him out of their Pasadena apartment. He had been subsisting on the odd hand-out and couch-surfing for the last six months. He had called in every favor he could think of and one of those favors was Ron – and look what happened to him.

Scotland thought about something for a second and she narrowed her eyes at Richard. "And, we're going to Mrs. Vasquez's house and you're removing that bug you put in her kitchen and wherever else you happened to stick one..." She pointed an accusatory finger at him. "Got it?"

Richard nodded and wondered how someone as beautiful as Scotland Yarde could be so pushy and mean when she wanted to be. He swallowed hard. "It's just the one in the kitchen..." He screwed his mouth to the side. "It's under the kitchen table."

Scotland nodded and looked at Carter. "Let's go now."

Carter looked at her wild-eyed. "You want me to come with?"

Scotland pulled her mouth to the side matter-of-factly. "You're the John Watson to my Sherlock Holmes."

Richard watched the volleying between the two gorgeous titans. He smirked and decided to chime in. "Technically, you two would be Cagney and Lacey..." He raised his eyebrows to them both. "If you want my opinion?"

Both Scotland and Carter discounted Richard's opinion with derisive eyes, and turned their duelling to one another once again.

Carter pursed her lips and interrogatively looked at her. "Why am I John Watson? I've got the look and smarts to be Sherlock Holmes."

Scotland looked at her and scoffed sarcastically. "Puhleeze..." She waved her off and pointed both of her thumbs at herself. "Dean's Honor Roll every year, and graduated summa cum laude."

Carter scoffed right back at her with contempt. "White House Press Secretary for four years." Her eyes penetrated her friend with added contempt to enforce the fact. "And, I come loud every night."

Scotland shook her head and twirled her finger in the air sarcastically like it was a big deal – which it was not, to her. "Whoop-dee-doo..." She snorted contempt for that fact. "I've been to the White House and have masturbated in the Lincoln bedroom..." She snorted a derisive laugh. "With your vibrator..." She playfully glared at her. "And, I was not thinking of you at the time."

Carter acted shocked but was not. "Hah..." She sneered at her. "Masturbated in the Oval Office." She pointed both of her thumbs at herself defiantly. "This girl right here."

Scotland's jaw dropped. "You do know there's constant video surveillance of the Oval Office." She opened her eyes thinking she knew that already – but apparently not.

 Carter's eyes had that deer-in-the-headlights look. "Say-what?" Her mouth went dry.

Scotland snorted a laugh. "Oh my god..." She guffawed at her. "You didn't know?"

Carter swallowed hard and thought back. "They only turn it on when the President is in the Office..." She had that quizzical look on her face that you could not deny. "Don't they?"

Scotland shook her head and was busting a satisfied smirk on her face.

Carter was now aware of those constant date offers from the secret service agents. "Hah..." Her mind started to race, and she now knew why she was so popular. She growled, perplexed at her faux pas, "No wonder."

Scotland narrowed her eyes at her inquisitively. "No wonder what?"

Carter looked at her surprised. "What?"

Scotland narrowed her eyes and took a breath. "Never mind." She turned to Richard and he was totally engrossed in their conversation and probably engorged. "I trust you're finished..." She pursed her lips at him. "We should go now."

Richard looked at them both. "Umm..." He forced a laugh. "We won't have to tell Mrs. Vasquez about that bug, do we?"

Scotland shook her head and leaned into him. "We don't..." She narrowed her eyes at him for even thinking that he could bug Mrs. Vasquez's house. "But if you cannot come up with a plausible reason for us being there, you are going to tell her..." She thumbed in Carter's general direction. "Or my Oval Office, masturbatory friend over there is going to tase the fuck out of you." She nodded to ensure he understood and saw him nod back in agreement.

Chapter 7

Mason piloted the Bentley down the street towards Mrs. Vasquez's house and he started to slow down. "Carter, Scotland." He headtossed at the young man as he ran out of the house.

Scotland looked out and recognized him immediately. "That's Emilio..." She had a feeling something was wrong. "Her grandson..." She scanned the area quickly and did not notice anything out of the ordinary. "Please pull over, Mason."

The Bentley sped up and Mason pulled it as close to the house as possible.

They all jumped out and wondered what was going on with Emilio. They could tell he out of sorts about something.

Scotland looked at him and he instantly recognized her. "Emilio..." She wondered why he was so agitated. "What's wrong?"

Emilio was anxious and frightened. "My grandma..." He teared up at what he found when he got home. "She's not breathing."

Carter looked back at Mason. "Mason, call 911, please!"

Mason already had his cell out and was dialling emergency service.

Scotland and Emilio started toward the house. "C'mon..." They raced back inside with Richard and Carter taking up the rear. "Let's see if we can help her."

They ran into the kitchen and Mrs. Vasquez was splayed out on the kitchen floor.

Emilio shook when he saw her helpless body on the floor and wondered what had happened.

Scotland got down and checked her pulse, her breathing and started CPR on her to see if she could revive her or stabilize her before the paramedics arrived.

She continued in vain and still could not find a pulse. She looked at an agitated Emilio. "Do you have a defibrillator?" He seemed preoccupied on his grandma. "Emilio! Do you have a defibrillator?"

Emilio shook his head. "No..." He swallowed hard and thought he would now be all alone. "We don't."

Scotland looked around and then her attention turned to Carter. "Carter. Your Taser..." She held out her hand. "Let me have it."

Carter sprang to action and pulled it out of her fanny pack and handed it to Scotland.

Scotland cracked the front of the Taser open to pull out the electrodes.

Carter instinctively got down and started to give Mrs. Vasquez mouth-to-mouth while Scotland worked.

Scotland pulled open Mrs. Vasquez's shirt and attached the leads to the correct spots by piercing the skin. "Carter…" She moved her hand to ward her away. "Watch out." She then triggered the Taser and watched Mrs. Vasquez's body convulse in an arch as the Taser was discharged.

Carter quickly checked her pulse and shook her head. "Again…" She pursed her lips and had a grim look on her face. "Do-it-again."

Scotland pulled the trigger and watched as her idle body arched from the Taser discharge and held it for another few seconds before releasing.

Carter checked again and smiled. She massaged Mrs. Vasquez's neck to get the blood flowing and they watched her chest rise from her breathing. She looked at Scotland and smiled and saw a return.

In the distance they could hear the sirens wailing as they rushed to the Vasquez residence.

Emilio watched with sadness but now hopeful that his grandmother could and would make a recovery thanks to Scotland and Carter. The ambulance attendants loaded her into the back of the ambulance, and he readied himself to hop in as well. He turned to the two women speaking to the police and he waved when he saw them look at him. For the first time tonight, he smiled.

Scotland and Carter waved to him as the two officers talked with them at length. Richard for the most part hovered in the background and made himself as inconspicuous as possible – having not been able to retrieve the bug because, in the commotion, he forgot it.

Carter and Scotland turned their attention back to the two officers who seemed out of place to be police and should instead be cover models for some fitness magazines.

Carter looked at the male officer, Nate Murdock, as he calmly jotted down her information. He held onto her driver's license. Occasionally, he would dart his eyes at her and pulled a smile and then a grin. It seemed like an inordinate amount of time to jot down some simple information but he seemed preoccupied with her look and so she grinned back helpfully.

Scotland on the other hand could not take her eyes off the rather tall, rather cross-fit shredded, and rather lickable female officer taking her information down. She towered over Scotland's five-foot-two frame by at least a good foot and had her brown hair braided up neatly. Her olive complexion had that caramelly goodness about it, and the more she looked at Officer Kate Hernandez the more intrigued and giddy she felt. She saw her pop-up her gorgeous brown eyes at her, and her grin was enticing to say the least. It is not like Scotland pish-poshed the idea of a relationship with a woman. She did occasionally experiment, loved the one she was with, and was very comfortable on her Kinsey Scale of relationships. She returned her grin with a smile and a twinkle in her eye because she was single and ready to mingle with the officer – if handcuffs were in play.

Two men casually walked out of the house with bags-in-hand and made a beeline to them all. Scotland side-eyed them and their ill-fitting, off-the-rack blazers and slacks gave them that detective-y look about them. Their LAPD issue three-point holsters that cradled their standard-issue Glocks and their shiny shields clipped to their belts, also gave them away as they cut across the lawn.

One of the men sidled up to Hernandez and there was a smirk on his face like he knew something secret and was about to share it with her. She was taller than him but by only a few inches. "Are you and Murdock done, Hernandez?"

Hernandez nodded, side-eyed him, and pursed her lips. She let out a formal murmur, "Yes, detective." She did not care for Detective Jake Hansen nor for his partner of over twenty years, Detective Gene Marx. They were douche-bags extraordinaire and had a questionable reputation no one, least of all Internal Affairs, could prove – but it had a heartbeat throughout the rumor mill.

Hansen nodded and looked as she handed the woman her driver's license back. He shook his head and the smarm started to bubble to the surface. He looked at Murdock as he did the same with the other woman's identification and he popped-up his eyebrows at Marx. "Excellent work officers..." He snorted a laugh. "You'll make detectives one day..." He saw Marx wince comically. "Just not today."

Hernandez turned to glare at Hansen and felt Murdock put his hand on her arm to ward her off.

Hansen came toe-to-toe with the Amazon and looked her in the eyes – but he had to tilt his head up a bit. "Is there a problem, Officer Hernandez?"

Hernandez swallowed and narrowed her eyes at him. She took a deep breath and looked through the man. Her Army Ranger training would make an example of him, but she knew it would be an end to her career. She had seen a lot and did a lot during her three tours in Iraq and Afghanistan and some pissant detective was not going to end it for her. She shook her head and pursed her lips as she stared him down. "No, detective..." She stepped back in line. "No problem."

Scotland and Carter took note of the tension and knew it was the expression of power and rank. They did not like that and made note of it for later.

Hansen flashed a smarmy smile at her and Murdock and side-eyed Marx as he stood there to support his partner and not the rank-and-file officers. "Good…" He headtossed to the house. "Now go check the house with the other officers and let us detectives take care of business."

Murdock nodded and touched Hernandez's arm to follow him and not hang around there. He knew what she could do to both of the detectives – he has seen her fight and it was not pretty for the receiver. "Yes, detectives." He nudged her to knock her out of her funk. "C'mon, Kate."

Hansen nodded at Murdock and simply smiled. He turned to the two women and he looked at their contact information. "Miss Carter Deklava and Miss Scotland Yarde…" He snorted a giggle and wondered who would name their kid that. "Scotland Yarde…" He was incredulous but in a sarcastic way. "Is that for real or some stage name?" His head volleyed because he did not know who was who.

Scotland narrowed her eyes and did not like him already. "I'm Scotland Yarde and yes, that's my real name."

Hansen nodded and could tell she was not one to be trifled with. He looked at her and he tilted his head to the side. "I'm Detective Jake Hansen and this is my partner Detective Gene Marx…" He looked her over and her friend and could not help but get lost in their beauty and their doppelgangerness. "I understand you and Miss Deklava assisted with reviving Mrs. Vasquez?"

Scotland nodded her head. "That's correct."

Hansen nodded and made a few notes in his notebook. "And, how do you know the lady?"

"I know her grandson, Emilio…" Scotland rattled off the information. "I teach English literature courses at the college. Aspen Hall Community College."

Marx piped up because he was intrigued. He did not care if he sounded heavy-handed or interrogative. "Do you always drop by your student's home with your friends?"

Scotland looked at him. "I've a vested interest in all my students but I dropped off Emilio at the other night because he was upset when his grandfather passed away. That's the first time I met Mrs. Vasquez."

Hansen was intrigued and looked at her squarely. "Then what were you doing here tonight?"

Scotland shot a look at Carter and saw that she narrowed her eyes. They would now be caught in a trap of question-after-question because there was no reason for them to be there a second night except to retrieve Richard's bug. She turned back to the detective and remembered that they carried out two evidence bags. Her mind raced and she could only assume they found something or some things that were out of the ordinary and were now playing sleuth. She looked at him squarely. "We were here to retrieve our friend's listening device that was somewhere in the kitchen. That's when we came upon Emilio frantically looking for help. We went inside and saw Mrs. Vasquez on the floor with no pulse or breathing and then administered CPR." She looked at him eyes-to-eyes.

Carter took a deep breath and rolled her eyes all the way around.

Hansen's mouth opened and he had a lost look in his eyes. He hoped he could catch her in a lie after he and Marx found the listening device duct-taped under the kitchen table, but the woman managed to beat them to the punch before they could unleash their punchy round of interrogative questions. He then went straight to his second-to-last question. "Do you know it is illegal to use a listening device in someone's home without a court order?"

Scotland nodded. "One – it's not ours. It's a reporter's. Richard Moranis' and he is over there. Two – I'm sure it was installed to ensure Mrs. Vasquez's safety."

Hansen shook his head at her. "A lot of good it did Mrs. Vasquez." He turned to Marx in a huff. "And we'll get to Mr. Moranis later, but we'd like your take on why the bug was necessary?"

Scotland looked at Carter's blank stare. Her attention turned back to the detectives. "Mr. Moranis had reason to believe that Mrs. Vasquez's husband was murdered and did not die of natural causes."

Marx snorted out a laugh and turned to look at Moranis and then back to them. "So, he's a detective now after bungling that news piece that got him fired?" He knew of Moranis and he did not care for him or reporters in general.

Scotland continued to do the talking because she was running through things in her head – 'what was in that other evidence bag?' "Richard was following up on a lead that he got from a county employee who worked at the medical examiner's office."

Hansen scribbled the note in his book and lifted his eyes at her. "And that would be?" He shook his head waiting for the name.

"Ron Little..." Scotland watched him scribble that down. "He was the janitor..." She saw him pause mid-scribble and offered the information freely. "He died of a heart attack recently."

Hansen looked up at her and there was a perplexed looked on his face. "Seems that everyone he meets ends up dying..." There was a glint in his eyes as he looked at Marx. "Maybe he's the connection."

Scotland shook her head. "Richard was with Carter and me all morning and afternoon when Mrs. Vasquez fell ill."

Hansen stretched out his hand to Marx and took the two evidence bags. He held them up for Scotland and Carter to see. "One of these has the listening device Mr. Moranis installed and I'm sure his fingerprints are all over it..." He held the other one up for effect. "This one has the insulin Mrs. Vasquez injected in herself either to administer her diabetes shot or..." He pursed his lips and took a deep breath. "Top herself because she could not live without her husband."

Scotland scoffed at that. "That's a lie for two reasons detective...." She pointed to the bag. "Mrs. Vasquez was not diabetic. That was for her husband because he did not have insurance to cover the insulin..." She saw him about to rebut her argument. "Yes, the bottle has her name on it because she needed to get the insulin in her name so her insurance would pay for it." Her eyes scanned the looks on the two detectives' faces. "And, the other night when I was here, Mrs. Vasquez did not look like a woman who wanted to commit suicide for her dead husband. She believed Richard and wanted to get to the bottom of it."

Hansen was at a loss for words and looked at Marx who had an equally quizzical and perplexed look on his face. He turned to Scotland and then looked at Carter. "Do you have anything to add, Miss Deklava?"

Carter's mouth dropped open and she side-eyed Scotland and she took a labored breath. "I'm really only here because my friend forced me to tag along." She forced a smile and saw Scotland tense up and growl at her.

Hansen turned to look at Scotland and he took a deep breath. The accident started to look more like attempted murder to him right about now so it was not case closed as he would have thought. "That's a lot of information to digest..." He screwed his mouth to the side and side-eyed Marx and then turned to look at Scotland. "Tell you what..." He forced a smile. "We'll be in touch with you and Miss Deklava..." He headtossed over to Richard Moranis who was still standing idly by with the lone police officer. "We're going to take Mr. Moranis down to the station and ask him a few questions to, you know..." His head tick-tocked to the side and he flashed a Cheshire-Cat grin. "See if his story corroborates with yours."

Scotland nodded and pursed her lips. The thoughts started to ruminate in her head about the insulin injection and that made her question all the information she knew so far about this case – something just did not seem right. "You have Carter and my contact information so contact us whenever."

Carter piped up once again. While Nate was a delicious distraction, being with the detectives made her sour to the thought of having to deal with the police again. "May I just say that I was an innocent party in all of this."

Scotland looked at her derisively. "I think they get it, Carter." She tilted her head at her and pursed her lips.

Hansen nodded and closed his notebook. He did, however, have to make a point of the two gorgeous women in his company and their striking doppelganger resemblance. "On another note…" His head cocked to the side and a smile curled over his mouth. "Did anyone tell you that you both look like celebrities?"

Scotland forced a smile and nodded. "Yes…" She laughed. "We get that a lot. It is Hollywood after all." She shrugged cutely.

Marx looked them both over and was perplexed. He looked at his partner and shook his head.

Hansen did not want to waste their time any longer and shook his head at Marx. "I'll tell you in the car, Gene. His attention turned back to the two women. "You're both free to go."

Scotland nodded and she looked at him comically. "Aren't you going to tell us not to leave town?"

Hansen snorted a laugh. "Umm…" He looked at her and sized her up. "That's only in the movies and TV…" He shook his head and looked at her intently. "But Marx and I always get our man…" His head tick-tocked from side-to-side. "Or woman in the end." A smirk curled over his mouth.

Scotland nodded and tilted her head at him knowingly. Her lips pursed with the added benefit of the detective's proviso. "Wow…" She looked at Carter and saw her shake her head slowly. Her friend knew her well and knew what was to follow. She turned to look at Marx and then back to Hansen. "That's why you're both detectives, then…" Her mouth curled up sarcastically. "Mazel Tov."

Carter closed her eyes and wanted this to be over soon. Preferably before Scotland got them both thrown in lock-up for some trumped up charge because she pissed off the detectives for some reason.

Hansen scoffed and snorted a giggle. "We'll see you when we see you." He casually saluted them, and he and Marx walked towards a wild-eyed Richard Moranis.

Scotland sidled up to Carter. She looked at her and their stares screamed volumes – they had known each other long enough to know what each other were thinking. "I wonder if he got that out of a fortune cookie?"

Carter snorted a giggle and shook her head. "C'mon…" She started on her way to her car. "I feel like Gorgio's for dinner, and you're buying."

Scotland groaned at her but followed her dutifully. She wondered about all the information that was floating in her head like flotsam. It would take her a while for her to put it all together and she needed some delicious Italian sustenance and sleep.

Mrs. Vasquez would get all the help she could at the hospital – with Emilio by her side. Richard Moranis would be safe at the police station and he could spill his guts on the conspiracy theory Ron Little drummed up.

All of that would have to wait until later for her organized mind to make something of all that disorganized information.

Carter waved her onward and there were plenty of people on the street looking at what was going on.

Scotland wondered if the person responsible for Mrs. Vasquez's condition was somewhere near as he or she would certainly be interested in seeing what their work did in making them a certain celebrity at the moment. She scanned some of the faces, but nothing seemed out of the ordinary.

Scotland got comfortable in her seat and smiled over at Carter who always managed to have a carefree and winsome grin on her face after such a hectic event. She took a breath and closed her eyes. She felt her hand interlace with Carter's as good friends do.

Carter gave it a squeeze. "She'll be alright…" She looked over at her best friend and smiled at her. "Mrs. Vasquez. She'll be fine. You saved her life, Scotty."

Scotland acknowledged her friend and smiled back at her. "Thanks for your help."

Carter wondered what was going through that head of hers. She knew Scotland was ruminating through all the information and wondered what she would do next. Whatever it was, Scotland could always count on her. She would never leave her friend hanging. "My pleasure…" She too wondered about the events. "I wonder who would target her like that."

Scotland shrugged her shoulders and she was still deep in thought.

Mason feathered the throttle and threaded the Bentley though the crowd.

Scotland knew she had to do something because, in her mind, something was not sitting right. Ordinarily, she would leave it up to the police to work on this case, but since it was a friend who was hurt, and she knew something was awry, it was up to her to make it right.

But all of that would have to wait because dinner was on the menu.

Chapter 8

It was a bright and sunny Monday morning in LA – as always. Scotland's weekday mornings always started with her personal trainer working her like a pack mule in her fully equipped gymnasium, adjacent to her aunt and uncle's main house in toney Beverly Hills. It was not for a lack of trying or anything that she could not afford, but when she told them she would be moving to LA they did not take no for an answer. It took six months of preparation time for them to custom build a pool-house that would rival many houses or mansions for that matter. Their Yarde estate took up a significant lot with streets and corners that touched Lexington Road, Glen Way, Oxford Way, and an alley that served as a service lane that looped up behind the Beverly Hills Hotel – another Yarde favorite. It also had the benefit of a separate entrance for their main house and one for Scotland's pool house. The construction of the gym was an added bonus as was the track installed for outdoor runs – just because she asked, and they could.

All their children were raising their families in the four corners of the planet, and the expansive property was too large just for the two of them and their loyal staff. They wanted Scotland to partake in the excess that only they could bestow on her. Since her parents were on the East Coast, her aunt and uncle would be her West Coast parents. They doted on her and gave her the freedom to decorate the interior as she saw fit and when she did arrive, the gorgeous poolside house was ready for her – all fifteen hundred square feet overlooking the Olympic-sized saltwater pool. It was a resort-like, verdant oasis for stress-free living in a metropolis like Los Angeles.

That was two years ago, and it would not seem right for her to move out even if she could conceive of a good enough reason. She stayed rent-free and all utilities were taken care of – she just paid for her own essentials – much like her personal trainer, Cross-Fit-Rob, who relished in punishing her to the nth degree because he had a certain look for her that she did demand, and his motto was 'Look Fucking Good Naked' which she certainly lived up to thanks in no small part to him.

After her morning ablutions she sat down to a well-deserved breakfast and sipped her Americano expressly made by her Miele built-in espresso machine. She managed to call the hospital early to check with the nurse and was a little concerned to find out that Mrs. Vasquez was in an induced coma and would remain that way until her doctor deemed it otherwise. She gave Emilio her word that all the hospital bills would be taken care of –

especially considering Mrs. Vasquez was a hospital guest in the Yarde Medical Center Intensive Care Unit.

She apprised her aunt and uncle about what had happened over the weekend, and they were aghast and could not wrap their heads around the very notion that a murder conspiracy could and would revolve around a pension fund. Scotland let on what she planned to do to get to the bottom of the mystery and they supported her like a doting Nick and Nora Charles.

She texted Carter and advised her too, and Carter responded that she thought she was out of her fucking mind but would be available to bail her out of jail if the need arose. Scotland sarcastically thanked her with a round of pointed expletives and inappropriate emojis to boot. A smile curled over her mouth when Carter responded in kind in only the best way she could – a picture of her flipping her off.

Scotland would have to do this on her own as Carter had a number of social engagements and sponsorships that required her undivided attention, and Instagram pictures for herself in some half-naked pose to satisfy their corporate hunger and the hunger of her eighty-million Instagram followers.

Scotland secured the pivot front door and waved to Juan and his crew as they expertly tended to the lush landscaping just outside Scotland's pool house – affectionately known as Scotland's Yard.

She got comfortable in the Bentley GT Convertible parked under her pool house porte cochère and fired up the beast's W12 powerplant. It growled to life and she felt that it was a top-down morning and proceeded to make it so.

She had managed to procure a last-minute audience with SoCal Management Company Incorporated and its CEO, Dirk Stafford. It did not take much as she only had to email him and follow it up with a call – it was that easy. She piloted the gorgeous car down the streets, and it ate the asphalt with gusto. The miles effortlessly disappeared quickly as she headed to their headquarters located in Century City in Tower One at Century Plaza Towers.

She wondered how she was going to ask Dirk about the goings-on that filled her weekend. She knew he would take the line of questioning well because he was in fact a friend of another friend of the family. She knew she had to proceed with caution and question him gingerly or there could be trouble on the horizon. She already advised her aunt and uncle and for good measure she spoke with her dad who always provided her with sound legal advice.

There was a hint of caution in her eyes hidden behind her Tom Ford sunglasses, and she pursed her lips and wondered what the best strategy would be to get this meeting successfully out of the way – and then head into work at the University. She chewed her thoughts and weighed all the options in her head and chose what she thought was best.

"You got us…" Dirk Stafford held up his hands to surrender. "We did it, Scotland."

Scotland marvelled at Dirk's playful and non-explosive reaction to her just coming out and stated what she knew already. Her eyes scanned the view from his top floor northeast office with a spectacular shot of the LA cityscape. She pursed her lips apologetically, and her head tilted to the side as if to offer her condolences for bluntly telling him what she knew. "I'm sorry, Dirk…" She saw him hold up his hand to stop her from apologizing, and he pouted and shook his head.

"No apology needed, Scotland – and no offence taken…" He sat on his commanding desk and unbuttoned his bespoke suit's jacket to get comfortable. "Being a fund management company for the largest pension in California I've heard it all, I've been accused of all, and I've seen it all."

Scotland was concerned he would take it the wrong way, but he was very polite and understanding especially when someone accused your company of conspiracy and, potentially, murder. "Dirk, there was just no way for me to beat around the bush and let you know what I know. It was not my intention to accuse or incriminate you in any way or your company." She pleaded with him with her eyes.

Dirk Stafford smiled and leaned forward. "Don't worry at all about it…" He popped up his eyebrows and smiled politely. "In fact, I'm glad you brought this to my attention. If there is any hint of rumor that this may or may not be happening…" He postured a reassuring thumb in his direction. "I need to know about it and see if it is true…" He picked up his coffee and took a sip. "I've a lot of employees and I need to know what each of them is up to, and if something like this is happening, I need to investigate it. Even if it is a rumor." His eyes had that conviction in them that he would indeed investigate it.

Scotland leaned forward with her cup of delicious coffee nestled in her hands. "It's all just conjecture, Dirk…" She licked her lips. "But I thought you should know."

Dirk gave her a reassuring nod and his look thanked her for bringing it to his attention – in-person no less. There was nothing he enjoyed more than a polite and beautiful woman sitting in his office. "You do me the honor of having you in my office, Scotland."

Scotland feigned embarrassment. "I just thought you should know the police are also involved in this."

Dirk tilted his head back and pursed his lips. "Yes..." His eyes narrowed and his mind raced. "I was wondering why I had a message from a Detective Hansen..." He shrugged politely. "Something to do with a Mrs. Vasquez. I've still got to call him back, though."

Scotland nodded and sipped her delicious coffee. "Yes. I ran into him and his partner on Saturday at her house..." She pursed her lips and wondered just how much he knew about what happened to her. "Did the detective elaborate?"

Dirk shook his head and had a pensive look. "Does Mrs. Vasquez have anything to do with this murder conspiracy you told me about?" He arched his eyebrow Mr. Spock style.

Scotland nodded her head. "Her husband died last week."

Dirk nodded and he was in a ponderous mood given that his company may have had something to do with it. "Was he a client?"

"I believe so." Scotland sipped her coffee to wet her whistle. "Juan Vasquez..." She pulled her mouth to the side. "Not sure if he had a middle name."

Dirk's eyes brightened up and he held his finger up like Yosemite Sam firing off a round. A smile curled across his mouth as he scooted to his computer. He let out an investigative sigh as he mumbled and typed on his keyboard – and hit enter. The screen lit up and there was an astonished look plastered across his face. "Here you are. Seems there are a lot of Juan Vasquez's but only one that retired in the last two years..." He studied the confidential file information and relayed what he could out loud. "Juan Emilio Vasquez. Worked in the Los Angeles County Sanitation Department. Hmm. Diabetic..." He cleared his throat politely and pursed his lips. "Did not take the longterm health insurance option. Wife – Esmerelda and grandson Emilio..." He almost pouted at the seemingly endless information only a man in his position would want to know. "Looks like there are no other family members."

Scotland shook her head. "Yes. Very small tight-knit family."

Dirk looked up at her. "I hope Mrs. Vasquez is alright after what happened."

Scotland shook her head. It was a lot more hope than before but still touch-and-go. "She's in a medically-induced coma."

Dirk looked shocked. "Oh dear…" His eyes were open wide with concern. "Well, I'm sure she is getting the best medical help especially with such a good friend as you, looking after her well-being."

Scotland smiled and nodded. "Yes. I'm good friends with her grandson Emilio."

Dirk nodded and smiled at her politely.

Scotland took this as her cue to leave the meeting. There was nothing else to talk about and she had to get to work. "Dirk, it was a pleasure talking with you. I'm sure you have a busy day."

Dirk smiled and got up. He took her cup and placed it on his desk. "Scotland, it was a pleasure meeting you and please extend my best to your uncle. If there is anything SoCal can do for Yarde Pharmaceuticals, please just have him call me."

Scotland smiled and shook his hand. "Thank you, Dirk. I will definitely mention it to him."

Dirk showed her out through the front and pressed the elevator button for her. "If there's anything else you would like to discuss, please feel to call me on my private line…" He grinned brilliantly at her. "I'm always happy to talk with you."

Scotland smiled as she stepped inside the waiting elevator. "I will, Dirk…" She waved. "Thank you for the delicious coffee."

The doors closed and Scotland smiled as she looked at the news monitor letting her know of some of the current events and good work SoCal does with a number of homeless charities, rehabilitation centers and the California penal system. Her eyes also glanced at the interior security camera indiscreetly housed in the ballistic cover.

Dirk passed his executive assistant and smiled at her brilliantly. His voice had that sing-song tone to it, "Marjorie…" He looked like his request was nothing out of the ordinary. "Please cancel all of my meetings for the rest of the day."

Marjorie nodded and had his calendar open. "Right away, Mr. Stafford."

Dirk strolled into his office and closed his doors.

He let out a miffed exhale as he marched to his desk and sat down. He picked up the phone – and dialled the number off by heart.

The voice on the other end answered in a monotone grunt, "Hello."

Dirk paused for half-a-heartbeat and pursed his lips. The meeting was not what he was expecting on a Monday morning because someone was sloppy. "It's me…" His mood clouded with a more serious tone. He was not a happy camper and he let the person on the other end of the line know it.

"We've got a problem…" His eyes and brow narrowed with an evil bent. "And, when I say we, I mean you."

The voice paused and breathed a sigh over the line. "Where do you want to meet?"

Dirk pursed his lips and let his breathing do the talking. There was a labored sigh as things got out of hand recently. For years it was going well – hand over fist kind of stuff. Now, for some reason there were questions – questions that should not have answers. "I have to pick up some flowers…" He thought for a moment and wondered if he should kill two birds with one stone and thought – 'fuck it.' He pursed his lips and let out another deep sigh. "Let's meet at the LA Flower Market."

The voice on the line paused. There was silence and then a murmur, "Fine. One hour…" The voice was also not happy and groaned out over the line, "The sighing isn't necessary and not appreciated."

Dirk closed his eyes and let his head tilt back and be caught by the Herman Miller headrest. "There wouldn't be any sighing or this call if your man wasn't so sloppy."

The voice paused and then the silence was broken once more, "Let's talk about it face-to-face and not over the line."

Dirk nodded and this time he did not care. He groaned out loud, "Suits me just fine. One hour."

"Fine."

Dirk narrowed his eyes as he sat up and leaned forward. "Fine, right back at you." He hung up the phone and looked at it. "Asshole." He chewed his thoughts and now he had to deal with this issue. He wondered, 'where did it start to go sideways?'

Dirk sauntered around the heavenly displays of flowers as far as the eyes could see. The scents assaulted his senses and he loved it. He waited until he saw his guest and decided to make the plunge on a rather full bouquet that just burst with color.

He paid and left the florist a healthy tip and then made his way to his guest who moved away from him to the Wall Street and East 8th entrance. It was a busy and noisy corner perfect for a clandestine meeting in case they were being monitored.

Dirk exited with his booty and saw his guest as he sat unceremoniously on a bench. His partner sipped a coffee, and he made his way closer to him.

Dirk sat down and leaned back not too worried whether the bench would dirty his bespoke suit. He had other things on his mind right now that would result in a prison-orange jumper for several life sentences – if convicted. He looked at Detectives Hansen and Marx with a derisive glare and waited for them to explain themselves.

Hansen had a perplexed look. "What seems to be the problem?" He had a matter-of-fact look plastered on his weathered face. "Huh?"

Dirk took a deep breath of the downtown LA air and he was almost pleased at the acrid smells as they mixed with the sweet smells of the flowers. "My problem is that Scotland Yarde showed up at my office this morning."

Marx sipped and swallowed, and he looked at Stafford with an impertinent glare. "LA is a little out of their jurisdiction." There was a smug look on his face as he rested his coffee on the bench beside him. He reached into his pocket and pulled out an open packet of Halls cherry flavored cough drops and toyed with it in his fingers. He unwrapped it and popped it in his mouth, and the cherry and menthol mixed with the coffee flavor. Even after all these years he still appreciated them but could not recall when he became addicted to their sickly, sweet flavor.

Dirk pulled his mouth to the side and narrowed his eyes at the pain-in-his-ass. "Not Scotland Yard the British police force..." He rolled his eyes at him for being a smartass. "Scotland Yarde the little lady and a formidable one at that..." He shifted where he sat and looked at Hansen and Marx. "She was at my office this morning asking questions about that Vasquez woman who should be dead as a doornail right now but seems to be in a medically induced coma."

Hansen piped up. "Which one is she again?" His head volleyed to Marx and then Stafford. "There were two of them there. Scotland and her friend Carter Deklava."

Marx just shrugged his shoulders and went back to his delicious coffee.

Dirk let out a low exasperated sigh. "The one that looks like Kristen Stewart."

Hansen tilted his head back and smirked. "Oh right..." He nodded his head comically and thought back to Saturday. "Her, but more smiley."

Stafford nodded. "Yeah..." He got back to the problem at hand. "So, how did your guy mess up?"

Hansen stewed for a second and curled his mouth up. He shook his head and was trying to figure out how they could extricate themselves from this mess. It was if the problems were slowly pointing in their direction so they could get caught. "He injected her with a rather large dose of insulin, but she was not diabetic."

Stafford looked at him quizzically. "Yes, I know. The husband was diabetic."

Hansen nodded. "Yes, but our man thought she was because the prescription had her name on it…" His head tick-tocked from side-to-side. "So, he assumed he could make it look like an accidental overdose and case closed."

Stafford interjected. "Yeah…" He narrowed his eyes at the two detectives. "Only not so case closed. In fact, case not closed…" His voice started to rise. "Case very much fucking still open."

Marx paused and snapped his head to the asshole. "Keep your voice down, Stafford."

Stafford looked squarely at him and levelled his angry eyes at Marx. "Just drink your coffee and suck on your cough drop…" His finger wagged between him and Hansen. "The grown-ups are talking."

Marx's eyes opened with hurt in them. He was about to get violent with the man, come what may but he felt Hansen's arm block him across the chest.

Stafford glared at Marx. "Still getting your dad to defend you, huh?"

Hansen looked at Stafford with a certain amount of public safety. He murmured to him matter-of-factly, "If you keep poking the bear, I'm going to have to let it claw the fuck outta you, Dirk."

Stafford did not care. He had a lot riding on this, and it was him that brought the two of them into the fold because they were desperate for fast cash. "I don't give a shit about him or you. We've got a loose end – that Vasquez woman…" He made sure Hansen and Marx knew where he was coming from with just a stare. "And we've got a loose cannon – Scotland Yarde." He glared at them both. "Question is what're you going to do about it?"

Hansen could not deny things were getting a little out of hand. These murders were supposed to look like accidents, and they should have been tied up with a bow. Instead, it was a hastily packed suitcase with wires sticking out of it. He pursed his lips and he looked at Marx and then turned to Stafford. "We've got to first tie up the loose end of the assassin who missed his mark."

"Ah, yes…" Stafford shook his head at the unclean and improperly prepared assassin. "Wile E. Coyote needs to disappear. I don't want that ex-con growing a conscience."

Marx shook his head. "It was his first assignment…" He glared at Stafford and then looked at Hansen with a pleading look. "He's just a kid."

Hansen shook his head. "He messed up big time."

Marx shook his head at his partner. "It wasn't his fault. For all intents and purposes, he did the right thing. How was he supposed to know the old lady wasn't a diabetic? Huh?" He looked at Hansen incredulously. "Her name was all over the prescription."

Stafford looked at Hansen and then at Marx. "So, you want to go to prison for his error?"

Marx blinked blankly at him. He did not like him, but he knew he was right. He could not have any loose ends to draw attention to their operation and especially to them all – the Star Chamber. He simply shook his head in agreement with them both. "So…" He let out an exasperated sigh and wondered how they should do it. "Do we make it clean or dirty?"

Stafford looked at them both. "Make it look anyway you like, just make sure he stays dead…" He smirked at them both. "For all our sakes."

Hansen nodded. "And what about the Vasquez woman and Scotland Yarde?"

Stafford looked at him. "There's no way we can touch them now. It'll make it too obvious…" He screwed his mouth to the side and thought about it. "Hopefully, if we plant something on Mr. Coyote, and the Vasquez woman wakes up maybe you can say it was a robbery meant to look like an accident."

Hansen looked at him perplexed. "Nothing was stolen. Why would he try to make a robbery look like an accident when nothing was stolen?"

Stafford dropped his head and groaned out loud. "I'm not the criminal mastermind…" He looked at them with angry eyes. "I'm just fucking spit-balling here."

Marx chimed in. "You brought us in on your little scheme so don't think you're not the mastermind behind this or innocent in what we've done so far."

"You needed the money because of your shitty investment skills of buying high and selling low…" Stafford pointed an accusatory finger right at him. "You needed cash – I had an idea. That's when chance meets opportunity. You and your partner were the muscle to make it all look like accidents…" He tilted his head. "And make it look like accidents you did."

Hansen held out his hand to calm them both down. "Okay…" He knew they were not getting anywhere arguing amongst themselves. They needed to just get shit done. "The ship has already hit the iceberg, there's enough blame to go around and we're all on this sinking ship together so let's figure a way to get off."

Stafford hemmed-and-hawed. "And the last thing we need to do is draw any more attention to our operation. We should shelve everything for a while."

Marx glared at him like he was talking shit. "And just how long is a while? Huh?"

Stafford narrowed his eyes and growled at him. "A year at least. We need this to blow over."

Marx was incredulous. "A year?" He scoffed at that tentative timeline. "Are you outta your mind? We've got a payroll of seasoned troublemakers that'll sell us out if we don't keep providing them with work."

Stafford held his hand up in protest. "Hey. You wanted to involve ex-cons in this scheme. I liked it when it was a homegrown internal operation."

Hansen looked at him with a perplexed look. "Do you know how big California is and how many people are retired and part of the pension fund you manage? Huh?" He shook his head. "There was no way to make enough money when it was just the three of us and I fucking hate travelling to shitholes to do a job..." He looked at Stafford. "Have you ever been to Hamburg Farms or Jamesburg?" He snorted a derisive laugh. "I ask you. Who the fuck decides to retire in shitholes like that? Huh? We should've just left them because those places are hell on Earth already."

Stafford looked at Hansen and then and Marx. "You know very well why. Those retirees had some of the richest pensions and their payments had to be curtailed."

Marx scoffed. "They could've retired in Boca or Miami..." His head tick-tocked from side-to-side. "I'd have gone and tied a little vacation time in on the side while I was at it."

Hansen looked at Stafford. "We're not shutting down operations. The Vasquez woman is an isolated incident..." He smirked a little. "An unforeseen circumstance. That's all."

Marx nudged him. "Tell him about the reporter."

Stafford sat up like a frightened ostrich. "Reporter? What reporter?" He could feel his blood pressure spiking. "No one mentioned anything about a fucking reporter." His head volleyed between the two of them.

Hansen poo-pooed his initial fright about the news. "He's a nobody. A washout. A has been." He shook his head not bothering too much about the incident and a little ticked Marx brought it up. "No one is going to believe anything he says."

Marx narrowed his eyes at his partner. "Scotland and her friend believed him."

Hansen closed his eyes and wished Marx would just shut the fuck up. He side-eyed him but it was too late. The cat was now out of the bag.

Stafford could feel his anxiety rise to Mount Everest proportions. He clenched his jaw and wondered what else the detectives were holding back from him. "Scotland Yarde and Carter Deklava know this reporter?"

Hansen nodded his head and now had to spill to Stafford. "Yeah, they know him..." He looked intently at Stafford. "So what?"

Stafford was incredulous. He let out a groan and rolled his head back like he lost all muscle control in his neck. "It means she is not letting on what she knows and is just fishing. That's what." He paused and then turned to them both. "Is there anything else you're neglecting to tell me?"

Marx looked at Hansen and he knew they should tell him about the other thing. "The reporter had a listening device in the kitchen, and it uploads the recording to the Cloud."

Stafford dropped his flowers on the ground and dropped his head in his hands. There was a low guttural groan coming from him and he wished he had a time machine. "For fucksake..." He play-sobbed because he could feel the walls closing in on them all. "You guys have to tell me these things. Plausible deniability doesn't work with us and what we're doing. That means the device could have taped everything that happened in that kitchen between the old woman and Mr. Coyote."

Hansen nodded. "Seems so..." He swallowed. "We're holding the reporter in lock-up for now. The worst part is over if we just take care of Mr. Coyote, then we can tie that loose end up."

Stafford had a worried look on his face. "Yes, but there are so many other loose ends." He groaned at them both, and half-heartedly kicked the bouquet into the street to take it out on something. "Just remember my friends. Anyone who has ever said that orange is the new black is full of fucking shit." He shook his head and now started to get worried.

Hansen piped up. "Okay. We'll take care of Mr. Coyote and then we'll worry about what to do about the reporter."

Stafford got up and looked at them both. "Okay." He adjusted his jacket and pursed his lips. "Let's hope we don't have any more of these surprises or you can kiss your pensions goodbye and we may be sharing a cell or worse."

Marx pursed his lips. "We'll fix this."

Stafford namasted each of them individually. "For all of our sakes I hope you're right, detectives."

Hansen nodded. He looked over at the kicked to the curb bunch of flowers in the gutter. "Aren't you going to be needing those?"

Stafford took a deep breath to collect his thoughts and glanced over. He shook his head. "They were for my girlfriend, but I'm just not in the mood anymore."

Marx looked at him quizzically. "Aren't you married?" He screwed his mouth up at him.

Stafford looked at him and Hansen matter-of-factly. "Aren't the both of you also married?" He cocked an eyebrow and tilted his head to the side to let them know he also knew about them, too. "Hasn't stopped either of you from your side pieces, has it?"

Hansen looked up at him and growled. "I think it's time you left before shit goes down, okay?"

Stafford volleyed his head at them both and pursed his lips. He let out an exasperated sigh along with a derisive command, "Just get this cleaned up." He buttoned up his jacket because that is the way a bespoke jacket should be done up. "Before this gets more out of hand."

Marx play saluted to him as he sipped his coffee. "Yes, sir..." He narrowed his eyes at him because he did not like him one bit. "Right away, sir." He felt Hansen put his arm across his chest.

Hansen looked up at Stafford. "We know what we're supposed to do, Dirk."

Stafford was about to say something smarmy again but just left them with a smug look on his face as a parting gesture.

He turned and walked away. No flowers and in no mood for an afternoon delight.

Marx growled as he watched Stafford walk away. "That guy is an asshole."

Hansen watched him too. His mind clouded with things he had to do because it was getting out of hand. His mouth pulled to the side and he thought of things that needed to be done to tie up some of the pending loose ends. "Mm-hm..." He scanned the street and let out a sigh. "A real asshole."

Marx finished his coffee and started to play with his cup. He side-eyed his partner and saw him deep in thought. He was always the planner and he looked to him for guidance. He would always support his partner no matter what. "What do you want to do first?"

Hansen curled his mouth up and looked at Marx. "Let's figure out a way to get rid of Mr. Coyote."

Marx nodded. "We're going to have to make sure that guy doesn't have anything on him to tie us to him."

Hansen nodded in agreement. "Yeah..." He thought long and hard. "Moranis is another problem and that fucking bug of his."

Marx nodded and he mumbled matter-of-factly. "The fucker won't talk. You know that."

Hansen looked him in the eyes. "Maybe we should make sure he doesn't talk at all..." He smirked. "Permanently." He snorted a giggle. "Just an idea."

Marx smiled and nodded knowingly. "We've done it before." He thought for a second and looked at Hansen. "What're going to do about Kristen Stewart and her friend Bella Hadid?"

Hansen jolted out of his thought pattern and what he was going to do to the reporter. "What?"

Marx looked at him and shook his head. "The two women..." He narrowed his eyes because he thought his partner would have realized the doppelgangers. "Scotland Yarde and Carter Deklava..." He smirked. "You know. Kristen and Bella." He snorted a giggle.

Hansen tilted his head back now that he realized who his partner was referring to. He took a deep breath. "Yeah..." He bit his bottom lip. "Those two are going to be a bigger problem."

Marx nodded. His eyes twinkled because he had an idea to satisfy their situation and one of their stand-by assassins. "We could get you know who to take care of them both." A smile curled over his mouth.

Hansen scoffed at the suggestion. "We're not using that fucking freak on anything, anymore understand?" He looked at Marx and was more forceful. "Understand?"

"Okay." Marx held up his hands and knew the guy's reputation. "Just thought it would be a good idea to make an example of them."

Hansen shook his head. "Example of them is right..." He shook his again head to try and put it out of his mind. "That would guarantee no open casket funeral for them that's for sure." He sighed. "C'mon. We better get back to work."

Chapter 9

"So…" Carter looked at Scotland as she sipped her coffee. "What happened?"

Scotland pursed her mouth and tick-tocked her head. "Surprisingly, he did not fly off the handle like I expected him to…" She looked at Carter's reaction. "Even after I just bluntly told him."

Carter chewed her thoughts and pulled her mouth to the side. "Yeah, that's odd."

Scotland looked at her anxiously. "So, what did your spiders find out about Dirk?"

Carter pulled out her iPhone.

Scotland looked at it and then at her. "Is that a new one?"

Carter nodded her head. "I didn't like the other one."

"Why?" Scotland was perplexed, as always, with Carter's purchasing power and shopper's remorse that she did not get the other one. "What was wrong with it this time?"

Carter rubbed the new phone. "This one's the Rose Gold…" She blinked at her blankly. "The other one wasn't."

"Well, that's as good a reason as any." Scotland shook her head and cocked an eyebrow up at her vapidness.

Carter found the email and she sent it to Scotland's phone. She started to read through it with delight and was shocked at some of the information on Dirk Stafford especially the highlights noted in the rather thick file of information her spiders garnered on him. She pulled her mouth to the side and murmured to Scotland who also scanned the information with zest and shock. "Hmm…" Her eyes were wide at some of the highlights and lowlights. "Seems our Mr. Dirk Stafford is a bit of a douche."

Scotland could not deny the information. He was a player throughout his highschool years right up until now. "Mm-hm…" There was a worried look on her brow as she read through the information and she shook her head at his less than stellar history which primarily involved women. "He's a misogynistic douche."

Carter looked at her friend with haughty derision. "And you want this guy to manage the Yarde Family Trust?" She scoffed readily at that suggestion. She growled in protest, "I-think-not." She pursed her lips and shook her head with playful disappointment.

Scotland looked at her sideways. "It was just a ruse to get into his office, Carter…" She pursed her lips at her, and matter-of-factly mumbled, "Calm the fuck down."

Carter's eyes dropped to the screen once more. She shook her head. "Seems he was into all sorts of mischief in University…" She pursed her lips, and her eyes told the story the more she read. "Hmm, there were a number of alleged assaults, no convictions because his family either paid them off or made them go away somehow."

Scotland could not believe what she was reading. "Seems like he's still doing it even to this day." She fumed at his behaviour and thought it was lucky she did not know of this information beforehand, otherwise it would have clouded her judgement of him then and there.

Carter shook her head in disgust, and she looked up at Scotland. She groaned out her distaste for the man and his family, "Fucking rich people." She let out an exasperated sigh, dipped her head and went back to reading the information.

Scotland's mouth dropped open and she simply looked at her friend and her hypocritical view of the world. She pursed her lips because she thought she should rebut that comment but thought twice and went back to finishing off the dossier on Dirk Stafford – surreptitiously procured by Carter's many spiders. "I can't believe your spiders got all of this information – and unredacted no less." She nodded her head with approval.

Carter smiled and shrugged. "My minions serve their purpose. What can I tell you?" She snorted and sneered at her power.

Scotland shook her head and cocked an eyebrow up at her. "By the way, I haven't heard from Richard, either."

Carter scanned the gorgeous UCLA campus and stopped. Her head snapped to Scotland and a devious smile curled across her mouth and her just-threaded eyebrows popped-up.

Scotland saw that and her head tilted to the side and she let out her customary groan. "Oh god…" She rolled her eyes at her with impertinence. "You've either got something smarmy to say, just thought of something devious to do, or just cut a silent but deadly one…" She glared at her with derision. "Which one is it?"

Carter scoffed comically at her friend. "Umm…" Her finger pointed to the air like she was counting a bouncing ball. "No, yes, yes – but earlier." She snorted a giggle.

Scotland simply closed her eyes and wondered why she egged her on. She let out an exasperated sigh and looked at her gorgeous friend. "Okay…" She pursed her lips with intensity. "What's your idea? Hit me with it."

Carter's eyes opened wide to lay it on her. "We contact those two officers. You know, the studly dude and that Amazon you had your goo-goo eyes all over." She popped-up her eyebrows knowingly.

Scotland scoffed at her. "What?" She acted like she forgot. "Which ones were they?"

Carter narrowed her eyes interrogatively. "Playing stupid with me isn't going to work, babe." She smacked her lips and thought of Nate, the rather tall and gorgeous Boris-Kodjoe-hunk of man and her salacious mind wandered.

Scotland feigned like she finally clued in. "Oh…" There was a slight smirk on her face, and she chuckled. "You mean those two."

Carter sneered and nodded her head sarcastically. "Yeah, those two. The ones that looked they were chiseled out of marble." She slid her hand over her body sexy-like and winked at Scotland. "I know you've been thinking of Officer Hernandez and what she could do to those perfect stems of yours if she split you open…" She acted like she had a reading from the future and comically gestured to her. "I see scissors sharpening in your future, Scotland." She snorted a giggle because she knew she was funny to the core. "A big pair…" She paused, pointed, and popped-up her perfectly groomed eyebrows at her. "And a small pair." She guffawed this time.

Scotland winced and screwed her mouth to the side. "She's not that tall." She smacked her lips and just wanted to talk about Officer Kate Hernandez some more.

Carter narrowed her eyes and knew she was full of shit. "Give me a break, Scotty…" She rolled her eyes at her for even suggesting such a dubious observation. "You're just scissor-sizing her up…" She pursed her lips and shook her head derisively. "You know perfectly well how tall she is vertically…" She looked at her unapologetically and with a hint of smarm. "You're just thinking about her horizontally, aren't you? Splayed out on that Hastens mattress of yours."

Scotland shook her head at her. "It's not all about sex, Carter." She leaned into her and went into lecture-mode. "It's about communication and compatibility. It's about the right fit."

Carter rolled her eyes even more this time and twice around. "Ugh. Blah-blah, blah-blah-blah…" Her body shivered in denial. "You sound like an eHarmony commercial…" She looked deep into her friend's eyes. "Just admit you want to put that English degree of yours to good use, and cunning linguist her until she blacks out."

Scotland snorted a laugh. Her head tick-tocked from side-to-side and knew Carter had her dead to rights. A salacious smile curled over her kissable mouth. "Fine..." She looked at her with conviction. "You got me, your honor."

"Phhhfft..." Carter shook her head at her. "Stop denying the inevitable, Scotty. She's fucking gorgeous and your parents will love her. Admit it. All six feet plus of legs, ass and shoulders of her."

Scotland reached over and squeezed her friend's hand and loved how understanding she was. She could not deny that Carter Deklava was also a gorgeous woman who men and women pined for and she knew it. "You're a really good friend..." She teared-up a little and let out a happy sigh. "And a bit of an asshole sometimes."

Carter shrugged and smiled. She returned the squeeze, and she would always be there to support her best friend. "You know me so well." She playfully batted her eyelids adoringly at her.

However, something behind Scotland caught Carter's undivided attention.

Scotland narrowed her eyes at her. "Just so we're on the same page of secretly lusting after someone..." She leaned into her because she saw what was going down that night, and if it were more private, it would have been Carter. "I saw you twirling your frosted extensions at Officer Murdock."

Carter moaned deliciously as her mouth watered and her eyes sparkled. "Mmm..." She licked her lips and smacked them. She let out a guttural groan to satiate her hunger. "I feel like some hot chocolate."

Scotland was aghast at her friend for thinking such a thing and there was a look of horror painted across her face as she decided she had crossed a line for her ribald thinking. "Carter Deklava the Fifth..." She shook her head at her disrespectful friend. "That is so inappropriate referring to Officer Murdock that way."

Carter paused and turned her attention to Scotland derisively judging her in that way for no reason. There was a perplexed look on her face as she looked through her friend. "What?" She reeled back not knowing what she was going on about, and she sized her up-and-down. "What're you talking about?"

Scotland narrowed her judgemental eyes at her friend who should know better than to make a reference such as that. "Referring to him as hot chocolate just because he's..."

Carter cut her off and looked at her with awestruck eyes as she pointed at the UCLA Java Stand that just put out a sign. "I want hot chocolate." She saw Scotland's freaked out look draw across her face as she turned around to confirm that there was indeed a sign.

Scotland's jaw dropped. 'Yep...fuck!' Her mind raced on how to save her reputation, but she was coming up blank. She turned back to Carter and saw her narrow her eyes at her. She swallowed hard and felt her face blush out of embarrassment. "Umm..." She watched her friend stay silent so she could squirm, but she swallowed and cleared her throat. "Did you want a large one?"

Carter blinked at her and pursed her lips. "Mm-hm." She nodded ever so slightly.

Scotland took a breath and felt her mouth go dry because Carter had her on the ropes. "With whip or without?"

She replied matter-of-factly because who the hell has hot chocolate without whip cream? "With."

Scotland piloted the Bentley over Highway 10 with the top down. In the passenger seat Carter was deliciously sipping her decadent beverage, and she kept side-eyeing her as she would take a small sip and lick the lid lasciviously. Her embarrassment did not relent, and her face remained flush.

Carter side-eyed her with a healthy smirk on her face. She giggled cutely and would let out a satisfied "Ahh." After each small and delicious sip, and generously smacked her lips.

She pointed to the cup and raised her eyebrows above her designer Tom Ford sunglasses. "This hot chocolate is delicious."

Scotland groaned and wondered when they would get to the Grand Central Market and meet up with the two gorgeous officers for a late lunch and some casual conversation. They did in fact confirm Richard Moranis was a guest at the LAPD lock-up mainly because of the listening device found in Mrs. Vasquez's kitchen. He could not and would not deny it. She shook her head and mumbled to Carter, "Who in their right mind places an 'if found, please call...' sticker on a listening device?"

Carter shook her head and wondered the same thing. She pursed her lips and gave a slight shrug. "He probably did not want to lose it because he probably thinks he'll need to sell it soon for the money..." She snorted a giggle. "That or both his kidneys."

Scotland pursed her lips and side-eyed her friend. "Just drink your hot chocolate."

Carter grinned cutely and leaned close to her friend. She responded in her little-girl voice, "Yes, mummy." And, giggled out loud.

Scotland just let out a playful and exasperated sigh.

The drive into downtown was quick and painless as traffic was surprisingly light for that time of day. Scotland headed down Hill Street and into the Grand Central Market parking lot just half a block down. Open-air, it was a perfect parking venue but she closed her roof just in case.

They strolled out back onto Hill Street and were surprised to see the two officers as they waited for them on the corner of 3rd.

Scotland beamed as she saw the two of them casually standing there like a couple of Blue Knights. She waved courteously and headtossed at the gorgeous Amazon. Her hair was perfectly braided and now in the early afternoon sun she almost glowed like a goddess. Her mouth dropped open and she saw her return her smile with some added teeth in a grin that would melt hearts and wet panties. She just let out a little schoolgirl like giggle and felt her heart flutter.

Carter smiled at the gorgeous Officer Nate Murdock and saw him wave and return her smile. She side-eyed Scotland and murmured, "Wipe your mouth, Scotty..." She took another sip of her beverage. "You're drooling."

Scotland nonchalantly swiped her arm up and surreptitiously did as she was told. She felt giddy and continued to giggle. She admired Officer Kate Hernandez and stood front-and-center with her and had to look up. "Hi."

Kate was lost in her smile and she acknowledged her with a nudge and beamed back politely. "Hi..." She licked her lips and started to giggle and be awkward. "I like your outfit."

Scotland smiled at her and giggled. "I like yours too." She always admired someone in uniform.

They continued to stare at each other, and the silence started to become awkward and deafening especially for that part of town.

Carter's head volleyed between the two of them and she side-eyed Nate who stared at her and wondered what he should do. "Okay..." She waved her hand in the general direction. "Shall we go eat?"

Scotland nodded and took the lead with Kate beside her. And she could not be happier. "Sure. Let's eat."

Carter rolled her eyes and pursed her lips. "Great idea..." She followed them with Nate beside her. She mumbled under her breath, "Now that we got that awkwardness out of the way."

Nate looked at her inquisitively, and asked her in a cool-sort-of-way, "So, what're you drinking?"

Carter nonchalantly held the cup and swirled the liquid left inside. Her head tilted invitingly at him. "It's hot chocolate and it's delicious." She tempted him with her look.

Nate smirked and comically leaned into her and responded matter-of-factly in a low murmur, "Just like me."

Carter's head tilted and nodded at his apparent coolness toward what she already thought and giggled at him. "Yes, you are." She playfully nudged him because there was chemistry there and some sexual tension and innuendo.

Nate acted surprised and was playfully shocked at her. He playfully mumbled to her. "You mean you agree that I'm like hot chocolate."

Carter curled her salacious mouth to the side and growled at him in a low tone. "Yeah..." She licked her lips because she had to tempt the god-like man as her ribald thoughts overtook her senses. "And I'm sure you're delicious."

Nate giggled and beamed at her. He was speechless.

Carter politely offered up her chalice of decadence to drink from, and he humbly accepted without question.

"That's a really nice car you have." Kate licked her lips and had to make small talk just so she could look at the gorgeous and diminutive woman – compared to her, of course – who was setting her senses aglow.

Scotland smiled and nodded. Her head leaned into her so she could invade her personal space and get a smell of the gorgeous woman that was making the butterflies attack her stomach. She felt antsy and she never felt like this before. "Thanks..." She played with her hair even though she did not need to. "It's new..." She perked up her eyebrows. "Perhaps I can take you out for a ride sometime."

Kate nodded and her eyes lit up. "I'd love to. I've never been in a Bentley before."

Scotland smiled up at her. "Maybe we can grab dinner sometime and I can drive – or you can drive it, Kate." She left it open to see if she would bite. It did not occur to her to even find out if she was in a relationship. It did not matter, she flirted with her and that was enough.

Kate nodded in agreement. "That sounds great, Scotland." She grinned from ear-to-ear.

Scotland's thoughts wandered at the possibilities of the date and she fist-pumped in her mind. 'Yes!'

They went inside and ordered something quick and sat down at one of the many available benches inside. It was Tacos Tumbras a Tomas for Scotland and Kate, and Egg Slut for Carter and Nate.

Scotland sat across from Kate and admired as she ate – it was the little things. "So, Richard is in lock-up?"

Kate nodded and pursed her lips. "He admitted to the listening device and unless Mrs. Vasquez decides to drop the charges, he could be looking at some time. It's a felony." Her head tick-tocked as she tucked in.

Nate chimed in. "I hope she's okay. We checked in with her grandson and he says that they have her in an induced coma for now."

Carter eyed him and Kate. "Do you have anything to go on? Was there someone there with her?"

Nate and Kate shook their heads.

"We don't know for sure." Kate washed her bite down with a sip of water. "As far as the detectives are concerned it was an accidental overdose."

Scotland shook her head. "Mrs. Vasquez was not diabetic. The prescription may have had her name on it, but it was for her husband. He didn't have any insurance, so she had the free clinic she worked at fill out a prescription in her name."

Kate looked at Scotland and Carter a little perplexed. Her eyes narrowed and she was concerned about that information Scotland just told her. "Are you sure?" She looked at her with an intense interrogative stare.

Scotland nodded her head. "Yes. On Friday when I was at her house, she told me that in front of Emilio."

Kate and Nate stared at each other like there was a piece missing and it was a glaring problem.

Kate leaned in and had a pensive look on her face as she looked at the two women. "That's interesting because that piece of information didn't make it into the detectives' report."

Scotland shook her head vehemently. "I told them that point blank when they questioned Carter and me on Saturday."

Carter nodded her head. She looked at them all. "Do you think they may have missed it by mistake? Or on purpose?"

Scotland tilted her head from side-to-side like a metronome trying to keep the beat of the story balanced. "It's possible they could simply say they forgot to include it, if questioned..." She looked at Nate and Kate. "Promise me you won't say anything to your captain. This knowledge could get you both in trouble and not in the good books with any of the detectives, let alone Hansen and Marx."

Kate and Nate nodded. They were not even supposed to see the report because it was not for their eyes, but they disliked Hansen and Marx so much they wanted to see what was cooking with the case. They managed to surreptitiously procure a copy and read through it with great interest.

Scotland looked at them both. "As soon as we can get access to that recording that Richard has, you can take it to the captain." She saw them both nod their heads.

It was Hansen's and Marx's case so they should not be meddling in it at all anyway. Nate and Kate both agreed.

Carter looked at Scotland. "How do we get access to that recording?"

Scotland had a perplexed look on her face. "Not sure how he kept the recording. Since he doesn't have a cell, I can only assume it uploads to the Cloud."

Carter looked at her and wondered what was going on in that head of hers. "And, how do you plan on getting access to that file with poor Dick locked up?"

"I'm working on it, Carter." Scotland pursed her lips and gave her an impertinent look.

Scotland hemmed-and-hawed and looked at the two officers. "Is he allowed visitors?"

Chapter 10

Hansen and Marx pulled up to the rundown motel and drove into the parking lot. Being that it was an unmarked police car, the hotel did not tend to look at them or for them when they happened to come around and question some of their patrons.

"Which one is he in?" Hansen took a breath and hated doing the wet-work but this one required their undivided attention because they trusted too easily and on someone too young.

Marx looked at him and murmured, "Two-twenty..." He craned his neck and pointed ahead. "There. Second floor around the corner."

"That's good..." Hansen pulled the car into a stall – which there were many because this was the type of motel that people who frequented it either did not have a car; or if they did the car would only be there for the hour because they rented the room for that long – but they only needed ten minutes; the rest was foreplay. "We should go around and make our way to his room, you know..." He smirked as he shut the car off. "Play it cool."

Marx shot him a look. "Do you even know how to play it cool?"

Hansen smirked and he took off his sunglasses. "I did once..." He recalled the days when he was good looking, athletic and desirable. Now he was an average detective with high-cholesterol and high blood pressure. "Way back when Louise still loved me, but shit happens, and time moves on." He gave him a shrug.

Marx opened the glovebox and pulled out the packages with his gloved hands. He slipped them into each of his blazer's breast pockets and pulled his mouth to the side and exhaled a sigh of despair. He said nothing because nothing needed to be said.

Hansen took a gander at him and shook his head. "You know it has to be done..." He gave him a determined expression and scanned the motel and side-eyed the office. "The kid fucked up."

Marx nodded. "Yeah, I know..." He pursed his lips and it was his idea to give the kid a break when he approached them. They did the cursory checks and he was legitimate – and he came recommended; not highly but recommended, nonetheless. "It's him or us, and we choose us."

Hansen nodded and slapped his arm. "That's right..." He pushed his door open. "Now get your head in the fucking game, Gene." He narrowed his eyes and pursed his lips aggressively because he knew he was in two-minds.

They sauntered over to the office and asked the guy at the counter a few questions, then invited themselves to his logbook. The manager knew them well and it was in his best interest to assist them and leave them alone. They then decided to take a walk around for no particular reason and without permission or a warrant.

Hansen took point and he walked around the first floor and randomly banged on a door.

Randomly, they went inside a unit to ask the occupants twenty questions then left promptly.

Marx kept a close watch on the room in question and he saw the blinds waver a bit. He mumbled to Hansen under his breath, "He's inside." He took a breath.

They continued to make their rounds and made their way up to the second floor.

Hansen side-eyed him and they went the long way around and came up to two-twenty from the other way. He sidled up to the door and scanned high and low and there was nothing to concern him. No one would see them go in, and no one would see them go out.

Marx tapped on the door and waited. He did not have to wait long because the door creaked open without the chain attached – because they were all friends. He entered first and saw the kid smile at him.

Hansen took up the rear and closed the door quietly.

The kid smiled and showed the condition of his poor teeth. "Hi, Marx…" He leaned over and nodded at Hansen. "Detective."

"Kid…" Marx nodded and smiled. "Anyone here with you?"

The kid shook his head and tweaked a little. "Nah, Marx…" He forced a smile. "You know I'm alone." He sniffed and wiped his nose.

Not one for believing anyone, Hansen walked past him and checked the closet and the bathroom. He scanned high and low and only then was he satisfied. He came out and looked at the drug paraphernalia scattered across the table – spoon, candle, rubber tube – you get the picture. "Kid?" He looked at him suspiciously. "You're on probation and you're not supposed to be using. You know that."

The kid got a little antsy. "I just need something to calm myself down, detective. That's all…" He swallowed and started to get nervous. He was high – not stupid. "It's just that I've never done an old lady in before, that's all."

Marx pursed his lips and shook his head. "Then that shit wasn't necessary kid because she's still alive."

The kid looked shocked and what little blood was left in his face drained to his nether regions. "What?" He shook his head defensively. "I gave her a huge dose, Marx…" He gulped. "I swear I did. I even checked afterward. She was not breathing and had no pulse."

Hansen glared at him and narrowed his eyes. "You a doctor now, kid?"

"What?" The kid almost scoffed at the implication. "No…" He shook his head repeatedly. "No, I'm not. But I checked to make sure and she was not breathing and had no pulse. I swear."

Hansen shook his head with disappointment. "Then why is she in the hospital…" He stared questionably through the little junkie. "Alive?" He looked at him appalled at his defense when he knew otherwise. "You fucked up, kid."

The kid shook his head and forced a laugh and wondered if the two detectives were joking with him, but neither was laughing. "That can't be…" He shook his head. "I watched the house and made sure I got out undetected and found a way to make it look like an accident. Her insulin."

Marx shook his head. "She wasn't diabetic, kid."

The kid shook his head. "Nah…" He pointed a finger at them both. "You two are trying to trick me. The prescription had her name on it."

Marx pursed his lips and stiffened his spine. "Wasn't hers. It was for her husband."

The kid processed the information but slower than a normal person would, and he held a hand out to both detectives. "Hey…" He now looked spooked. "You can't blame me for that. It was a clear as day. Her name was on there and so I took the opportunity. Just like you showed me."

Hansen looked at him disapprovingly. "So, let me get this straight, you're saying it is Detective Marx and my problem you fucked up?" He leaned into the kid. "Is that what you're saying?"

The kid simply shook his head guiltily. "No sir…" He looked to Marx for support but got nothing in return. "Did she talk?"

Marx shook his head and crossed his arms. "She's in a medically induced coma."

The kid looked at him and forced an excited smile. "That's good then, right?" His head volleyed between the two of them.

Hansen shook his head critically and pursed his lips. "No…" He glared at the kid so he could understand the ramifications of his poor performance. "Not good. Do you know why?"

The kid did not know if it was a trick question and shook his head. He was feeling queasy and was a little sweaty. "No, sir."

Hansen took a deep breath and eyed the stupid ex-convict. "Because she's still alive, that's why."

The kid tilted his head back and now understood. "Oh..." He forced a smile and hoped it would diffuse the tense situation, but it did not. "Well, what do we need to do?"

Marx scoffed at him and snorted a laugh. "We?" He looked at him like he was pulling their leg. "It's not we, kid. It's just you. We told you the consequences and you understood."

The kid stiffened his spine and looked at them both. He shook his head and the defiance started to grow inside of him. "No..." He looked at each of them. "You said that you'd have my back if something went sideways. I arranged for it to look like an accident and it worked. How was I supposed to know she wasn't diabetic? Huh?" He shook his head some more and volleyed his head at both of them. "We shook on it that you'd help me out of any bind..." His eyes drilled into both of them. "So, help me."

Hansen could not believe the junkie's chutzpah. He looked at Marx and shook his head. "Jesus..." He turned to size the kid up. "The balls on you." He scoffed. "We shook on it?" He snorted a laugh. "So, first you were a doctor, now you're a lawyer? Is that it?"

The kid gulped and wondered if he went too far. "Umm..." He side-eyed them both as he thought furiously about a way out. "I could just disappear..." He laughed. "Yeah. Just go someplace that's not here."

Hansen smirked and tick-tocked his head. "Yeah..." He looked at the kid and saved the best damning evidence for last. "It seems some reporter placed a listening device in the kitchen. Question is, did you talk with the old lady when you were in there?"

The kid swallowed hard and he sweated some more. "Umm, well, yeah. That's how I got a seat at the table and like, we chatted for a bit and then I saw my chance and I kind of talked to myself."

Marx groaned. "Oh, kid..." He shook his head. "Why'd you do that?"

The kid moaned out, "C'mon, Marx. I was nervous, okay?"

Hansen took a breath and he looked at Marx. He shook his head. "The kid's right, Gene..." He shrugged. "We got to help him."

The kid smiled and knew the detectives would come through in the end. He smiled and felt less nervous. "What do you want me to do, detective?"

Hansen thought about it for a second and then he turned to the kid. "Detective Marx and I have to make it look like the old lady was just an accident. She came across some homeless kid..." He point to him. "You..." He pursed his lips and thought some more. "That she let into her house and gave him something to eat and drink. The kid saw an opportunity held her down, gagged her, and injected her with her own insulin hoping she would just die accidentally..." He pointed to Marx who pulled out a small purse that they took from the scene. He watched him open it and tossed it recklessly onto one of the armchairs. "He stole her purse and ran back here after buying drugs, and then he overdosed."

The smile on the kids face disappeared and he volleyed his head between the two detectives and could not believe they were contemplating such a thing. "But..." He looked at Marx and then at Hansen. "But that means I'd have to be..." He gulped and his eyes were wide open with horror. "Dead."

Hansen nodded and smiled. "Yes..." He lunged forward with the Taser and zapped the kid. He watched the kid convulse, and he dropped like a rag doll to the floor. Satisfied he was unconscious he smiled with satisfaction. "You were right, Gene, kid was a little smart." He looked at his prostrate body.

Marx reached into his other pocket and pulled out the other package. He emptied the contents onto the table and picked up the tube. "C'mon..." He side-eyed Hansen. "Let's get him into the chair.

They picked him up and dropped his unconscious body into the chair. Marx arranged it just so and moved the items on the table to look like he was in the process of using. He pulled out another syringe and stuck it in his arm and pushed the plunger down. He pulled it out and snapped the cap back on and stood over the kid.

Hansen stared and made sure things were going as planned. He then saw the kid's chest rise and his body heaved up in an arc and then slumped back into the slouched position. He took a breath and smacked his lips and looked at Marx.

Marx checked his pulse and checked his breath. He looked over at Hansen and nodded. He then loosely wrapped the tube around his arm and picked up one of his used syringes and stuck it in the same red-spot he administered the lethal dose. "It's done."

Hansen did a cursory scan of the crime scene and was satisfied it looked legitimate – a murder that looked like an accidental overdose. He looked up at Marx and shook his head with approval. "You still haven't lost your touch, Gene."

Marx pursed his lips and smiled at Hansen. "It's like riding a bike." He shrugged and snorted a laugh.

Marx talked with the coroners as they took the kid's body out on the stretcher – the body bagged and zipped up snug as a bug in a rug.

Hansen looked at the sergeant as he came inside.

"Detective." The sergeant nodded his greeting.

"Sergeant…" He looked around. "We'll finish the paperwork at headquarters. We were around interviewing some leads on a case and came across this dead junkie…" He flicked at the door. "We had to break the chain after the manager unlocked the door."

The sergeant shook his head as the body was taken out. "Poor junkies…" He took a breath and took a cursory look at the crime scene and was satisfied nothing looked out of place. There were two detectives here so his job was practically done for him. "Wonder if there are any next of kin?"

Hansen shrugged. "Leave it with us…" He smiled at the sergeant as he was about to leave the scene. "Marx and I'll take care of it."

The sergeant nodded and smiled at him. "You always do, Hansen." He turned and walked toward the door. "You always do."

Hansen watched him exit and he looked at Marx. There was a sly smile on both of their faces. He mumbled softly to himself as he put his notebook away, "Just like riding a bike."

Chapter 11

Scotland and Carter walked into the LA County Lock-up and followed their procedures to get an audience with Richard Moranis. They had to sign the requisite papers and leave their belongings with the guards at the front, and dutifully proceeded though the scanners, and then into the waiting area.

Carter leaned over to Scotland and murmured in a low tone so none of the other visitors could overhear them. "I'm nervous and I didn't even do anything." She popped-up her eyebrows and had a wide-eyed doe-look.

Scotland looked at her and narrowed her eyes comedically. "Are you sure?" Her head tilted to the side and there was a judgement in her eyes that was undeniable. "I've known you my whole life and what I know about you would get you the gas chamber..." She snorted a cute giggle and gestured with her finger to make her point. "And a lethal injection just to make sure you were dead." She cackled in her face.

Carter rolled her eyes at her. "They don't use the gas chamber anymore, Scotty."

Scotland smiled at the visitors across from them. Even though they were being quiet you could hear a pin drop in that room. She leaned closer to Carter and whispered, "The governor would bring it back especially for you. Because he, like me, would love to see you suffer."

Carter glared at her derisively and forced a laugh – and stopped. She mumbled in a low tone derisively, "Fuck off."

Scotland pulled her mouth to the side and her eyes twinkled – she nudged her lovingly. "I'm only joking. Calm the eff down." She winked at her and only got a blank glare in return.

The guard called out and enunciated with purpose, "Yarde and Deklava to see Dick Moranis."

Scotland and Carter stood up and saw a sea of giggling and snickers from the other visitors. They just rolled their eyes at their infantile behavior.

Scotland looked at them and scolded them all, "It's his parents' fault, not his. That's his name." She scanned them all and simply got playful shrugs and dropped heads.

She felt Carter tug her toward one of the interview rooms.

They sat across from Richard and he looked a little frazzled to say the least. His eyes were red, and he looked like he did not get much sleep.

Scotland smiled at him. "How're you doing?"

Richard blurted out bluntly, "How do you think I'm doing?" He glared at her and growled, "I'm in jail." He pursed his lips at her.

Scotland was taken aback and she turned to look at Carter who was equally as stunned at his outburst. She turned back to him. "Whoa, Richard..." Her hands were up in surrender. "We're just here to check in on you. To see how you were doing."

Richard forced a smile and he showed it to both of them. "Sorry. I'm just dandy, thanks." He nodded his head aggressively at them both. "How the hell am I supposed to feel? They've locked me up."

Carter narrowed her eyes at him and aggressively pointed her finger derisively, so he understood. "Look, Dick..." She felt Scotland place a steady hand on her arm, but she continued. "We weren't the ones who decided to bug an old lady's house and..." She looked at him wild-eyed and forced a maniacal laugh. "Decided it was a genius idea to put his name on said device." She made a point by pointing in thin air just for effect. "Then got busted for the crime while being at the crime scene." She narrowed her eyes at him. "I know you're uncomfortable trying to not get ass-raped in here, but you brought this on yourself, dummy."

Richard started to tear-up and blubber at his sad state of affairs.

Scotland looked at him uncomfortably as he whimpered. Her mouth was open, and she did not know what to say to him. She turned to an equally shocked – but not by much Carter – and waved her hand at Richard. The evidence was clear and present. "Now look what you did, Carter."

Carter rolled her eyes all the way around. "Jesus..." She groaned out loud and her head tilted back like a Pez dispenser. She took a deep breath. "Richard..." She moved her head to see if she could get his attention by looking in his teary eyes. "Richard, look at me. Stop crying – you're a grown-ass man. This is LA County Lock-up. Not prison. They only rape you in prison."

Richard only continued to whimper and blubber his way through their meeting because he was sad and apparently a sad individual.

Scotland looked at Carter and shook her head derisively. "What's the matter with you?"

Carter was perplexed. She shrugged her shoulders at her. "I was only trying to help."

Scotland knew that when Carter Deklava tried to help, it only made matters worse. She tilted her head towards Richard. "Does it look like you're helping?" Her eyes said it all. Richard blubbered like a little kid who dropped his ice cream and he was not going to get anymore. Her lip curled up because she was getting more uncomfortable by the second. She turned again to Carter. "How is it you made it four years as White House Press Secretary and didn't start any international incidents?"

Carter stared right through Scotland and leaned into her offensively. "It's because I've got an ass that won't quit and I'm fucking delightful."

Scotland looked at Richard and then awkwardly at the guard standing nearby. She forced a smile and presented Richard to him like there was nothing she could do to stop him from crying. She cutely shrugged her shoulders.

The guard looked at Richard and then at Scotland and said matter-of-factly, "It happens more than you think." He turned and looked forward because there was nothing he could do. He was not a babysitter.

Scotland waited patiently and eyed Carter. She pursed her lips at her friend to tell her to be quiet and stop helping. She just wanted him to cry and blubber himself out before she asked him some pointed questions.

After what seemed like an eternity, Richard stammered and wiped his tears and nose dry. "I'm sorry..." He gasped for a breath without breaking down again. "I've never been in jail before."

Scotland looked at him and kind of felt sorry for him. "Look, Richard..." She searched her pockets and found some napkins from the coffee shop and handed it to him. "How do we access the voice recording from your bug?"

Richard looked at her. "It loads to my iTunes account."

Carter nodded and smiled. "Now we're getting somewhere."

Scotland turned to him. "You have to give us access, Richard."

He looked at each of them blankly and blinked, and slowly shook his head. "You guys have to get me out of here first. I didn't hand it over to the detectives and that's why they locked me up. I told them they needed a warrant first."

Scotland namasted him to plead for the access. "We just want to get the sound bite from that night, Richard..." She leaned into him. "We need to know if Mrs. Vasquez was alone."

Richard shook his head in defiance and pleaded with the women. "I'm sorry but I can't do that. That's the only bargaining chip I have left."

Scotland pleaded with him again. "Once they get that warrant, you won't have anything to bargain with."

Richard shook his head and looked at both women a little perplexed. "I don't want to bargain with the detectives. I meant with you..." He looked at her blankly and then turned to Carter. "That recording is all I have to force you to bail me out of here. And both of you have the means."

Scotland felt her temperature and blood pressure rise. She clenched her jaw with the perfect overbite and growled at him offensively, "Why-you-little-motherfucker..." She stopped mid-sentence and saw the guard lean toward her and wave at her but not so much to disturb the two gorgeous women.

"Umm..." The guard was apologetic for even interrupting. "No swearing, ma'am." He shook his head slightly and smiled appreciatively at them both. He had let the first few slide, but he had to draw the line somewhere no matter how good-looking they both were.

"Sorry about that, officer." Scotland smiled appreciatively and turned back to the little fucker that she wanted to murder right then and there.

Scotland's tendons in her jaw popped out and she showed her clenched jaw to Richard. "We're trying to help you, Richard. But you're making it very difficult for us to do it."

He leaned back and crossed his legs and his arms. "Well..." He stared at both of them and shook his head matter-of-factly. "I don't feel you're doing everything you can or I wouldn't be in here."

Scotland seethed and her breathing took on a whole new level. She turned to Carter and looked to her for support. She tilted her head at Richard for her to say something to him.

Carter could see what Richard was doing and it made Scotland angrier by the second. "Hey..." She held up her hands. "I tried and you warned me off. This is on you now, Scotty."

Scotland rolled her eyes and let out an exasperated sigh. She turned to Richard. "Look. You give us the access code and we promise to get a lawyer for you..." She looked at him with stars in her eyes. "Deal?" She smiled at him and nodded.

Richard weighed his options and his head volleyed between the two of them and he pulled his mouth to the side as he chewed his options. He leaned forward because he was in the better negotiating position. "No deal."

Scotland and Carter were escorted out the interview area. They were surprisingly treated with respect as they were asked to leave – and never return. The guards were in front and behind them as they marched them through the hallway to the exit for them to collect their possessions.

Scotland looked remorseful as she picked up her things and packed them in the requisite pockets. She looked at the guard as he watched her. "Umm..." She swallowed and was nervous. "Once again I apologize for punching the prisoner."

The guard held up his hand and waved her off. "It's okay. We didn't see anything and unfortunately for him he doesn't have a lawyer yet to say otherwise, so we consider it a non-issue."

Scotland looked at Carter and she had a smug look on her face but remained quiet unless they wanted it to look like a particularly aggressive episode of the Real Housewives of Beverly Hills inside the LA County Lock-up. She turned back to the guard. "Again, I apologize."

The guard pulled his mouth to the side and shook his head. "It's okay. It happens more than you think." He nodded matter-of-factly.

Scotland pursed her lips in thought for her past actions as she marched out the exit to the parking lot with Carter in tow.

Carter got in the passenger seat and remained quiet and did not want to poke the bear, but she had to. She looked over at a regretful Scotland and saw her turn to her for her comeuppance. "I don't think it was particularly helpful for you to punch poor Dickie in the face like that, Scotty." She pursed her lips to the side to lament at the turn of events inside the interview area.

Scotland chewed her thoughts and softly banged her head against the steering wheel of the Bentley. She groaned loudly at having lost her patience inside there. "That guy is such a jackass."

Carter nodded but she understood what he was trying to do. "He's desperate and wants us to get him a lawyer." She gently rubbed her back to console her for her faux pas.

Scotland turned to her as she rested her head on the steering wheel. "Really?" She pursed her lips almost perturbed by her. "You're the voice of reason all of a sudden?"

Carter shrugged her shoulders and grinned. "One of us has to be the bigger person here." She snorted a laugh. "The look on poor Dickie's face when you decked him was priceless, though." She guffawed and howled in the car.

Scotland fired up the beast and fumed.

Scotland had to now get the pain-in-her-ass a lawyer on her dime, otherwise the next person she would have to deal with would be his court-appointed, pissant, public defender who would just love to come after her for assault.

She pulled out the parking area and asked Siri to dial the number of her family law firm in Los Angeles. It would be an easy ask and they could get the freeloader released so he could get them access to the iTunes account.

A block away, a lone individual sat surreptitiously in his heap of a car. It did not look like much but it was a wolf in sheep's clothing – if that sheep had dents and rust. He let out a heady bellow of vape steam and checked – and made sure it was the correct Bentley – which should not be difficult, but he confirmed the license plate number anyway.

He smiled with a mish-mash of Jabberjaw teeth and seethed contently at the thought of having to hurt the helpless women in their fancy and expensive car. He looked to the passenger seat and marvelled at his loaded semi-automatic shotgun resting peacefully. At a distance the steel-shot would make small work of metal and glass. Up close it would kill in the most heinous way imaginable. These shells were banned but he had them, was ordered to use them, and was chomping at the bit to try them out.

He cranked the key and the engine blared to life, which was a problem for the occupants in the Bentley. The muscle-car engine was made for speed and his suspension was tuned for racing. The incessant growl the more he revved it brought a smile to his weather-worn face.

He checked his mirrors, signalled, and gave chase.

Chapter 12

Carter side-eyed Scotland as she piloted her way through traffic. A content smile curled over her mouth and crinkles creased her eyes as she pulled her sunglasses down her nose. She wondered how long it would take her to notice and ask what she found so delightfully amusing.

Scotland took a breath and pursed her lips. She had caught sight of the smile, but she could not smell anything – especially with the top down. She smacked her lips and kept her attention on the road but had to ask anyway. "And what do you find so amusing?"

Carter feigned shock. She poked her sunglasses all the way up and sat up still amused at how her brain worked. "I'm just replaying the interaction you had with the Amazon goddess, that's all."

Scotland shook her head slightly and let the bus in ahead. "I don't think she'd appreciate you referring to her as the Amazon goddess."

Carter scoffed at her. "Have you seen how small you look in comparison to her when you're standing beside her?" She marked a line on her chest with her hand. "At least you're at tits level..." She snorted a giggle. "But they would hardly be classified as tits."

Scotland's jaw dropped open. "That's horrible."

Carter screwed her mouth to the side and tick-tocked her head. "The girl is jacked..." She held her hands up to make her point. "I get it..." She side-eyed Scotland's physique. "You're jacked too. Kind of wonder who'd win in a wrestling match." She snorted a giggle.

"Why is that when I'm interested in someone, you think we're going to end up wrestling in bed?" Scotland pursed her lips derisively but continued to pay attention to her driving. "Huh?" Her eyes were covered by her sunglasses, but they checked her mirrors, and out in front of her.

"It's just how my dirty mind works." Carter simply shrugged. "I think it'd be sexy. You know, loser comes first and all." She childishly grinned like a little girl.

Scotland snorted derisively and smacked her lips, "In all these years, we've never wrestled." She pulled her mouth to the side in a salacious smirk and her pornographic memory thought back at their sexual history together.

Carter nonchalantly glanced over at her with her head resting on the headrest. She snarled matter-of-factly, "That's because you knew you'd lose if you tried." She lusciously bit her bottom lip.

Scotland snorted derisively and smiled knowingly. She murmured in a low tone, "Maybe."

Carter snickered and licked her lips as she scanned Scotland in her lounged, driving position. "By the way…" She pouted and had to rescan Scotland's insane body once more. "Kudos to Cross-Fit-Rob." Her hand waved at her awesome body in recline. "I could bounce a quarter off that ass of yours."

Scotland grinned enthusiastically. "I'm hoping Kate does." She giggled like a lovesick schoolgirl.

Carter smiled at her. "I'll make sure she has a handful of them for your date."

They both cackled as traffic started to move once more.

Scotland side-eyed Carter. "So…" She grinned because, you know, tit-for-tat. "What do you think of Nate?" She growled at her and had to nudge her friend. "That man is packing. And I don't mean his Glock." She almost felt sorry for the state Carter would leave him in when they did hook up. She was a stubborn alpha in bed, but she needed a man like Nate to tempt her. Problem is she would break the man.

Carter snorted a giggle, and she licked her lips at her new friend-with-benefits. She let out a guttural growl, "Mm-hm…" She turned to her and murmured lustily, "Mummy-like." Her salacious mind wandered, and she knew what she was going to do to him and with him. "I almost feel sorry for him."

Scotland looked at her quizzically. "Jesus, Carter. You sound like a vampire."

Carter looked at her matter-of-factly. "Well…" She smacked her lips and had a shit-eating grin plastered across her face. "Someone is going to get sucked dry…" She comically pointed both thumbs at herself. "And it isn't going to be this girl." She snorted a giggle.

Scotland almost felt sorry for Nate. He obviously did not know what he was getting himself into with Carter. She was a force to be reckoned with and a sexual dynamo. She was a gorgeous woman who would make men and women do a double-take and leave them breathless but pining for more. She mumbled to Carter inquisitively, "Is there something wrong with us?" She pulled her jaw to the side to chew her thoughts.

Carter wondered that too. If there was one person she could confide in, it was Scotland, and she would return the favor. "Perhaps."

Scotland pursed her lips and put the thought out of her head. She went back to focusing on the road.

Carter nodded her head and smiled some more. Her look went blank, and she turned to her friend. "Scotty…" She smacked her lips. "Far be it from me to criticize your usually excellent driving, but why are we going this way?" Her look turned pensive and then concerned, because Scotland only did something like this when something was awry.

Scotland caught sight of the muscle-car after they left the LA County Lock-up and it had been tailing them ever since. She did not make her route obvious with turn-after-turn but started to lead the tail away from the main traffic-light controlled streets to more open road in the industrial areas southeast of downtown, and if necessary, the freeway. It piqued Carter's interest understandably when they should have been heading West. "We've got a tail and it has been following us since we left the jail."

Carter pulled the visor down and slid open the vanity mirror. She adjusted it just so to look at the sparsely spaced traffic that was still with them, but she made out the car in question. Her mind raced and she noted the license plate – in reverse – and committed it to memory. Her mind clouded with concern – was it there just to watch them or do them harm. The anti-terrorist training she picked up when she worked for the White House gave her pause. No one tails someone in a muscle-car unless they want to chase you. She pursed her lips and prepared herself, and murmured to Scotland, "Hmm...I think this tail means trouble."

Scotland toyed with her mouth and she also felt the same way. "Mm-hm." She started to increase her speed and watched in the rear-view mirror as her pursuer started to pick up speed too. It started to pass the other cars on the street. Her eyes perked up as the railway cross-arms came down and the red-lights flashed of a pending train and she missed her opportunity to pull through and was now caught.

Scotland's mind raced as her left foot held the brake down and her hand pulled the gear lever back to 'Sport' – her right foot touched the accelerator – her eyes focused on the rear-view mirror.

The muscle-car driver rolled his window down as he sidled up behind her and waited for the slow-moving train to approach. He gritted his teeth and bided his time for when the train would block the car completely and it would be like shooting fish in a barrel. A content smile flashed across his mouth, as he readied his weapon to unleash its fury. The train came closer-and-closer – but what he saw attached to the fancy and expensive Bentley on the trunk was what spooked him – the surreptitiously placed, built-in, rear-view camera to accompany any forward facing dashcam. His eyes had that startled look in them because he was being recorded and he reacted like a caged animal – instinctively and without thinking.

He shoved the shotgun out the driver's side window and rested it on the door frame, and his trigger finger squeezed back.

Scotland's startled eyes opened wide by what she saw in her rear-view mirror and it did nothing to stop her reflexes from acting. "Jesus-down!" She pulled Carter down with her for cover – deeper into the cabin.

The shotgun boomed three times in rapid succession and the aimless blasts tore at the trunk, driver, and passenger area. Metal, wood, and leather were shredded and splintered from the impacts.

Scotland slammed the accelerator down hard and the Bentley lurched but was held by the brake as the tachometer climbed and the engine let out a gruff, rapid-fire, chugging snarl. She let the brake release with a snap and the massive car fired itself across the tracks with a howl and snapped the cross-arms like sticks. It forged straight ahead past the train as she held the steering wheel at the bottom – still hunkered down for safety on top of Carter.

The muscle-car roared and jumped the tracks, but the rear was clipped by the train's front end and twisted and crunched the backend like an accordion. The driver growled at having been caught off guard by the resourceful women. It should have been an easy kill and a closed casket funeral, but now they just made it harder for him. He filled the inside of the car with expletives as he regained his composure and righted his car on the other side as the train continued, and he chased after the Bentley at full speed. The engine snarled loud and the muscle-car ate tarmac.

Scotland popped her head up over the dash, and kept the Bentley headed in a straight line. Satisfied they were in the clear she sat up and white-knuckled the steering wheel. The engine growled and her eyes assessed the condition of the interior and it looked grim – bits and pieces of the luxury interior were either missing or shredded to ribbons. She yelled out to Carter, "Are you hit?"

Carter shook her head and kept her head down. "No!"

Scotland checked the wing mirrors as they were the only things that could tell her if they were being pursued.

Carter swallowed hard as she assessed the front cabin and thanked Scotland's quick-thinking. The blasts would have done to them what it did to the interior – the luxury parts were shattered or shredded to pieces. The rear-view mirror was missing and there was a hole in the windshield – giving the Bentley redneck air conditioning. The headrests offered some protection but were collateral damage against their assailant. That was the only damage she could see but she was more concerned if they were being chased. She would have used the vanity mirror but that too suffered the same fate as the other mirrors and part of the top section of the windshield.

She turned in her seat to look back and her eyes opened wide at the muscle-car in hot pursuit. "It's still after us!"

Scotland continued to white-knuckle the steering-wheel at nine and three and kept her eyes peeled forward. Even though they were being buffeted by the wind blowing through the massive hole in the windshield she was more concerned about getting to safety – wherever that may be. Her eyes scanned and darted, and she blurted out to Carter, "Are-you-okay? Are-you-hit?"

Carter shook her head. "No!" She looked at Scotland and checked quickly for any injuries. The adrenaline was coursing through her body and she was sure it was coursing through Scotland's. "Are-you-okay?"

Scotland nodded her head and she swallowed but her mouth and throat were dry from the adrenaline coursing through her. She expertly sped past cars – doing over the speed limit – that seemed like they were standing still. In the background she could hear the growl of the muscle-car echoing off the buildings on either side of the dragstrip – it was now a Death Race and they were at an extreme disadvantage.

Carter looked back and saw the muscle-car cut in-and-out of traffic as it tried desperately to catch up with them. The Bentley lurched forward as there were cars ahead that slowed for a light and her eyes wondered which was the best way to get out of the way of the car barrelling down behind them.

The muscle-car did not stop. He kept his foot firmly pressed to the floor and ran other cars off to the side of the street with little regard for their safety or his.

Carter shot her eyes back and they were wide with terror as she saw him approach. "Here he comes!" She could see the look in his eyes and the shotgun pointed out of the driver's side window. "Five o' clock!"

Scotland slammed on the brakes hard and the Bentley ground to a halt in a very short time. The tires screamed in protest. She yelled out for their safety, "Get-down!"

They heard the blast for the shotgun and stayed down for cover. They heard the splintering of glass and metal impacting metal.

Scotland popped her head up and floored it. She cranked the wheel to the left and mounted the sidewalk to make it onto a street perpendicular to the one she was on. The tires once again howled in protest at the sudden turn at full speed but the car instinctively obeyed and carried them to safety.

Carter looked up and the passenger wing mirror and passenger side windows were shattered and missing – pieces of glass peppered her but she took no notice. The passenger side of the windshield had a massive hole to match the one in the middle, and the windshield pillar was badly damaged from the blast.

Scotland planted her right foot down to the floor and covered the brake with her left. The surge of the W12 engine pulled the beast across East 4th Street. Her eyes did not deceive her and up ahead was the bridge that crossed over the Los Angeles River. Cars slowed and she was going to swerve toward the bypass that would lead her away from the bridge.

Carter pulled at her and covered her with her body. "Down!"

The shotgun blast was aimed lower than before and it hit the Bentley point blank in the trunk. The muscle-car driver was happy with that shot and pulled the trigger once more hitting the car almost in the same spot. The steel-shot would surely penetrate the cabin this time and he smiled, but it disappeared when he saw two heads pop back up – his attempt at whack-a-mole was unsuccessful. The backend of the Bentley took the brunt of the shots and the car started to look like a jigsaw puzzle with missing pieces.

Carter looked back and the backseat was shredded from the blast as was the trunk.

Scotland swerved toward the bridge and mounted the sidewalk and gunned the engine. She had no choice and scraped cars idly driving with traffic. She swerved to the left at oncoming cars who blasted their horns in protest, to let her know she encroached into their lane but they swerved out of her way just in case.

The muscle-car kept up with them and swerved to hit the Bentley's tail. The driver's grin said he was having a good time terrorizing the women as they made their way across the bridge.

Scotland swerved to the right and came up along his passenger side and used the weight of her car to return the favor. She pursed her lips with conviction as she slammed into his passenger side. The weight of the Bentley bullied the muscle-car relentlessly as metal crunched against metal.

The muscle-car driver pulled the shotgun out of the driver's side window opening and pointed at her through the passenger side and aimed low this time. He did not care that his car would also take the brunt of the steel-shot as his callous nature spoke to his conviction to maim the women – as ordered.

Carter pulled Scotland down and the blast ripped through the muscle-car and tore up the driver's door and front fender of the Bentley.

Scotland braked hard and came up from behind the muscle-car and fuck-tapped him hard bumper-to-bumper, and she accelerated. The Bentley pushed him faster-and faster.

The Bentley's surge shoved the muscle-car forward and smoke rose from between the two vehicles in combat and the smell of burnt rubber filled their nostrils.

He braked but was still being forced forward. He knew this gave his brakes a workout and they started to smoke, and smoulder and he felt the brake pedal fade and drop to the floor. The screeching sound and the smell of burning rubber filled his nostrils and he veered to the left toward East 4th Street and hoped it would break him free of the woman who shoved him now. However, he was surprised when she anticipated his move and followed along and shoved him and continued to give his brakes an undeserved workout. Smoke and flames started to come from his wheel-wells and he tried shifting down but the Bentley was too bulky and their engine too powerful, compared to his muscle-car which seemed exhausted and taxed from the chase which had now made him the pursued.

He pointed the shotgun out the back and fired. The blast shattered his own rear window and trunk and hit the Bentley square in the hood – gnashing a hole through the metal.

Scotland slowed down and noticed the warning lights that lit up on her instrument panel like a Christmas Tree. She clenched her jaw, and growled out loud, "Shit!"

Carter knew it was trouble and the engine had sustained a hit. She saw him swerve left down South Alameda Street, but Scotland did not give up that easily. She followed him to the end.

Scotland corrected her course and accelerated at the muscle-car. The engine now protested but she kept her foot planted to the floor. She closed the gap and pulled up along his passenger side. She swerved and smashed into his car again, and the gnashing and crunching of metal against metal protested loudly but the two drivers continued in a race toward superiority.

The muscle-car driver was deeply frustrated that he had not been able to kill them already or force her off the road. He dished it out but did not take it well and decided he would have to regroup and kill them later. He aimed the shotgun down at his passenger door and squeezed the trigger. The steel-shot tore through it like it was paper.

"Fuck!" Scotland felt the aggressive pull of the steering wheel and felt the Bentley lurch down on the corner. Smoke poured from her hood and she simply floored the car and swerved hard left into the muscle-car. She felt the Bentley almost submerge under the muscle-car and slammed it precariously toward the buildings on the left. She swore she heard him scream as he lost control.

The customers at the gas station could see the trajectory of the muscle-car and Bentley as they raced down the street. They ran for cover just in the nick-of-time.

The muscle-car driver gasped in terror as his car bounced off the sidewalk at a high rate of speed and flew through the air directly into the gas station – and the fuel truck filling up the tanks. His arms went instinctively across his face at the pending crash and there was nothing he could do. He had no brakes because he was in the air and he was out of control like an aimless missile. The muscle-car smashed into the tanker and detonated in a massive ball of fire.

Scotland swerved hard to the right then left as the Bentley fishtailed wildly. She tried desperately to get the badly damaged Bentley under her control. She felt very little steering feedback and slammed the brakes as hard as she could. The Bentley swerved violently from the high rate of speed and she fought with the wheel to correct the misguided swerve and tried her best to make the front-end hit head-on whatever she was going to crash into.

Carter gasped and her body tensed up at the pending impact. She felt the heat from the initial explosion when the muscle-car careened into the fuel tanker; but she was more concerned about them now as the building got closer-and-closer.

Scotland tried her best to correct the dangerous skid and swerve and she was wild-eyed at the pending crash.

Both women knew it was now up to fate and physics, and they prayed out loud, "Fffuughk!"

The Bentley bounced hard against the sidewalk and lifted its front end up and impacted the warehouse wall – hard. Quicker than a blink of the eye, the seatbelts retracted immediately as well as the multitude of life-saving airbags that deployed in the front, sides, and knee areas – as the car came to a smashing halt in a very short distance.

The secondary explosion from the fiery car crash into the fuel truck ripped through the LA sky and the sound rattled windows. Onlookers ran toward the Bentley, but some tried to get to the other car that impacted the fuel tanker, but it was impossible. The heat was extreme, and they tended to the women because they seemed in better condition.

Scotland shoved her airbag down and looked over at Carter as she did the same. She was breathing so that was a good sign.

Carter shoved her airbag out of the way and took a deep breath and coughed from the smoke. She looked over at Scotland and mumbled, "Ow!" Her eyes rolled because her brain was rebooting from the crash.

Scotland's eyes were open wide with fear that her friend had been shot or was injured in another way. "What?" She swallowed hard. "Are you hit or injured? Can you move your legs?"

Carter was still a little groggy as she pointed to the front of the car. "No..." She moved to make sure she was okay. "You just drove us into a wall, Scotty."

Scotland looked at her derisively. She glared at her with impertinence. "Would you've preferred the fuel tanker?"

They winced when they heard another explosion and felt the heat from the blast – everyone in their vicinity did. They managed to turn in their seats and surveyed the condition of their assailant as he roasted away.

Carter looked at the condition of the muscle-car and themselves. She rolled her eyes and rested her head on what was left of the headrest. "Fine..." She moaned as she heard voices from outside the car come up to them to tend to their injuries. Questions started to fly but she could only hear Scotland's voice as it cursed at her in a low mumble. "You win this one."

Scotland rested her head back on what was left of her headrest and it felt hard and uncomfortable, but she did not argue with its support – such as it was.

Carter surreptitiously reached into her fanny-pack and pulled out a Snickers bar. She callously tore the wrapper with her teeth and took a half-chomp of the delicious bar. She chewed and handed the remainder to Scotland.

Scotland stuffed the other half into her mouth, and gingerly stuck the spent wrapper into the cup holder trash can. She took a deep breath and waited for her strength to return.

They both flinched when another explosion rang out.

Chapter 13

Scotland and Carter watched from the ambulance as the firemen sprayed foam over the burnt-out wreckage of the muscle-car and fuel tanker. The attendants continued to check them over to make sure that they were okay.

The ladies took a breath and scanned the beehive of activity as every conceivable emergency vehicle was dispatched to that area and were now doing their part to control the situation. They then saw some familiar faces approach them. Two smiled to acknowledge they were happy to see them. The other two looked like they had bugs-up-their-butts.

Kate grinned and she looked down at Scotland being treated by the paramedic. "Hi, Scotland..." Her eyes creased and she curled her lip. "Are you okay?"

Scotland nodded. "I'm fine..." She nudged Carter who murmured something unintelligible. "We're both fine."

Nate simply smiled at the gorgeous Carter Deklava. "I'm glad you're both okay."

Hansen put his hands on his hips and growled at them both. "You two ladies have caused quite a mess here." He was gruff and shook his head at the scene. "A high-speed chase? Property damage? Crashing into a fuel tanker and almost destroying the city block?"

Marx nodded in agreement and wonderment at the raucous scene.

Carter looked like a startled ostrich and glared at him. There were no words for what she felt for the detective, but her brain was formulating a response with a string of well-chosen expletives.

Scotland beat her to the punch and threw the icepack to the ground and scowled at the detective. She yelled at him derisively, "Listen here, detective-shit-for-brains..." Her eyes took on a fiery-red that surprised everyone within earshot. She pointed to the burnt-out muscle-car being pulled out of the tanker's side by a tow-truck. "That crispy-motherfucker over there was shooting at us..." She growled some more at him, "And we weren't about to stop and let him use us for target practise, got it?" She narrowed her eyes, so he understood where she was coming from.

Hansen swallowed, held up his hands in surrender and backed off. He cleared his throat and rubbed his neck. "Umm..." He blinked and was trying to say and do the right thing now that he was rebuked in front of everyone after his initial outburst. "I hope you're both okay."

Carter looked up at him and snarled sarcastically, "We're fine..." She nodded and looked at Scotland. "Thanks for asking." She too narrowed her eyes at the detectives. Her eyes softened when she caught Nate looking at her and she pulled a sideways smirk.

Kate looked at the detectives with impertinence, and then turned to the two paramedics. "Are they okay?"

The paramedic nodded and smiled at the officers. "They're both okay. Just a few bruises and some mild whiplash..." She headtossed at the Bentley being pulled out of the wall which took the brunt of the assault. "They're in considerably better shape than their car." She snorted a chuckle. "That's for damn sure."

Hansen looked at Scotland. "Do you know why anyone would want to kill you both?"

Marx was stunned and looked at them. "Yeah..." He shook his head derisively. "What's so special about you two that someone would want you dead?"

Scotland glared at him now and her eyes once again took on that fiery-red glow. "Oh, I don't know, detective..." Her head tick-tocked and she looked at Carter and turned back to him. "I've been told I mark tests pretty hard, and well..." She tilted her head at her compatriot. "Carter's kind of like a Kardashian..." She looked at him with surprise. "So..." She shrugged her shoulders matter-of-factly. "Why wouldn't someone want to try and kill her."

Carter shot Scotland a contemptuous look and did not appreciate that reference. She growled at her with haughty derision, "Fuck you, Scotty..." She pursed her lips. "I'm much hotter than a Kardashian." She pouted defensively. "All of them."

Nate and Kate smirked at Carter and then at Scotland. They were a gorgeous bickering couple that deserved to be together but for their sakes – were not.

Hansen looked at her interrogatively. "This is hardly the time to be flippant, Ms. Yarde..." He shook his head with impertinence towards her making light of the situation. "This started right after you went to see Richard Moranis at County."

Scotland looked at him quizzically. "So, you're keeping tabs on who's seeing him?"

Hansen nodded. "Of course..." He offered a slight matter-of-fact shrug. "Why wouldn't we."

Scotland eyed him inquisitively. "This happened way too soon for it to be a coincidence..." She chewed her thoughts. "This hit took some planning and not just because I've been asking Moranis questions."

Hansen looked at her. "Just who've you been asking questions?" His eyebrows popped up. "Hmm?"

Marx shook his head and agreed with his partner. "You should be leaving the detective work to the detectives."

Carter scoffed at that. "That leaves me with very little confidence, detective."

Hansen narrowed his eyes and leaned into the two of them. "Stay out and off this case or we'll have you arrested for obstruction..." He looked at both gorgeous women aggressively. "Understand, ladies?" He nodded his head so they could understand where he was coming from.

With that said, Hansen and Marx looked at one another, took another look at each of them, and took their leave to talk with the other investigating officers by the fuel truck.

Scotland and Carter watched them walk away and they both instinctively flipped them double-handed birds.

Nate and Kate smirked as they too watched the detectives walk away.

Carter mumbled to Scotland derisively, "What a couple of fucking assholes." Her eyes narrowed and she shook her head.

Scotland murmured back to her friend in agreement. "On that we agree, my friend." Her lips pursed and her mind raced.

Kate and Nate looked at what was left of the Bentley as the tow-truck yanked it out of the wall with a crash of stone, glass, and metal crunching, smashing, and screeching. They felt sorry for the wall and the car. The three-hundred-thousand-dollar Bentley was now a tangled and twisted heap – ready for the scrap yard. They both groaned with disappointment at the state of it as it was dragged across the sidewalk and onto the street. The large trailer truck was ready to accept it because there was no way it was going to move on its own – let alone be towed behind a tow-truck.

Kate mumbled in a low tone to eulogize the condition of the once gorgeous Bentley, "Oh my god..." Her eyes teared up at the condition of the car she fell in love with – after Scotland Yarde of course. "That was such a beautiful car."

Scotland pursed her lips and shook her head at her once gorgeous Bentley. She almost whimpered when she saw what was left of it. It was unrecognizable. She mumbled forlornly, "I waited months for that car." She feigned a whimper and sniffed and hoped for some sympathy to her 'one-percenter' problem.

Carter scoffed at her as she saw the tangled mess. Her mouth dropped open. The car saved their lives because it took the brunt of the shotgun blasts and the crash. She smacked her lips and stared at it as it screeched and ground its way across the sidewalk and slammed onto the street with a crash. "Don't worry, Scotty…" She smirked at her friend's sadness for losing her bespoke lover. "A little Turtle Wax and Armor-All and most of that will buff right out." She snorted a maniacal cackle.

Scotland slowly turned her head to her friend. "You know…" There was a perceptible and palpable anger behind her narrowed eyes and pursed lips. "You're so lucky you're sitting in an ambulance right now, Carter."

Carter nudged her friend because she did enjoy busting her balls in her time of need. It was hilarious to see her reaction and she revelled in keeping her down to earth when the need arose. "C'mon…" She leaned her head on her friend's shoulder. "You can always buy another car."

Scotland perked up and knew Carter was right. Her rich people problem was nothing compared to being killed by the shotgun blasts. "Yeah…" She pulled her mouth to the side. "You're right."

Kate and Nate looked at them both and wondered what they managed to get themselves into. It was only a short time since they saw them and had lunch, and now they managed to escape an assassination attempt in a matter of just a few hours.

Kate looked at Carter and then turned to Scotland. "Did you get anything from Moranis?"

Scotland shook her head and smiled up at the gorgeous woman. "He held out and wanted me to get him out of lock-up before he'd give us the code to his iTunes account." She huffed. "The little fucker." She still could not believe he extorted her into helping him.

Scotland's mind raced. If there was one assassination attempt – would there be two? "You don't think someone would want to kill him too…" She cocked an inquisitive eyebrow up. "Do you?" Her mouth pulled to the side.

Kate was shocked. "In lock-up?" She shook her head derisively. "You'd need a big set of balls to be willing to murder someone with so many guards watching you."

Carter was surprised. "Scotland managed to punch him in the face…" She giggled. "And all she got was a slap on the wrist…" Her eyes perked up. "Oh, and we're not allowed back in…" She cleared her throat. "Ever."

Nate looked shocked. "You did what?" He could not believe someone would even consider doing that in an interview room.

Kate giggled. "You've got a lot of chutzpah doing that. You could've been arrested for assault." She shook her head and admired the alpha.

Scotland pursed her lips and shook her head. "Yeah, not my finest hour…" Her head tick-tocked from side-to-side. "But he kind of deserved it."

Carter nodded her head and pointed at Scotland. "On that I can agree with her..." She too nodded and pursed her lips. "He was asking for a punch in the face."

Scotland thought about it and wondered if Kate could help. "Do you mind doing something for us?"

Kate smiled generously and leaned into the gorgeous woman. "I'd do anything for you."

Carter looked at the two women cavorting with one another with her and Nate so close. It looked like they should be chaperoned just in case things got out of hand quickly. "Okay..." She smirked and pointed her finger back-and-forth between her and Nate. "You two need to know Nate and I are right here, so dial it back." She looked at them with wild eyes.

Scotland snorted a giggle and turned her attention back to Kate. "Can you ask the guards to keep an eye on Moranis?" She perked up her eyebrows at her. "As a favor to me?"

Kate hemmed-and-hawed. "It's the detectives' case and we'd be stepping on their toes if we officially ask."

Carter interjected. "What about asking someone unofficially." She popped-up her eyebrows.

Kate nodded and smiled back at both women. "Nate and I know a guard who we can ask off the record."

Scotland reached out and touched her arm. "Thanks, Kate."

Kate smiled and went to the side and pulled out her phone.

Carter looked over at Scotland. "You don't think he's in danger, do you?"

Scotland let out a worried sigh. Her mouth dropped open and wondered that too. "If someone was crazy enough to try to kill us..." She looked at her friend with troubled eyes. "It'd be easy to get him in lock-up."

Carter screwed her mouth up with a hint of concern for the little creep's well-being. "And here I thought the worst thing that could happen to him is he'd get his asshole shanked in there."

Scotland stared as the Bentley was hauled onto the trailer with noises that protested it being moved in any direction. "Getting ass-shanked would be the least of his problems."

Nate looked at them both and was a little surprised at the two ladies talking about someone getting raped in lock-up. His expression said it all and he caught both of their attention.

Carter looked at him blankly and murmured, "We're only kidding." She shook her head derisively. "Lighten up, Nate."

Nate's jaw dropped and somehow, he was beholden to the gorgeous woman telling him what to do.

Kate came back to them and put her phone away. "My friend will keep an eye on him..." She smiled at Scotland. "It's dinnertime for them. Nothing bad happens at dinnertime." She shrugged cutely at her and gave her a wink.

Nate looked at the two paramedics. "Are they okay to go?"

They nodded and one chimed in. "Just take it easy. Remember, you were in a pretty bad crash."

Scotland nodded at her. "Thanks."

Kate tilted her head to the cruiser. "C'mon..." She led the way and turned to Scotland. "Nate and I'll give you a ride back..." She smiled at them both. "Anywhere you want to go."

Chapter 14

Richard Moranis sat quietly in his holding cell – alone. He shook his head in disgust at the conditions inside the cell and made it a point to write an article about his experience once he was released.

He scanned the confined conditions and wondered how long someone could be locked up in here and not lose their mind.

He heard the guards outside as they paced back-and-forth and the murmurs and mumblings from the other prisoners as they awaited trial or their release. His mind was made up when he forced Scotland to get him a lawyer – a good one – and not one of those court-appointed ones right out of school.

He got up and fumed as he checked the condition of his mouth where Scotland hit him. He looked at his blurred image in the metal mirror that was scratched and distorted. It was uncalled for and he stewed and made sure the bleeding had stopped. He pulled his mouth to the side and winced at the pain. He swore he could feel a loose tooth somewhere in his mouth, but he did not want to risk making things worse. He snarled his lip and mumbled under his breath, "Bitch."

He was startled when the viewing door slammed open and a guard checked to see where he was.

"Dick Moranis!" The guard chided him, and the sound echoed throughout the area.

Wild uncontrolled laughing and hooting could be heard throughout the jail area.

The guard looked around outside and he fumed as he yelled out loud so the other prisoners could hear him, "Shut-it!"

It immediately went quiet and he pursed his lips satisfied that his power reigned supreme. He turned back to the prisoner he came to see. "Someone wants to see you, Moranis. Now."

Richard marched down the hallway toward the interview area once more and hoped it was good news. "Is it my lawyer?"

The guard did not care to be questioned and was gruff and in a foul mood. "Just keep walking."

Richard thought long a hard and hoped it was not Scotland Yarde to hit him in the face again. His thoughts darkened as he thought he would have to defend himself this time, but that would take all of two seconds before she really went to work and kicked the shit out of him. His pulse raced as he approached the interview area and his spirits lifted as he caught sight of his guest.

He excitedly sat down and looked her up-and down and smiled at her – bewildered. He wondered why she would be visiting him, but he was happy just to see a familiar face. "Joanne..." He smiled but winced in pain. "I'm so happy to see you."

Joanne's eyes were wide with shock. "Oh my god..." She tried to reach out but saw the guard shake his head for her to keep her hands to herself. "What happened? Did you get into a fight?" Her look was grave at his condition.

Richard shook his head. "It was Scotland Yarde."

Joanne looked at him confused and her head tilted to the side. "I don't think they have jurisdiction in LA, Richard."

Richard shook his head and looked her in the eyes. "No..." He took a breath because he knew he would have to explain it to her. "Not Scotland Yard." He narrowed his eyes to make his point clear. "Scotland Yarde."

Joanne headtossed at having been improperly told what-was-what but there was still a confused look on her face. "What?" She cocked an eyebrow at him.

He groaned and knew it was going to be a long day, but he was in lock-up so that really did not matter. "The woman I was with on Saturday when I came to see you."

Joanne's look brightened up and she knew the two women he was with but was still unsure. "Umm, the one that looks like Kristen Stewart or Bella Hadid?"

Richard fumed and growled because he was in pain when she punched him for no good reason. "Kristen-Damn-Stewart." He pursed his lips and let out a pained sigh.

Joanne was shocked she would even do that to him. "Oh my god..." She shook her head in disbelief. "Why would she do that to you?"

Richard fumed some more and wondered that himself. He mumbled under his breath, "Because she's a bitch."

Joanne was aghast. "Richard..." She shook her head in disagreement. "It's impolite to refer to women in that way."

Richard was shocked and should have known better and his look turned apologetic. "I'm sorry, Joanne. I'm not sure why, but I'm in a bad mood..." He looked up and around and growled in a sarcastic manner, "Oh, because I'm in jail. So, you'll have to forgive my manners."

Joanne scoffed at his fake apology. "No need to be snarky, Richard." She huffed at him.

Richard paused and took a deep breath to calm himself down. He held up his hands in surrender. "You're right. I'm sorry." He looked at her and wondered. "Why're you here?"

Joanne smiled and tried to be as cheery as possible. "I work part time here and I saw your name in the entry log, so I decided to drop by and see how you were doing."

Richard perked up and was a little happy that there was someone who cared for him. "Thanks, Joanne." He smiled and did not care his mouth hurt. "That's awfully nice of you to stop by and see me like this."

Joanne nodded. "It's my pleasure. It's at the end of my shift so I decided I should at least stop by and see how you are..." She pursed her lips and noted how swollen his lip was. "And by the looks of it you're not faring too well, Richard."

Richard rolled his eyes and pursed his lips and winced. "Like I said, it wasn't a prisoner..." He let out an exasperated sigh. "They're a far sight more congenial and welcoming than that bi..." He saw Joanne look at him rather gruffly. "I mean Scotland."

Joanne smiled at him. "Well..." She nodded and started to feel awkward. "I just hope you're doing okay and will be doing better once you're out, that's all."

Richard smiled and nodded. "Thanks, Joanne..." He looked up at her and admired her beauty and vitality. "It's nice to know I have at least one friend."

Joanne waved that comment off. "I'm sure you have plenty of friends, Richard."

"Not one that would take the time to visit me and not want something in return." Richard smiled at her and his growing affinity for her.

Joanne smiled in an awe-shucks kind of way because she felt for him and it showed. "Is there anything I can do for you?" Her eyebrows popped-up to question if there was any help needed. "Anything at all."

Richard groaned. "Unless you have a lawyer handy in your purse, I'll be okay for now."

Joanne nodded. She sat there awkwardly and teared up for him. "It's hard seeing you like this Richard. I only wish I could do something for you."

Richard smiled graciously. "I want to thank you for giving me that letter from Ron the other day."

Joanne waved it off politely. "That's okay. It was addressed to you." She smiled awkwardly again at him and wanted to continue the conversation. "Was it important?"

Richard nodded and then tick-tocked his head. "Yes and no." He pursed his lips mysteriously and hoped she would ask more questions so he could at least continue the conversation.

"Oh…" Joanne had a confused look flash across her face. "I don't understand. I'm sorry."

Richard chuckled politely. "Sorry…" He pursed his lips and he forgot about the pain in his face. "The information was important, but it kind of got me where I am right now."

Joanne looked shocked. "Oh no…" She gasped. "I hope you didn't get arrested because I gave you the letter."

Richard shook his head aggressively to prevent her from thinking that. "Oh no…" He almost reached out to comfort her but heard the guard warn him off. He looked at him and forced a smile to apologize. He turned back to Joanne and smiled to put her at ease. "No. Please don't think that. The information Ron gave me just confirmed a few things he told me. It was the listening device I put in someone's house that got me arrested."

Joanne gasped. "What?" Her eyes had a shocked look in them. "Richard…" She licked her lips nervously. "How could you? You can get into some serious trouble for that."

Richard rolled his eyes and held his hands up and waved them around at his surroundings. "Well, no-shit, Sherlock." He saw her narrow her eyes at him and he slowed his roll.

"But is that the reason they locked you up?" Joanne pressed him some more.

Richard's head tick-tocked from side-to-side. "Hmm…" He pursed his lips to the side and darted his eyes around. "I also won't give the arresting detectives the password to my iTunes account where the file is saved."

Joanne looked at him perplexed. "What file?" She was intrigued.

Richard snorted a giggle thinking everyone should have been up to speed on his case. "Oh. The voice recording file from that person's house. We think someone poisoned her to keep it quiet."

Joanne looked at him oddly. "Keep what quiet, Richard?" She stammered nervously, "You're scaring me with this cloak and dagger stuff."

Richard took a breath and wondered if he should even be telling her any of this. If she knew too much, she could be a target too – and he did not want that. "I shouldn't tell you. You could be in danger if you're involved."

Joanne shook her head and looked at him with a burning desire to help. "I'm already involved when I gave you that letter…" She sighed for his safety and her head tilted to the side. "Let me know how I can help you."

Richard hemmed-and-hawed and chewed his thoughts as his mind raced. "It has to do with a pension management company assassinating pensioners so they can keep all of their pension value in the fund without having to pay them out..." He side-eyed the guard and then continued. "They make the murders look like accidents, so the police aren't suspicious."

Joanne processed the abridged version and her mind raced and there was a quizzical look on her face. She shook her head. "That can't be, Richard..." Her head tilted and her eyes darted to put the pieces together. "To what end?"

Richard looked at her. "The pension management company gets paid a percentage of the fund base and so the larger it is the more money they make."

Joanne narrowed her suspicious eyes at him. "No one in their right mind would even conceive of something that bold..." She shook her head in disbelief and it was plastered across her face as well. "It's, umm..." She was trying to find the word or words. "It's inconceivable..." She looked at him blankly. "That's the most diabolical thing I've ever heard..." She scoffed and simply saw Richard nod. "Over what? Money?"

Richard's eyes opened wide and he nodded in agreement. "A lot of money. Tens of millions of dollars a year..." He pulled his mouth to the side. "People have killed other people for a lot less."

Joanne could not believe the conspiracy, but she also knew if there was little basis to Richard's story he would not be in here right now. She took a deep breath and pursed her lips. "Okay..." She tick-tocked her head. "Let's say this is true. What can I do to help you?"

Richard looked at her and there was a shocked look on his face. He had few friends he could trust, and he was not sure what he could do where he was right now that would help him. He looked at Joanne's innocence and wondered if she could be trusted. He would have trusted Scotland and Carter but he was hangry, and she punched him so they were on his shitlist. He wondered if he should involve Joanne. He already blurted out the conspiracy theory and wondered what she would do if she had the information? Take it to the police or send it to his old publisher? He did not know and wondered if he should trust her. She had always been so kind to him, and he had only known her for the last few months but there was something pure and innocent about her and he had to trust someone. He stammered because he was out of options, "Umm, can I trust you with something?"

Joanne nodded and her eyes were wide with excitement and adventure after having been told the secret conspiracy. "Yes…" She smiled obligingly at him and wished he would trust her. "Anything. Just let me know how I can help you, Richard. Please." Her eyes implored him to trust her.

Richard was understandably nervous. The information he was going to trust her with would blow the conspiracy wide open. He had already written the story and combined with the information Ron Little gave him and the recording from Mrs. Vasquez's house he knew the story had legs. "Okay. I need you to write this information down…" He watched her pull out a pad and pen and readied herself to be Erin Brockovich. She nodded that she was ready. "My iTunes account is ricmoran1341@icloud.com and my password is sinarom!7293." He watched her write it all down.

Joanne showed him what she wrote, and he nodded his approval.

Richard bit his bottom lip and winced at the pain because he forgot about it. "There is an email address you need to send the information to. It's my old boss, Gavin McLeod at the LA Times. His email is gavmcleod@latimes.com." Richard let out a sigh and felt that he had just confessed all his sins to a priest and now his mind and soul were free – which is odd since he was an atheist.

Joanne smiled and nodded. "You can trust me with this information, Richard." She pursed her lips and put her stuff back in her handbag. "Leave it with me. I'll make sure he gets it."

Richard smiled and pursed his lips. "Thanks, Joanne. I feel a lot better now."

Joanne chuckled and shyly looked down and then turned to him. "I'm glad I made you feel better. When you get out, we need to go get coffee, okay?" Her eyes lit up about the prospect of them meeting up.

Richard perked up too and things did not seem so bleak right now. He had a good feeling that Joanne would get the information out. "I'd really like that Joanne." He smiled.

Joanne could feel the awkwardness build again and she giggled. "I guess I better get going before traffic really gets bad." She slowly stood up and politely waved to him.

Richard nodded, got up and returned the wave.

He watched her walk out and he waved to her once more and saw her return the favor and then she disappeared.

Richard walked back to his cell and was just in time for dinner. He felt his appetite come back regardless of what they had in store for him. He looked forward to it.

He went inside and the guard shut the door. The lock slammed into place.

Richard waited patiently and the slot slammed open and his tray of food was placed on the ledge for him to take. "Thank you." He smiled as he looked at the tray's contents and it was more than what the server did to respond to his thank you. 'Nevermind.'

Richard walked back to his makeshift built-in table. After the customary side-eye from the guard, he heard the slot slam closed. He mumbled under his breath, "Sure isn't Musso and Frank's that's for sure."

He looked at the meal and saw a wrapped sandwich, juice box, a Cup of Noodle and lukewarm water to go with it. He grumbled under his breath again, "Wow..." He sighed and peeled the lid of the Cup of Noodle back. "Definitely isn't Musso and Frank's."

He pulled his mouth to the side and poured in the lukewarm water to get it ready now so after he finished his sandwich, he could probably enjoy it. The water filled it and it bubbled as predicted and he closed the paper resealable lid to keep what little heat there was in the water inside the cup. He pushed it to the side and started to unwrap his sandwich which looked kind of appetising, but he was being generous.

He wondered if Joanne would follow through on his instructions and he hoped she did. He did look forward to meeting her for coffee when this was all over, and he smiled contently. He chuckled as he bit into the sandwich and was pleasantly surprised at the taste. He murmured to himself. "Hmm. Not bad. Not bad at all." He wondered if a little lukewarm soup would add to the piquant nature of the un-Martha-Stewart-like sandwich, and he peeled the lid back a tad to expose the savoury soup.

He noticed small, soft bubbles forming in the water like it was boiling. He pursed his lips and thought that was odd. He waited for a few more seconds and then it foamed up oddly. His jaw dropped open and eyes had an instantaneous startled look of terror. He gasped, then...

"Kaboom!"

Chapter 15

The next morning, Mason piloted the Bentley Flying Spur to the County Lock-up after Carter and Scotland received calls to meet the detectives there. They heard the news about Richard Moranis and were aghast to hear that he had been killed last night.

Carter looked over at Scotland and popped up her eyebrows. She flashed such a smug smirk that you would need to use a brick to wipe it off her face. She did have a glow about her that was unmistakable for someone who had the best evening of her life – after almost dying.

Scotland side-eyed her and knew she wanted to spill her guts to her, but she was biding her time because she knew she was busting at the seams with some salacious news. She groaned and knew she was going to regret the blow-by-blow account. "So…" She pursed her lips to the side. "What'd you get up to last night?"

Carter beamed and she turned to look at Scotland so she could see how satisfied she was after her late evening cavorting. "Nate and I hooked up."

Scotland feigned surprise. She looked at her and could see she enjoyed herself – maybe a little too much. "Really? Quelle surprise."

Carter looked at her funny. "Be happy for my happiness, Scotty." She pouted.

"I'm sorry." Scotland looked at her and this time she was a little more open about her pending story. "Please. Continue." She motioned with her hand.

Carter smiled wholesomely and put her hand on her friend's arm. "So, we came back to my place because his roommate was home, and we couldn't…" She tick-tocked her head from side-to-side and her eyes rolled. She air-quoted but it was unnecessary. "Hook up."

Scotland looked at her funny. It was always amusing when Carter would go into highschool mode when she would tell her about her conquests. "You mean fuck." She had a matter-of-fact look on her face. "We're adults, Carter."

Carter snorted derisively and simply shook her head and continued. "Anyways…" She pulled her tongue out at her cutely. "After forty-five minutes of heavy-petting and foreplay, we got hot and heavy and between inches eight and nine as he slid into me, I kind of passed out for a bit and then it really got feral."

Scotland narrowed her eyes out of concern for her friend. "Jesus…eight and nine?"

Carter nodded appreciatively. "The boy's big..." She nudged her friend and groaned comedically, "Lemme tell you." She forced a wink and giggled. "So, as we were ripping pages out of the Kama Sutra and him bending me into every pretzel shape he could think of..." She pursed her lips and had a quizzical look on her face. "I come hard, and he comes and calls me Gwen." She had a dubious look on her face. "And then he does this rapid-fire-moan-and-groan like he's having a seizure and gagging on something – because let's face it, I'm that good in bed." She curled her mouth up and her eyes went blank. "Needless to say, I was..."

Scotland's mouth dropped open, and she interjected. "Concerned?"

Carter shook her head, and her inquiring eyes were wide open. "Perplexed."

Scotland looked at her funny and narrowed her eyes. "Perplexed? That's what you were?"

Carter nodded her head. "Yeah, I'm complicated. No man has ever called me someone else's name because..." She waved her hand over her body and circled it around her perfect Brazilian nether region. "C'mon..." Her eyes had that what-the-fuck look about it. "Who'd cry out someone else's name when you're doing all of this? Huh? I ask you?" The quizzical look on her face was completely unnecessary to the casual observer, but necessary in her opinion.

Scotland shook her head and mocked her lovingly. "That fucker..." She raised her hands in despair. "What was he thinking?" She looked away and rolled her eyes all the way around – twice.

Carter could not and would not see the sarcasm. She was too much of a narcissist for that. "So, I shove him off and ask him who the fuck is Gwen."

Scotland loved her bluntness. It always cut through the bullshit. "And he said?"

Carter paused and looked up at the Alcantara headliner and she had to take a moment – reality show-style for dramatic effect. She exhaled with purpose. "His roommate."

Scotland's eyes were wide open, and she now understood what was going on with Officer Nate Murdock. "His roommate is his girlfriend?"

Carter grabbed onto her like she was a life-preserve. She clenched her jaw and growled, "His soon to be ex-wife."

Scotland gasped for real. "Wait..." She narrowed her eyes and could not believe Nate's audacity. "Soon to be ex-wife?"

Carter nodded critically. "Uh-huh." She looked perturbed but still had a delectable afterglow about her and she was not going to just let that go after having put in the effort. "He said that they could not afford to live apart so they're sharing the one-bedroom condo until things settled." Her eyes rolled in amazement. "A one-bedroom!"

Scotland looked at her quizzically. "And when would that be?"

Carter shrugged and held her hands up vacantly and yelled, "Who-the-fuck-knows?" She screwed her mouth to the side. "If he didn't make me come those six times and stick his thumb up my ass – and you know how much I love it when they do that to me – I'd be more pissed off!" She sat back in a huff now because she realized she had been used and then duped – but she still enjoyed the sex.

Scotland looked at her sideways and pursed her lips as she sized Carter up. "Hmm." Her studious look yelled volumes. She wanted to say something more but thought otherwise – to be on the safe side.

Carter turned her attention from the cityscape to her friend. Fortunately, her arms were crossed so she did not have to recross them. She growled at her, "Hmm...what?" She pursed her lips so hard they were turning blue.

Scotland took a short breath as her mouth dropped open and wondered if it were the right time to bring up certain things – she had noted and stored away for future reference about Carter's many carefree dalliances – and how they ultimately ended for her – and that would be not so well. "Umm...not to be critical, babe..." She tried to formulate a diplomatic response. "But you seem to have a penchant for hooking up with married men..." She paused and corrected herself. "Whoops. Married people." She popped-up her eyebrows out of concern and not to gloat – but it may not have come out that way.

Carter scoffed at that and then thought about all her relationships. She wondered why all the ones she enjoyed having sex with were always married and not single. Her mind raced and she lived through each and every one of them in a blink of an eye and the sordid ending. "Hah." Her jaw shifted to the side and she tapped her porcelain veneered teeth – deep in thought. Her eyes saw the light, but it was not the first time they had this conversation. Scotland would often have to remind her of every sordid detail – when the need arose. She tilted her head like she thought of a time where he or she was not married. "What about..." She paused for a moment to reflect once again. Her mouth screwed to the side and she thought twice about that time. "Hmm." Her lips pursed and she discounted that example.

Scotland could hear the wheels in her head turn. "Don't worry. It's not all on you. They're also responsible." She smirked because there was the one example she swore she would never bring up again – ever – but she rarely kept that promise because it was so amusing.

Carter saw the satisfied smirk and she looked at her with a derisive glare. "What? Are you thinking about that time with him and her in the place and that thing?"

Scotland politely shrugged her shoulders, and she had a smug look of defiance on her face. "Maybe."

Carter narrowed her furious eyes at Scotland and pointed an offensive finger in her direction. "Look..." She shook her head derisively. "It's not my fault the First Lady liked to watch and participate, okay?"

Scotland playfully shrugged her shoulders and held her hands up. She pursed her lips confidently. "You brought it up."

Carter huffed and saw that they were there. Mason always made the trip seem short. Fortunately, he was the type of driver who drove and did not hear the conversations in the car – he was that good and well compensated for his troubles.

Scotland and Carter walked into the County Lock-up without having to scan through or leave their possessions behind. They were escorted in with Hansen and Marx, and at the end of the hallway there were swarms of police officers and crime scene investigators. There was an acrid smell of smoke which could not mask the stench of urine, excrement, and vomit. Hopefully, not from what happened last night but who knows?

Scotland held her nose and wondered how anyone would be able to survive in these conditions and she shook her head sadly. She wondered why there was no noise from the other prisoners, though.

Hansen walked casually with his partner as they led the ladies towards the crime scene. "Watch your step, ladies."

Scotland's eyes opened wide when she saw the twisted metal door torqued away from its hinges and the scorch marks from the flames that haloed the doorway. It looked like the gateway to hell had been ripped open. All around was a dampness obviously from the sprinkler system but in a concrete tomb such as this, why would they need a sprinkler unless concrete suddenly was now flammable. She let out a muffled mumble, "Jesus Christ..." Her jaw dropped and she could not believe the amount of damage. She pointed as Marx turned back to see if she saw something she was not supposed to. "He was in there?"

Marx nodded and pursed his lips. "Afraid so..." He turned and shook his head and kept walking. His eyes scanned the damage the explosion and fire caused. "I don't think he suffered..." He paused and did not know himself. "Much." He shrugged a little as a consolation.

Carter looked at Scotland with wild eyes. First an attempt on their lives and then a successful one on Richard Moranis. She gasped and felt sorry for him. "Oh..." Her eyes saw the carnage the explosion caused and hoped he did not suffer but Marx did not help one iota. "Poor, Dickie." Her lips pursed and let out a sorry sigh.

They came up to Kate and Nate already there at the scene and the investigators were packing up already.

Kate headtossed to them and smiled as she saw them arrive. She marvelled at Scotland, "Hi." She grinned at her and licked her lips – happy to see her.

Scotland smiled back. "Hi, there." She turned to Nate and smiled and nodded. He uncomfortably smiled and turned away nervously. Her thoughts clouded. 'That's right I know...turn your head in shame. Shame!'

Carter glared at Nate and stared right through him and she growled low. Her eyes narrowed derisively at him for good reason.

Hansen stopped and scanned their faces and had an exasperated look on his face. He looked at Scotland and Carter. "We've got to stop meeting like this..." His head tilted and took solace in the fact that they were at least safe. "Wish I could say the same for Mr. Moranis." He pursed his lips and rubbed his neck. The tension was getting to him and it showed.

Scotland gasped as she looked inside the cell. The interior was all scorched and the fixtures looked like they had been through fifteen rounds with a sledgehammer. "Jesus..." She gasped at the condition of the interior and wondered why anyone would want to kill Richard that way. "What did this?"

Hansen curled his mouth up and could not believe it himself. "The preliminary reports corroborated with the video footage suggested he was killed by an explosive in his meal. A Cup O' Noodles." He raised his eyebrows. "We believe it was activated with the addition of water which may have been laced with a chemical reactant." He scanned their faces. "We're looking for the person that delivered the food because this was a targeted assassination."

Carter scoffed comically, "For fucksake..." She murmured, "I knew those things were bad for you, but c'mon."

Scotland ignored her and gasped. She felt remorse for hitting him. She started to tear-up and felt Carter wrap her arm around her and pull her in for comfort. "Jesus. Poor Richard." She let out a gasp and sniffed. "I can't believe I was the last person he saw, and I punched him." Tears dribbled down her cheeks.

Kate felt sorry for her and pursed her lips. "You couldn't have known, Scotland." She tilted her head and wanted to hold her but that would be inappropriate.

Hansen looked at Marx and then turned to Scotland. "You weren't the last person to meet him." He eyed her reaction. "Another woman met with him just before he was taken back to his cell..." He waved at the damage. "And then this happened."

Carter looked at him smugly and mumbled. "Did she punch him in the face?"

Hansen looked at her surprised. "What? No..." He screwed his mouth up. "Why would she do that?"

Carter shook her head at him. "Then I think you see my point." She tilted her head at Scotland who was still remorseful.

Hansen's mouth dropped open and wanted to say something but closed it and shook his head in disbelief. "We're still trying to find out who she was and what she was doing with him."

Scotland whimpered as she wiped her eyes dry. She took a deep breath of the smelly air and almost gagged. She turned to Hansen and Marx. "I'll pay for his funeral costs."

Marx nodded and smiled. "That'd be appreciated. We contacted his ex-wife, and she slammed the phone down on us." He shrugged.

Carter was surprised and mumbled in a low tone, "Poor guy made friends everywhere he went apparently."

Scotland nudged her and groaned at her bluntness, "Carter."

Hansen smiled. "I'm sure he would've appreciated you paying for the funeral like that..." His face screwed up a little and he winced at the initial walk-through of the crime scene when he and Marx attended. "Umm..." He paused and blinked blankly. "It may take the medical examiner a few days to put the parts of him they could find back together but the stuff they had to scoop up with the shovel may have to be cremated, so..." He heard Scotland start to cry some more and his eyes grew exponentially wider with every sob as Carter tried to console her. "Uhh, perhaps we can go to the..." He pursed his lips because he hated when women cried in front of him. "Umm, someplace that's not here."

Carter glared at him and shook her head with disapproval. She saw a blank look on his face and wondered how he delivered bad news to other people. Her lips pursed at his objectionable comment and she turned to her inconsolable friend. "C'mon, Scotty..." She smiled at Nate and Kate as she took her away from the area. She murmured to her politely, "Let's go find you a quiet place to blubber so the others don't see you ugly-cry, okay?"

Scotland simply nodded in approval and went where Carter led her — away from there.

Carter pursed her lips and let out a sigh. She groaned at her, "C'mon, sweetie. Not in front of all the people..." She shook her head for her friend. "You know you look like Chloe Grace Moretz when you cry."

Carter handed Scotland a bottle of water that the guard was kind enough to get for her. "C'mon..." She smiled at her friend. "Have a little sippy-sip of water and we can get something stronger later, okay?"

Scotland nodded and felt a little better. She looked around and she started to cry again.

Carter looked at her wide-eyed and wondered what was now wrong. She groaned out loud, "What?"

Scotland blubbered uncontrollably as she sat there. "This..." She pointed down, remorseful. "This is where we sat when I punched him." She bawled again.

Carter looked at her and the guard who looked uncomfortable as he stood quietly. She was aghast and let out an exasperated groan, "Oh-for-fucksake..." She looked around. "C'mon..." She took her and walked her to another seat. "Sit here..." She moved her carefully in her fragile state. "No. Here. I don't want you looking at the seats and bawl again, okay?"

Scotland sat down and took another sip of water. "Thanks..." She took a breath and wiped her eyes and nose on her sleeve. "You're a good friend, Carter."

Carter was aghast but forced a smile. "Yes..." She handed her a tissue. "Umm..." She dabbed her eyes and thanked god she used mascara that did not run, or she would look like Pris from Blade Runner right about now. "C'mon. Don't use your sleeve on that designer-knock-off, honey."

Scotland sniffed and let out a sad exhale. She shook her head compassionately for Richard Moranis. "I can't believe that was the last bad thing that happened to him..." She pursed her lips and looked blank. "Me..." She shook her head disagreeably. "Punching him in the face."

Carter tick-tocked her head and had a pensive look on her face. "Hmm..." She screwed her mouth up. "I think the Cup O' Noodles were the last thing that fucked him over, Scotty. You had nothing to do with that. He could've been out if he was a little more cooperative, but he chose to be defiant and he was a sitting duck in here."

Scotland sigh deeply and she narrowed her eyes at her. "Honey..." She tilted her head to the side and looked her in the eyes. "I know you're trying to be helpful but you're making it worse."

Carter scoffed at that. She too narrowed her eyes and glared at her friend with impertinence. "Look, Scotland Yarde..." She poked a finger in her breastbone and avoided her tiny tits. "You had nothing to do with Dick getting killed. He was an adult and made decisions that he was responsible for. You cannot hold yourself liable for his poor decisions. Understand?" She glared at her once more to ensure she understood what she was saying and saw a tiny, frightened nod.

Scotland was shocked at her forcefulness but agreed. She saw her tilt her head with her crazy-eyes look and waited for her to answer – not just a gesture. She murmured sheepishly, "Yes. I understand." She gave a salutary nod.

Carter nodded and was more content now. "You help people as best you can. You have always helped people who could not fend for themselves. You're not responsible for how they got into that mess in the first place, but you always did whatever you could to help them out of the mess that they made."

Scotland lamented and nodded her head. "I guess you're right."

Carter pursed her lips. "Damn right I'm right." She could tell Scotland needed helpful reminders. "Remember in highschool when Amanda Cleaver was being bothered by that atrocious, troll Brent Partridge? Huh?"

Scotland nodded her head and recalled the sordid incident from inception to finality. "Yes. What a jerk."

Carter nodded. "Exactly..." She pointed at her for effect. "And the rumors he was spreading around school about her family that were only partially true?" She saw her nod hesitantly. "And-what..." Her eyebrows popped-up. "Pray-tell did Amanda's saviour, Scotland Yarde, do?"

Scotland murmured embarrassingly, "I punched him, and told him to shut the fuck up."

Carter nodded and pursed her lips. Her eyes had a maniacal look to them. "Damn straight, you punched him and told him off."

Scotland looked at her funny. "But, uh..." She curled her mouth up and her eyes darted. "Her father was arrested by the FBI for being the Baton-Rouge Strangler..." She winced a little as she recalled the sordid incident. "He's serving twelve life sentences."

Carter nodded. "True, but the point is Amanda didn't do it and Brent should've shut the fuck up."

Scotland pursed her lips. "Thanks for helping..." She darted her eyes a little as she thought through Carter's process. "I think."

Carter was happy with herself and sat beside her and threw her arm around her for comfort. "Point is, you help people in need and regardless of the consequences that they got or get themselves into, you can't control everything and you're not responsible for everything that happens to them or the people around them."

Scotland looked at her friend and leaned her head on her shoulder.

Carter smirked and added, "Unless that person is me, then you need to do whatever the fuck you need to do to get me out of the mess I got myself into."

Scotland took a deep breath and blinked blankly. "I think that's a given." She just stayed in her special place on Carter's shoulder.

Hansen came inside with his phone out. Marx took up the rear dutifully. He sat beside them and showed them the CCTV picture of Richard's guest just before he died. "This is her."

Scotland and Carter stared at the picture and gasped. They could not believe she had anything to do with his assassination, but they went with Occam's Razor and did not leave any stone unturned.

Scotland murmured to him, "That's Joanne from the Medical Examiner's Office..." She looked up at Marx and over to Hansen. "She's the receptionist."

Hansen nodded his head. "Seems she also works here part-time and signed in as Joanne Middleton and visitor of Richard Moranis."

Scotland narrowed her inquisitive eyes at Hansen. "It only proves she said hi to Richard. She is..." She caught herself and gasped a little. "Was interested in Richard as more than a friend the last time we ran into her at the ME's office."

Marx nodded and side-eyed his partner. "She may have just visited him because she knew he was here, Jake."

Hansen screwed his mouth up and tick-tocked his head as he thought through all the details. "True, but we should talk with her anyway."

Carter looked at him. "Yeah, and if she gets upset..." She tilted her head and pulled her mouth to the side. "Go easy on her. She may be in a fragile state. Okay?"

Hansen looked at her like she had two-heads. "What's that supposed to mean?"

Carter snorted and looked at him in the eyes. "It means you'll be the last person to write Hallmark Get Well cards, okay?"

Hansen scoffed and got up. He was in a bit of a huff after that comment. His wife did say he was a little robotic but what the hell did she know? "I'll make a note…" He snarled at the gorgeous woman. "Thanks for the advice."

Carter smiled smugly at him. "Any time. You know where to find me."

Scotland and Carter walked out towards the car and Mason was standing by to usher them inside. They saw Kate and Nate beside their patrol car.

Kate waved and walked up to them. She smiled at Carter and looked at Scotland and her sad eyes. "Are you feeling better?"

Scotland nodded and smiled up at her. "Thanks for asking."

Kate gave her a crooked smile and wished she could make her feel better. "There was nothing you could have done, Scotland."

Scotland nodded and tried her best to perk up, but the feeling of remorse preyed on her thoughts. "I wish I could apologize for what I did to him, that's all." She shrugged.

Kate nodded. "I understand. We sometimes say and do things we regret and wish we could take it back but sometimes we can't. That's what makes us human. Our flaws."

Scotland side-eyed her and smiled. "You know what would really cheer me up?"

Kate's eyes twinkled at her. "What? Tell me."

Scotland playfully rolled her eyes and invaded into her space. "Go out to dinner with me…" She grinned toothily at her. "Tonight. I'll take you to Spago."

Kate was impressed with the venue and melted when she saw her cute overbite and brilliant smile to go with her gorgeous looks. She nodded and her eyes lit up. "Only if it'll make you feel better, though." She playfully acted bashful.

Carter watched the two women toy with each other and she groaned and rolled her eyes all the way around at the two of them cavorting with her so close. She eyed Nate and he was as far away as he could be, and she narrowed her angry eyes at him. A growl emanated from deep inside of her. 'That's right…look away.'

Scotland beamed at her and licked her lips. She suddenly felt a lot better than before and was convinced that she needed to find Richard's killer to make amends. "Here…" She handed her phone to Kate and could not help but touch her hand in the process. It sent chills throughout her body and she felt herself get wet in all the right places. "Put your cell in here and I'll text you."

Kate did as she was instructed and handed it back to her making sure she touched her again and she felt wet in all the right places.

Scotland smiled and texted her and she watched Kate take out her phone and smile at her message. She loved how she giggled.

Kate nodded. "Seven sounds great. We can meet at the LAPD station."

Scotland nodded and was a little hesitant. "You don't want me to pick you up at your place?"

Kate pursed her lips, and her face went blank. "It's a long story..." She looked into her eyes and wanted to tell her then and there, but it could wait. Everyone had something preying on their mind and she was no different. "Is that still okay?"

Scotland nodded. "Of course. Seven it is."

Kate grabbed for her hand and squeezed it. "I'm looking forward to having dinner with you, Scotland." She felt the electricity when there was skin-on-skin contact with the diminutive alpha. She gave her one of her best sideways grins just to seal the deal.

Scotland licked her lips and felt the electricity flow as she squeezed her hand, and her G-string was now swamped. She could only guess what the beautiful woman could do to her in bed and she desperately wanted to find out. She was by no means a slouch and she would make her work for her body, but she would welcome the defeat. "I'm looking forward to dinner, too."

Carter smiled and watched them awkwardly hold hands and it seemed like ages before they parted ways. She mumbled to herself in a low whisper, "At last." Kate waved to her and Carter acknowledged her with a smile and a wave.

Mason helped them in, and they got comfortable.

Carter turned to Scotland. "My god. I felt like I just got scissored listening to the two of you set up that date." She comically rolled her eyes and saw Scotland simply grin back at her – in a much happier mood.

Chapter 16

Hansen parked the car in the Medical Examiner's office parking lot and grabbed at Marx's arm before he could get out.

"What?" Marx was startled and thought something was wrong.

Hansen had said nothing on the drive from the lock-up to the ME's office because he was deep in thought, and Marx was on the phone with his bookie. He chewed on his thoughts and was the thinker of the two of them. "We need to have a word with Stafford and why he called that hit on Yarde and Deklava, and then the one on Moranis." He took a deep breath and grumbled under his breath, "I don't like it when he goes off script like that and doesn't advise us."

Marx's look clouded and he narrowed his eyes. "Seemed like a good idea to take them out before they got to close to the truth."

Hansen rolled his eyes at his naïve partner. "Yes, if the assassin was successful and yes, if the women were nobodies." He let out an exasperated sigh and growled with a clenched jaw – and a pointed finger for effect. "Not when they're her and her." He pursed his lips so his partner would understand. "We don't need to know when he is about to do something foolhardy like wear socks with sandals…" He pulled his mouth to the side because he was a little upset. "But we need to know when he's about to do something fucking insane like try to kill Scotland Yarde and Carter Deklava."

Marx put his hands out to brace himself. "Okay…" He exhaled to calm his partner down and show he understood where he was coming from. "Jesus. I get it now. He probably thought he was doing us and him a favor, that's all." He rolled his eyes to agree with the effort not the result.

Hansen pursed his lips. "His effort is going to get us caught because now there are too many questions. You don't pull a three-hundred-thousand-dollar Bentley out of a wall owned by two dynastically rich women, and not have the Chief of Police and Police Commissioner asking questions…" He narrowed his eyes because he was concerned the house of cards was in a windstorm. "That chestnut who roasted himself over an open fire was a nobody, and no one gives a shit that he was the only fatality. But add Kristen and Bella to the equation and now we have a problem." He sighed out loud.

Marx screwed his mouth to the side and knew his partner had a point. They were good at diverting attention away from their operation but any hint of a conspiracy or questions that involved them could make their lives very difficult. "You're right. We should talk with Stafford and find out why he's such an asshole to not tell us."

Hansen opened the door and sighed with a huff. "We know why he's an asshole..." He popped his eyebrows up at Marx. "We just need to know why he didn't tell us."

Marx snorted his approval with a chuckle and got out too. "I'll set it up."

The detectives walked inside the ME's office and smiled at the receptionist.

Hansen checked her nametag and his eyes lit up. 'This will be easy.'

He smiled at her and saw her force a smile back at him and Marx. "Hi..." He pulled out his badge and side-eyed Marx as he did the same. "Detectives Hansen and Marx to see Joanne Middleton."

Joanne gasped and put her hand to her mouth and her eyes were startled at the unexpected visit. "Umm..." She gulped as she eyeballed both badges to confirm they were who they stated. "I'm Joanne Middleton..." She volleyed her eyes between the two detectives. "How may I help you, detectives?"

Hansen smiled at the confirmation. "Is there someplace more private we can go, Miss Middleton?" He popped-up his eyebrows.

Joanne's eyes teared-up a little as her hand trembled. "Am I in trouble, detectives?"

Marx saw that she was a little scared of being interviewed by them. "Oh..." He held his hand up to calm her. "Detective Hansen and I just want to ask you a few questions about Richard Moranis, ma'am." He smiled to make her more comfortable.

Joanne seemed a little more at ease, but her hand still trembled. "Umm..." She looked down at her partner for the day at the front reception desk. "Louise, can you cover for me?"

Louise dutifully nodded and thanked her lucky stars she was not being interrogated. She also enjoyed handling the desk herself because Joanne was too much of a perfectionist and she just liked talking with the couriers and ambulance drivers. "Sure, Joanne..." She beamed at them all. "I can handle it. Take your time."

Joanne nodded and escorted the detectives to the small meeting room around the corner. "We can talk in here..." She scanned her keycard for the door and showed them inside. She made a cursory glance at Louise who made a gesture wondering what it was all about, and Joanne simply shrugged apologetically. She turned back to the detectives. "Make yourselves comfortable."

Hansen got comfortable and watched Joanne casually sit in a chair, but she was demure and a little hesitant as she took her seat. She bundled herself up with her sweater and sat patiently and waited for the detectives to ask her about Richard Moranis.

Joanne stammered as her head volleyed between the two detectives. "So…" She licked her lips and pushed up her glasses. "You were going to ask me about Richard?"

Hansen nodded his head as he pulled out his notebook. "Yes…" He clicked his pen and readied himself. "How do you know the deceased?"

The color in Joanne's face drained immediately and there was a look of horror plastered on her face. She yelled out in alarm, "What?" She started to breathe heavy and tear-up. "What do you mean deceased?"

Hansen's jaw dropped and he side-eyed Marx who usually made these egregious types of errors – and he saw him purse his lips and shake his head with disapproval and disappointment. He turned to Joanne who was sobbing now. His eyes were wide with embarrassment, and he understood what Carter Deklava now meant. "Uhh…" He gulped and did not know how to extricate himself from the mess he just made. "I'm sorry Miss Middleton. I thought you knew."

Joanne looked at him with tears dribbling down her cheeks and she shook her head with sadness. "No…" She pulled out a tissue from the box nearby on the table and dabbed her eyes. "I didn't know. I just saw him yesterday and he seemed fine."

Hansen forced a smile and nodded. "Yes. I'm sorry to have to tell you that it happened last night during dinner time."

Joanne shook her head in disbelief. "How did it happen? Was he assaulted?"

Hansen screwed up his mouth. "Umm…" He shook his head and did not know how to tell her. "He was killed with an explosive device."

Joanne was aghast. "That's horrible." She breathed heavy like she was trying to come to grips with what happened.

Hansen nodded. "Yes…" He looked at his partner and then turned back to her. "How did you know Richard and what did you discuss yesterday?"

Joanne took a breath and dabbed her eyes and nose once more. "He used to come in every so often and speak with our janitor Ron Little."

Marx's eyes popped up. "Yes, we understand Mr. Little died of a heart attack recently."

Joanne looked at him and nodded. She paused and sized them both up and had an epiphany. "Wait. Were you the two detectives who arrested him?"

Marx held out his hand. "We held him for his own good, Miss Middleton…" He tilted his head, side-eyed Hansen and then narrowed his eyes. "He was being uncooperative."

Joanne scoffed at him. "Well, I hope you can live with yourselves, detectives…" She shook her head in disappointment. "You may have contributed to his death."

Marx was flabbergasted and let out an aggressive growl, "Now look…" He felt Hansen's arm go across his body to cut him off and stay out of the fight.

Hansen turned to Joanne. "Miss Middleton, that's unfair. We needed to know about some vital information he supposedly had on some questionable deaths and he was obstructing us at every question."

Joanne crossed her arms and while she may have been sad a few minutes ago she was now defiant and angry at them both. "So, putting him in lock-up satisfied your lust for going by the book but put his life at risk?"

Marx scoffed and looked at her as he leaned forward. "We don't even know if he was safer on the outside."

Joanne was perturbed by the little man playing detective and she leaned forward with her hands on her hips. She growled at him in an aggressive and impertinent manner, "Well, we'll never know now will we – because he's dead!" Her eyes were wide open and as angry as they could be for such a submissive woman.

Hansen held his hand up to stop the bickering that was getting them nowhere. "Miss Middleton. Did Richard say anything to you?"

Joanne glared at Marx and did not care. She turned to Hansen and nodded. "He told me to get some information to his old editor at the LA Times…" She pursed her lips and leaned at Marx and made him flinch a little. "Something to do with a supposed conspiracy."

Hansen was floored and he leaned over. "And what did you do with that information, Miss Middleton?"

Joanne looked at him matter-of-factly. "I sent it to him…" She looked at him blankly. "The editor. Last night."

Hansen and Marx groaned out loud and shook their heads.

Hansen looked at her aggressively. "I wish you hadn't of done that, Miss Middleton. There was some sensitive information in there that the police should have reviewed first."

Marx glared at her. "You could be in a lot of trouble for doing that."

Joanne postured to him and yelled out at him with impertinence, "Then arrest me, detective!" Her eyes rolled at him because she did not care for his attitude. "We all know your track record already for keeping someone safe in jail!"

Hansen stood up and looked at his partner. He growled out matter-of-factly, "Okay, we're done here..." He turned to Joanne who had her angry eyes fixed on Marx. "Let's go Marx. Miss Middleton, you've been very helpful."

Joanne pursed her lips and narrowed her eyes at the stare down she was having with Marx. She growled out in an aggressive tone, "My pleasure."

Marx stood up and looked over at Hansen. "Aren't we going to arrest her for something?"

Joanne stood up and postured at him. "Try it, gumshoe!"

Hansen grabbed Marx by his arm and pulled him toward the door. They hustled out of the lobby in a hurry and did not even look back.

Joanne yelled at the top of her lungs as they tried to hustle away from her. "That's right, Laurel and Hardy! Run away! If you have any more stupid questions, you know where to find me!" Her voice echoed throughout the foyer.

People in the lobby wondered what that was all about and stared in wonder at the scene which looked like a stone had been thrown in a still pond and everyone was now caught in its wake.

Chapter 17

Scotland steered the Bentley Bentayga up South Main Street. She was looking forward to her dinner with Kate and she did not let Richard's death cloud her mind. With her convertible a write-off she took to borrowing her Uncle's back-up SUV instead.

She had texted Kate and advised her that she was mere minutes away and she would meet her in front of the Express News. Her eyes lit up for two reasons: 1. There was a parking spot she could easily slip into. 2. Kate was looking especially lovely and quite different than when she was in uniform. Her yoga tights from top to bottom accentuated her shredded musculature and she looked like an Olympic athlete – a sprinter or a pole vaulter – she looked that good.

Kate approached the driver's side as the window rolled down and she beamed at the gorgeous driver. She looked at the vehicle and was impressed, and comically rolled her gorgeous, big, brown eyes. "Of course, it would be another Bentley. What else would it be?"

Scotland pulled her sunglasses down her nose and gave her a playful scan from top to bottom with her stunning blue eyes. "Hey, beautiful..." She headtossed at her and checked left-and-right to make sure the coast was clear – which it was not because there were police everywhere. "How much for the whole night?" She popped-up her eyebrows and had to take another look at the gorgeous woman as she stood there.

Kate giggled cutely. "For you?" She leaned against the open driver's-side window sexily and purred at her. She pursed her lips and named her price which was non-negotiable. "Can't do it for less than a hundred."

Scotland looked shocked. "A hundred, huh?" She cocked an eyebrow at her. "So, what do I get for a hundred?"

Kate grinned lustily. "Everything you see here." She winked at her playfully. "And a little bit more."

Scotland nodded. "That sounds tempting." She giggled as they continued to cavort on the street. "Got any references?"

Kate backed up a bit and put her sexy body on deck for the potential customer to gawk at. She stood and posed for her and turned seductively around so she could properly showcase her tangible assets. She turned back to her and growled in a salacious way, "All my references are right here, baby." She ran a hand from her chest down her body to her crotch and eyed her customer seductively. "You like?"

Scotland nodded and had to wave herself cool with her hand. She let out a satisfied huff and nodded her head in approval. "Well, I'm sold..." She stopped and playfully glared at her derisively. "Wait. Are you a cop?" She tilted her head to the side and comically side-eyed her suspiciously.

Kate playfully played along. She narrowed her seductive eyes at her and giggled. "Would that be a deal breaker?"

Scotland shook her head. "Absolutely not. It would make it even hotter."

Kate nodded and flashed and endearing grin at the gorgeous alpha sitting so regally in her expensive vehicle. She giggled cutely and felt submissive to Scotland for some reason even though most people would regard her as the alpha. Her thoughts clouded a bit, but she pushed them out of her head – for tonight at least.

Scotland giggled and flashed her cute overbite at the gorgeous Amazon. She got wet as she looked at her and thought about the sexy way she just moved. "You look beautiful by the way."

Kate bit her bottom lip gingerly and looked at Scotland. She was impressed how beautiful she looked all glammed up. With minimal make-up she was a gorgeous Lipstick, and she felt lucky to be able to get a date with her. She did however note that as far as the way they were dressed, they seemed to be light-years apart. She hesitated, "I think I'm a little under-dressed compared to you."

Scotland brushed it off and she shook her head amicably. "You look gorgeous. Don't fret about it..." She tilted her head to the passenger side. "Hop in. I'll give you your hundred bucks inside."

Kate giggled and got comfortable in the passenger seat, and she decided to lean in and give Scotland a hug just because she wanted to. She did not feel any resistance and wrapped her arms around her and gave her a tight squeeze. She had an unmistakable muscle-tone to her body that proved she worked out a lot, and she wondered just how hard she would have to work to break her. She had a feeling she was a tenacious and stubborn lover, but she knew Scotland would eventually yield to her – she would make her. A salacious smile curled over her cute mouth and she let out a moan as she continued to hold onto the woman who rested her head onto her shoulder, and she felt Scotland's arms curl around her to reciprocate.

Scotland felt Kate, and the girl was jacked – that was for sure. Her muscles had muscles and she had a lean litheness reserved for Olympic athletes. She could feel herself swamping her panties and she felt a light-headed dizziness the longer she held onto the gorgeous Amazon. She knew she would have to hold out as long as she could when they fucked, but she was not going to make it easy for her. She would not give up easy and she would be damned if she cried out for mercy – she was just that type of lover. She thought long and hard about it to confirm that amongst all her lovers. 'Ask anyone of them. Hell, ask Carter. She'll tell you.'

They were both startled by the police cruiser that pulled up beside them and flashed their lights. The squelch of the siren blared out at them and snapped them out of their love-stupor.

The officers in the squad car shook their heads and commanded them over their loudspeaker, "Move it along and get a room, you two!" They burst out laughing and sped away.

Kate smirked and shook her head as she watched the taillights disappear. "Dickheads." She pursed her lips.

Scotland smirked and looked up at Kate. "Friends of yours?"

Kate narrowed her eyes and nodded her head slightly. She mumbled under her breath. "Unfortunately." She just loved how Scotland giggled cutely at her.

Scotland pulled the Bentayga up to Spago on North Canon Drive. She saw the valets snap to it in their usual efficient way and waited for them to open their doors. They knew this regular customer would tip them generously for their efforts.

Kate looked up at the restaurant and murmured to Scotland as she came around to her and took her hand and laced her fingers into hers. She knew they were past the point of acting coy and she admired how the alpha took charge of her because she could, and she would. She shook her head almost apologetically and murmured to her, "I'm really under-dressed for Spago, Scotland."

Scotland gently tugged on her hand and shook her head. "You're not under-dressed..." She looked at her figure as it cut a swath in her skin-tight yoga pants and top – once considered an athletic accessory only relegated to gyms – but in Beverly Hills, de rigueur especially if you had the body for it – which Kate definitely did, and in shovelfuls. "Especially with a body like yours." She almost drooled as she scanned her from head-to-toe and then back all the way up again. She smiled approvingly, and seductively growled at her, "I like, a lot."

Kate smiled sheepishly at her and fell in love with Scotland again for the second time this evening. She was amazed how comfortable she made her feel, which was a treat, considering her last girlfriend was the exact opposite – a lot more controlling and into mind-games. She looked at her date and she admired her fashion sense. Head-to-toe she was the epitome of style, grace, and sexiness. She wondered if she bit off more than she could chew. She felt she was well outside her league and social standing with Scotland. "You look really beautiful, Scotland." Her eyes danced as she lost herself in Scotland's grace and the skin-on-skin contact was making her lustful – dinner be damned.

Scotland popped up her eyebrows at the gorgeous woman as they made their way inside. She licked her lips lusciously and growled at her beautiful date in a low tone, "I have to stop looking at your body because I'm soaking my G-string."

Kate snorted a laugh and felt her squeeze her hand. She would have let her blow off dinner and head straight back to her place to let her do whatever she wanted to her, but she had never been to Spago – and she knew she could always fuck Scotland. "Maybe after a drink, we can go to the bathroom and you can let me see just how wet I make you."

Scotland's jaw dropped down and she looked at her stunned. "Officer Hernandez..." She playfully gasped at her forwardness. "That's a great idea."

They both giggled as they entered and had the maître d' show them to their reserved table. A generous tip was given for her effort for placing them at one of the best tables.

Kate looked around the restaurant and was floored at the luxury and opulence of the interior. It was felt expensive, looked expensive and smelt expensive. The linens were crisp and white. There was not a hint of anything out of place that she could see. There was priceless art on the walls and large and irregular shaped sculptures in and around the interior to pique someone's interest. It was definitely reserved for the one-percent and she fucking loved being in there because Scotland made her feel special. Her eyes zeroed in on the large sculpture in the middle of the room that could easily have been replaced by a banquet sized table, and she wondered what made a bell an art display. "Hmm..." She got comfortable and her face had a quizzical look on it. "That's a rather big bell."

Scotland looked over and smiled. "Uh-huh..." It was suspended off the floor precariously on sleepers because hanging it would be impossible. It ceremoniously hovered in the air for all to see. It had become a party piece in Spago for the well to do to take a selfie beside as they dined. "It was donated by my aunt and uncle who are regulars here."

Kate got comfortable as she took the menu and thanked the maître d'. She looked at her and pursed her lips. "Is it an art display?" There was a quizzical look on her face because she really did not understand art.

"Uh-huh..." Scotland nodded and smiled at her. She just loved her look out of uniform and her ribald mind wandered about what she would look like naked. Given the skin-tight clothing she had on there was not much left to the imagination – it just made the gift more desirable. "It's made by the same bell-makers who made the Liberty Bell."

Kate nodded in approval. "Hmm, that's umm…" She pursed her lips and stared at it wholesomely. "Really cool."

Scotland giggled. She nodded at the menu. "Look the menu over and order…" Her salacious eyes narrowed, and she gingerly bit her bottom lip. "That first drink is anxiously waiting to wet your whistle." She forced a comedic wink at her just for effect because they knew what that meant.

Kate giggled and licked her lips. She sheepishly looked down. She could not look away from Scotland too long and then her eyes drifted back up to meet hers once more and she lost herself in Scotland Yarde's penetrating stare. She again giggled cutely at the offer and would take her up on it.

They ordered and their cocktails arrived. They looked at each other lustily as they sipped, cavorted, and shared their histories with one another.

Scotland was fascinated with Kate's military background and she seemed destined to be a police officer and probably a detective. "So, you grew up in the Valley?"

Kate nodded and smiled. "Both of my parents passed away a few years back. I went into the military right after high school."

Scotland admired her dedication. She held up her glass to toast her. "Thank you for your service." She saw Kate giggle and clink her glass with hers.

"Thanks, Scotland."

Kate was fascinated with Scotland's upbringing and family history.

"So, your family gets royalties from prescription medication patents?" Kate did not even know that existed.

Scotland sipped her drink and nodded. "Yes. Everything from ibuprofen, acetaminophen…" She popped-up her eyebrows. "Even acetylsalicylic acid…" She leaned closer to her and licked her lips. "Yarde Pharma holds the patents to a number of prescription medications. It's kind of like the 3M of prescription drugs."

Kate sipped and stopped. Her eyes narrowed suspiciously and she put down her drink and swallowed. "All prescription drugs?' There was a suspicious tone in her question.

Scotland swallowed and looked at her and detected the interrogative question. She shook her head politely. "Except OxyContin."

Kate smiled and was relieved. "That's good to know my date's not a world class drug dealer."

Scotland looked at her wild-eyed as she took a sip because she was hiding something that she thought she should know. She swallowed nervously. "Umm..." She cleared her throat politely and looked at her. "We do hold the patent to Viagra."

Kate looked at her horrified. Her mouth opened and she was in shock. "Well..." She shook her head and looked at her intently. "I can get a lady-boner on command."

Scotland choked on her drink and started to laugh at her. She felt comfortable with her so much so that her body butted up against her and she was practically on top. She looked deep into Kate's eyes. She salaciously growled at her, "Do you want to kiss me, Kate?"

Kate swallowed hard and she blushed. Her pulse raced and she noticed how hard she was breathing at that very moment at that very question. "Uh-huh. Umm, sure." Her head bobbed up-and-down nervously. She looked at the gorgeous alpha and she had a patient look waiting for her to make her move. "Oh..." She looked at her stunned. "You mean right now?" She could not believe she was being outsmarted, outgunned, and outfoxed by the diminutive alpha who usurped control over her – a woman who served multiple tours in Afghanistan and Iraq, and was a captain in the Military Police long enough to not take shit from anyone.

Scotland wrapped her arm around her toned gun and could smell her delicious vanilla scent and noticed her nervousness – and knew she had Kate right where she wanted her – in her control. Her eyes had a commanding conviction and she hypnotized Kate with her Dracula-stare and she threw down the gauntlet because she now owned her – every part of her. "Uh-huh." She nodded slowly but definitively. There was only one woman who never fell under her control like that but took control of her – and that was Carter Deklava. Her Van Helsing.

Kate swallowed hard and she licked her lips and dipped her head down and kissed the gorgeous alpha like she asked her to. Their lips caressed, and then their tongues came out to play.

Scotland licked her lips and smiled as she sat back and smiled up at the gorgeous woman. She was going to make a move and drag her to one of the private bathrooms and let her taste her amuse bouche, but their appetizers arrived and cock-blocked her.

She pouted at Kate and lifted the soup-spooned sized appetizer and clinked the spoon with hers as they dug into the delicious morsels of food.

Kate giggled and the delay only made them desire each other more. They knew if they were not allowed to release some of the pent-up sexual energy the evening would end up as one feral and brutal fuckfest that one of them may not survive.

Dish after dish came and they savoured the delicious food. They felt like they were at their limit when the ultimate dessert arrived at their table to share.

Kate's eyes lit up at the gorgeous softball-sized orb covered in gold leaf with a chocolate funnel cone at the top. And, to the side was a small jar filled with a raspberry sauce. Her heart fluttered at the extravagant dessert. A grin curled over her mouth even though she was full she had to try it because of its decadence.

Scotland looked at the dessert with some hesitancy and looked up at the waiter who was different from the one that served them earlier. She knew Kate was happy with it, but she wondered if it was for another table. "Umm…" She tried to get the attention of the waiter, but he was sheepish and did not meet her gaze. "I don't believe we ordered this."

The waiter smirked and murmured. "Compliments of Spago, Miss Yarde."

Scotland nodded appreciatively. "Okay, thank you." She looked over at another table as they were digging into their desserts and saw the look on their faces. She nodded and popped-up her eyebrows.

Their neighbor looked at her dessert and pointed to theirs. "We didn't see that on the menu." She was a little perturbed at their special treatment. 'Fucking Wolfgang!'

Scotland shrugged and rolled her eyes helplessly. "It was a surprise dessert."

The neighbour forced a smile and went back to enjoying hers but a little less now.

The waiter picked up the small jar. "May I?" He did not meet their gaze and simply waited to pour. A smile curled over his mouth as he waited for his cue.

Scotland looked at Kate and saw her nod. She turned to waiter and nodded. "Yes. Please proceed."

He paused slightly before he poured and mumbled a little louder. "Wait a few seconds before digging in as it takes time for the flavors inside to meld and froth up."

Scotland popped-up her eyebrows and nodded. "We're looking forward to it."

The waiter smiled and nodded. "It'll be a delicious surprise…" He paused once more just as he held the spout to the funnel. "I can assure you." He tipped the red liquid into the funnel and tapped it gently to make sure all of it went inside the orb, then placed it down on the tray and took his leave.

Scotland waited for something to happen as she and Kate looked at the orb but did not see anything. She did see the waiter make a beeline toward the front door and not back to the kitchen for some reason and then her heart started to race. Her mouth went dry immediately and a cold sweat formed on her brow.

Kate looked at the orb and noticed nothing was happening and wondered why the waiter went the wrong way and she too started to get nervous.

Scotland looked around and she fidgeted. What scared her was the small puff of smoke that spewed out from the funnel and her eyes grew large. She yelled out to Kate, "Don't touch it." She slid out of the booth one way and Kate slid out the other.

Many of the guests around them looked at them oddly as they continued like nothing was going on.

Their waiter returned and looked at the women standing out of the booth, and the dessert that was spewing some smoke out the top. He pointed at it. "Where'd that come from?" There was a quizzical look on his face.

Scotland scanned the restaurant and her eyes zeroed in on something that would help. She picked up the tray and ran with it toward the bell.

Kate followed her immediately and knew there was going to be trouble.

Scotland shoved the dessert under the bell and got against the side and shoved as hard as she could, but it would not budge.

Kate slammed against the side too, and she shoved as hard as she could.

Murmurs in the restaurant started to pick up and chatter started to fill the open space as they wondered what the two women were doing with the bell.

Scotland shoved and felt the bell jiggle a little. She looked at Kate. "On two..." She saw her nod and then she muttered. "One-two."

The two women put all their weight and strength into it and the bell leaned to the side – the sleepers unable to hold it in place. It clanged loudly and it fell over and covered the spewing dessert with a loud bang.

Then what followed was a loud, muffled explosion inside the bell and the building shook violently which shocked everyone in the restaurant. Smoke billowed out from beneath the bell and everyone's ears were ringing.

Hansen walked up to them inside the restaurant and shook his head disagreeably. It was Beverly Hills and not in his and Marx's jurisdiction, but they needed to be there because when they heard who was involved it just made sense for them to show up. He stared at Scotland and Kate sitting at a table being seen to by emergency personnel. He shook his head and curled his mouth up. "First the incident with your car and now 'la bombe surprise'…" He glared at Scotland with impertinence. "I don't think someone likes you, Miss Yarde."

Scotland side-eyed him and simply let the comment glean off her back. She simply took the Fifth.

Marx looked at Kate and smirked. He shook his head slightly.

Hansen looked at Kate blankly. "Are you okay, Hernandez?"

Kate nodded and said nothing.

Mason pulled the Bentley as close to the restaurant as possible and Carter Deklava bolted out the back and hustled out and through the police line.

"Umm, ma'am…" The police officer controlled the scene but seemed to not be able to control the gorgeous woman as she stormed toward the restaurant's entrance.

She did not even let him finish and was blunter than ever. She yammered out her command, "No." She held up her hand with authority and she saw him simply back up.

She stormed into the restaurant liked she owned it and looked around. She saw Scotland and made a beeline toward her friend.

"Jesus…" Carter crouched down and stroked her head and looked into her eyes. "I leave you for a couple of hours and someone tries to kill you?" She scoffed at the scene and wondered what had happened. She turned back to her friend and growled matter-of-factly, "Again?"

Scotland playfully untangled herself from Carter and looked at her derisively. "It's not like I go looking for it."

Carter looked up and glared at Hansen and Marx. She yelled at them interrogatively, "Why does this keep happening to her?" She pursed her lips and crossed her arms. "Huh?"

Marx shrugged his shoulders, smirked, and pointed to Scotland. He sarcastically murmured, "Ask her."

Scotland looked at Marx wide-eyed and then at Carter, and groaned, "Oh god." She dipped her head slightly to get out of this blast zone.

Carter narrowed her eyes at the detective. "Are you being flippant with me, detective?" She stood and moved toward him. "Your childish shrug, though comical to yourself and a handful pre-pubescent knuckle-draggers, does little to instill confidence in the general public when something like this happens to an innocent woman..." She presented Scotland as evidence and tilted her head and widened her eyes. "With-very-little-fashion-sense-I-might-add..." She saw Scotland's shocked ostrich expression but turned back to Marx. "And it only gives credence to the foolhardy to enforce their Second Amendment Rights because some dimwitted detective could only shrug his shoulders, because he doesn't know if he's going to number-one or number-two when his pants are down around his ankles." She crossed her arms and tap-tap-tapped her Jimmy Choo on the floor.

Marx blinked and pursed his lips. "Wait, what?" He had a lost look painted across his face. "Was that an insult?" He looked at Hansen who just shook his head, and he turned back to the alpha female. "Was it?"

Carter glared at him comically and growled at him, "I don't know." She shrugged her shoulders up high, had a smug look on her face and pointed to Hansen. Her response was droll, "Ask him."

Scotland reached out to her. "Carter, c'mon..." She took her hand and squeezed it. "It's not their fault."

Carter narrowed her eyes at both detectives and turned to her friend to make sure she was okay. She looked over at Kate and smiled at her. "Are you okay, Kate?"

Kate nodded and smiled back at her. "I'm fine..." She pursed her lips and sighed. "If it wasn't for Scotland, there would have been more fatalities than just the bell." She pointed to Exhibit A as the crime lab boffins worked on it.

The Beverly Hills detective came over to them all and held something in his hand. He headtossed them all to get acquainted. He looked at Scotland and he had a satisfied smile on his face. "I'm Detective Kelso. You did the right thing getting that explosive under that bell..." He held out his hand to them and showed them what they found. He rolled the debris around so they could get a good look. "This is steel-shot. That explosive had this in there and if it went off in this open room it would have sprayed it everywhere. It would have killed a lot of people..." He looked at Scotland and Kate. "Not least of which would be you."

Scotland closed her eyes and leaned against Carter for support. "Jesus Christ..." She moaned. "Whoever is doing this is seriously deranged."

Hansen nodded and side-eyed Marx. "Thanks. Looks like you have it in hand, and thanks for the call, detective."

Detective Kelso nodded and went back to his crime scene investigators.

Hansen looked at Scotland and Kate. "Will you two be okay getting home?"

Scotland nodded. "We'll be fine, detective."

Hansen nodded to them. "I've advised the Beverly Hills PD about your other brush with an assassin and they will be keeping an eye on your place and doing a routine drive around."

Scotland nodded and smiled. "Thanks again."

Kate murmured to Scotland, "Be right back."

Scotland nodded as she went over to the other police officers from Beverly Hills.

Scotland watched as Hansen and Marx hustled out of the restaurant at a pace that was similar to the bomber and wondered why they were in such a hurry.

Scotland held Carter's hand and smiled at her. "Thanks for coming over when I called."

Carter nodded and smiled back at her best friend. "There's no place I'd rather be." She saw a salacious smirk across her face, and she had seen it many times before – her eyes darted to Kate. She turned to look at the gorgeous Amazon as she talked with some of the Beverly Hills officers, and she turned back to Scotland. There was a shocked look on her face, and she knew exactly what she had in mind. "Scotland Yarde..." Her jaw dropped. "Both of us? Don't you want to be with her by yourself?"

To Scotland, nothing made her hornier than a Victoria's Secret model – been there and done that, many times – or the thrill and adrenaline rush that was coursing through her right now. She grinned at Carter and murmured, "C'mon. There's no way I can fuck her by myself and not yield to her eventually..." She bit her bottom lip gingerly. "If you're there, there's no way she'd survive the night without begging for mercy."

Carter scanned the Amazon's curves and her salacious mind wandered. All of a sudden she felt wet and knew Scotland would need help. A wry smile curled over her mouth. She turned to Scotland. "The girl is definitely jacked..." She giggled at the things they were going to do to her. "And it's been a while since we tag-teamed someone together."

Scotland nodded at her and smiled. "But we've done it before and quite successfully I might add."

Carter scoffed in approval. "Oh yeah..." She smiled and narrowed her eyes deviously. "I almost felt sorry for the last one."

They both looked at each other, smirked and murmured in unison in a dry and playfully unforgiving way, "Almost."

They both saw Kate turn to them and wave, and they both innocently waved back at her.

Carter whispered to Scotland. "I wonder if she knows what we're thinking of doing to her tonight."

Scotland snorted a giggle. "Do you think it'll help her?"

Carter pursed her lips. She could tell Kate could hold her own in a fight, but when it came to fucking, she wondered if she could best Scotland and her together. That would be tough, and they were unmatched and unrivalled having lost count of their victories and zero – count them – zero losses. "I doubt it." There was a smug smile of victory on her face already. "You still have that bed bondage restraint?"

Scotland smiled and watched Kate giggle with her colleagues from another jurisdiction. She just mumbled to Carter. "Uh-huh."

Carter nodded her head. "And you have those things and that other vibrating thing in the nightstand drawer?"

Scotland snorted a giggle and nodded. She replied without question or hesitation. "Oh yeah."

Carter smiled. "Then the poor woman doesn't stand a chance."

They paused for a moment as they watched her say her goodbyes to the officers and start on her way back to them.

"Carter..." Scotland's eyes had a hint of concern in them that gave her some pause.

"Hmm?"

"Do we sound like a couple of serial killers?" Scotland thought long and hard about that.

Carter pursed her lips and she almost lost her lady-boner. She blinked blankly. "Yeah, a little."

Scotland looked at her. "But you're still interested, aren't you?"

Carter looked at her matter-of-factly and almost scoffed at her suggestion otherwise. "Phhhfft, uh, yeah."

Kate came up to them. Her eyes had that innocence about them as she looked at the two incredibly gorgeous women standing before her deep in conversation. "Interested in what?" Her head volleyed between the two and she could not or would not decide who was more beautiful.

Scotland smiled at her and tick-tocked her head. "Just Carter and I being silly that's all." She snorted a giggle.

Carter laughed with Scotland, and then turned to the gorgeous Amazon. "Scotland is horny after almost dying and suggested I come home with both of you. And then she and I are going to go full-lesbian on that body of yours, and tag-team you until your eyes roll back into your head..." She leaned into her personal space offensively, palmed her between her athlete's tits and slowly slid her hand down to her abs until it reached her bellybutton, and playfully glared at her. "And you better dare not beg for mercy because neither of us will grant you your wish." She salaciously smiled and narrowed her wanton eyes at the beautiful Amazon. "Are you interested?"

Scotland groaned and dipped her head down at her bluntness. Once more she let the cat out of the bag and defeated their element of surprise. She only moaned out in protest, "Oh, Carter."

Kate was stunned and looked at Carter and then at Scotland. Her lesbian thoughts churned in her head at the possibilities of the evening and what untold sexual adventures awaited her. There was going to be some feral fucking and she did not know if she could defend herself against both of them at once. One at a time – of course, no problem – but both of them? She thought of every move they would make against her and her countermove against them. She knew they had the element of knowing their surroundings and she was at an extreme disadvantage in that regard. Strategically, they would be able to attack her easily and she would defend herself admirably but not for long. They would have instruments for her sexual gratification, but she would not yield easily. She would fight against the torture they would surely inflict upon her body. They would break her constantly until she screamed with every delicious orgasm they would grant. They would mercilessly fuck her into oblivion. She volleyed her head at both of them and sized them up – they had done this before and were experienced, and she was not. She gulped because combined they were a sexual force to be reckoned with and they were going to throw everything they had at her body. It would get her mind off the incident, that was for sure. She shook her head and pursed her lips at them both and murmured, "Of course I'm interested." She scoffed at them for even suggesting she would say no. Her eyes were wild with anticipation.

Scotland's head popped up like a startled ostrich. A salacious smile curled over her mouth and her wanton thoughts preyed on her dirty mind and she fist-pumped at them. 'Yes!'

Chapter 18

Scotland drove Kate to work the next morning. Carter simply rolled over and stayed in bed. But before they left, they made sure she was comfortable after splaying her to the mattress with the same bondage restraint they used on Kate and driving dildoes deep into her salacious holes until she cried out and blacked out. Satisfied, they left her to reconsider and rethink her many choices in life.

Kate was quiet on the ride back to downtown. She smiled and turned to Scotland who had a satisfied smile on her face. "I had a really, really good time last night and this morning, Scotland."

Scotland giggled cutely as she drove and squeezed her hand just because it needed to be squeezed. "I did too..." She licked her lips and recalled all the ways Carter and she tortured the poor girl, because she needed to be punished. "I had a really good time."

Kate swallowed and side-eyed. "I'm sorry I..."

Scotland held up her hand and shook her head before she could finish. "Don't worry about it..." She smirked salaciously. "It happens."

Kate shook her head and looked down in shame. "Not to me..." She pursed her lips and looked at her apologetically. "I've never done that."

Scotland had a shocked look on her face. "You've never squirted before?" A wry smile curled over her mouth. To her it was an occupational hazard even when she masturbated. Thank god for that mattress liner or she would have to buy a new Hastens every time she and Carter played with someone.

Kate shook her head. "Never. Not with guys or women."

Scotland was playfully aghast. To her it was natural, and she had set records for the number of times she had done it during sex – the top three was with one Brazilian underwear model and twice with Carter. "Beautiful girl, you need to let loose a little more." She grinned at her. "Let go of your inhibitions. It's just sex. Uninhibited, toe-curling, skin-on-skin, no strings attached sex. We're not writing the Declaration of Independence."

Kate snorted a laugh and smiled at her. "You and Carter are good together."

Scotland smiled and thought of her bestest friend in the whole world. Someone who saw her and inspired her to be herself and she in turn reciprocated that back. "Yeah..." Her mind recalled all the good times they had together and the excellent times they had together. "She's the most important person in my life."

Kate looked at her perplexed. "How come you're not together?"

Scotland's mouth curled up in a salacious smile that you would need a brick to wipe off, and her Tom Ford's hid the twinkle in her eyes. She turned to her passenger for a second and growled seductively, "What makes you think we're not?"

Kate snorted a laugh and understood their dynamic. "Got it." She pursed her lips and watched the highway get eaten up by the Bentayga. The smile wore off as she recalled the incident and almost dying last night. It started to prey on her thoughts, and she was happy she at least got to feel what it was like to be alive again after having sex with Scotland and Carter together.

Kate got out of the Bentayga and came up to the driver's side. The window dropped down and she licked her lips and took a good look at the beautiful woman who owned her body last night in so many ways, during so many times, that she lost count. "Thanks again for last night, Scotland."

Scotland reached out and squeezed her hand. She pulled her close and kissed her at least a couple of times and made sure there was enough tongue to tantalize her and make her want some more. "You have an excellent day, Officer Hernandez."

Kate nodded and smiled back at her. She waved as Scotland pulled off and headed down the road. Her smile disappeared from her face and she chewed her dark thoughts. There was some place she needed to be, and it was not here – but she had to get to work and make things look normal even though they were not. She took a breath and headed inside to get it over with. She had something on her mind she needed to do but that would have to wait until later.

Scotland dropped the keys in the bowl by the kitchen and a smile curled over her mouth. She wondered if Carter freed herself or was she still helplessly tied to the bed.

She walked down the hallway and did not hear anything. The door was still ajar, and she pushed it open and was delighted to see her still tied to the bed and as helpless as ever – just the way she loved her. She took a moment to get comfortable and wash her hands and made her way to the bed.

Her hand caressed Carter's face and she dipped down and kissed her bestest friend and her lover – and felt her stir and return the love. Lips caressed lips and tongues lashed and came out to play with one another – French-style.

It was not a secret to the Deklavas or the Yardes – but they did not air their laundry for the public because it really was not any of their fucking business. They loved who they were with and their respective families respected their choices because they were old enough to take responsibility for their actions.

Carter stirred even though the dildoes pinned her deliciously in her salacious holes and the four-point restraint held her right where she should be – beholden to her lover. It was sometimes difficult to determine who was more alpha and they knew each other for so long and so well that they would take turns and this time, here-and-now, it was Scotland. She purred deliciously to entice her lover and she could feel her wetness spurt out around the dildo buried deep in her pussy. "Hey, Scotty…" She licked her lips and deliciously writhed on the mattress for Scotland to appreciate. She moaned as the dildoes punished her gently from deep inside and she pulled on the restraints so they could strain and sing to her Dom. Carter wanted her to punish her. She purred deliciously at her, "Do you want to fuck me?" She drooled because she knew how good Scotland would treat her this morning.

Scotland looked down and slowly ran her hand down her breasts and across her abs. Her hand rested on the shaft of the dildo and she flexed what was not buried inside her lover until she heard her guttural moan through her clenched jaw – her cute overbite accentuated her sexy look. A devious but wanton smile curled over her mouth and she knew she had to punish Carter. She nodded and got up to undress and smiled at her. "I'm going to finish what I started last night…" She licked her lips and gingerly bit her bottom lip. "And you better not beg for mercy this time."

Carter swallowed and licked her lips. She loved it when Scotland undressed in front of her and it only made her wetter and prepared her for the toe-curling orgasms. She purred obediently and submissively at her lover, "I won't, Scotty…" She had a wanton look in her eyes as she eyed Scotland's incredibly delectable, groomed, toned, and muscled body. She moaned lustily at her, "You know I won't."

Scotland leaned over and kissed Carter on the neck, cheek and had to kiss her on the lips – once more. She giggled as she nuzzled her and sat beside her to enjoy a later than usual continental breakfast. She dropped open her mouth as Carter offered her a piece of ice-cold cantaloupe that burst with flavor just like her lover, and she chewed and savored the succulent bite as she smiled at her. She poured herself a cup of coffee from the carafe and sipped its deliciousness. "Mmm…" She leaned back into Carter and nuzzled her. "I love when you come over. Your coffee is always delicious."

Carter smiled and leaned her head on Scotland. "You know I love coming over…" She eyed her again. "Fffuughk, babe…" She let out a satisfied exhale that lingered, and it was more of an exultation of how she felt after having Scotland work her body in so many delicious ways that only she knew how. "You really worked me over."

Scotland took her hand and kissed it. "You know how horny you make me."

Carter cocked a sultry eyebrow. "Really?" She narrowed her eyes. "Was it me or did juicy-girl get your motor running?"

Scotland giggled cutely and she looked into Carter's eyes. They had a lot of fun with her last night and into the wee hours, and Carter this morning was just another outlet for Scotland. "She may've had something to do with it…" She tilted her head into Carter's and looked into her gorgeous aquamarine eyes. "But you know how much I love you."

Carter reciprocated and looked into Scotland's deep blue eyes and wrapped her hand around her head and tangled her fingers in her hair. She pulled her in and kissed her deeply and seductively like she knew how she liked to be kissed. She knew she had to reward Scotland for the way she twisted, flexed, and bent her body, and made her come and spout in tongues in the multiple languages she knew how to curse in. She would have said something funny or sarcastic, but this time right here and right now she was lost in her lover and her bestest friend forever.

Scotland's eyes moved over to the LA Times sitting on the table and she picked it up and looked at the front cover story. Her eyes took on a grave look and wondered where the story came from. "Did you see this?" She showed Carter the front cover.

Carter nodded and smirked. "Seems Richard managed to get his story out to the press before he died."

Scotland scanned the information, and it was all of the things that they already had seen including some additional lists and other compromising tidbits that Richard had been keeping until the time was right. "He never told us he had this information." She scanned quickly through the article and her eyes took on a fiery glow. "That little asshole…" She caught herself and looked up apologetically. "May he rest in peace."

Carter nodded and pouted. She narrowed her eyes. "Keep reading…" She raised her perfectly groomed eyebrows up. "You're going to take that back in a minute."

Scotland flipped through the story and continued to scan through the exposé. Her eyes narrowed and widened with every word and paragraph, and her jaw clenched, and her breathing went from shallow to labored as the information spilled into her. "Just where was this guy getting all of this information?" She looked it over again and could not believe the volume. "This stuff goes back over fifteen years."

Carter nodded. "There is no way Bob Woodward over there managed to get all of that information by himself..." Her mind raced thinking of the information she read through and he either had help or they were missing something – the keystone to lock this all up.

Scotland gasped and looked up. "Someone else wrote this story and handed it to the LA Times."

Carter nodded. "Yes. Seems there is another person working this angle, but I am not sure to what end or who it is?"

Scotland pouted and narrowed her eyes. "It couldn't be extortion? The moment the story was released there goes that person's advantage of getting money out of this." Her mind started to race and wondered what other motivation people have for exposing the truth. "So that leaves whistleblowers or revenge."

Carter's head tick-tocked. "Could be someone at SoCal..." She pursed her lips. "Whistleblower could've grown a conscience and wanted to expose Dirk Stafford's dirty deeds."

Scotland looked at the story snippets – her eyes gleaned over mysterious heart attacks, gas explosions, falling off boats, falls in showers and dying from exposure – just to name a few. All were deemed accidental deaths and the cases were closed. All of them were pension members. She thought out loud. "So, in order to not pay and keep the money in the fund and still get their fee, SoCal conspired to have them killed in various stages of their retirements and keep the money?"

Carter nodded. "Seems that way and pretty tidy. Make it look like accidents and make the spouses die afterward and a small remaining pension balance contribution to the estate, but the bulk stays with the pension and the fund manager gets paid..." She shook her head. "That's devious."

Scotland gasped. "Murder by natural causes." And shook her head at the conspiracy.

Carter smirked and shook her head. "I always have to ask, why now?" She looked at Scotland with a perplexed look.

Scotland nodded too. "Yes. What was the catalyst to get this freight train moving on SoCal and expose Stafford? There has got to be a reason. He's been doing it for a very long time but why now?"

Carter plunged her fork into another tasty tidbit of cantaloupe and stuck it in her mouth. She dipped the fork once more and craned it over to

Scotland who simply dropped her mouth and she fed it to her like a baby bird. "There's no sense in us speculating. Now that the information is out, we should talk to Hansen and Marx..." She snorted a laugh. "They must be choked that the information is in the paper already."

Scotland nodded her head. "Yeah, they must be pissed." Her brain scrolled furiously through all the information and events that they knew already, and she was busy putting the pieces together but there were still some missing pieces to the whole puzzle.

Scotland thought about something and she knew they were going to need some equipment. "Carter, are you still on speaking terms with the Toy-Maker?" She cocked an eyebrow at her.

Carter nodded. "Of course." She smiled because she was thinking the same thing, too. Her eyes lit up and she nodded in agreement. "Capital thinking, lover."

Scotland saw Carter get up and undo her robe. "What're you doing?" She knew Carter's lust for life and sex, but she thought she had worn her out to the bone already. "Again?" There was a quizzical look on her face, but it did not stop her from getting wet just thinking about breaking her friend yet again.

Carter looked down at her and smirked. "Scotty, I love it when you fuck me but give me some credit. I can turn myself off from you..." She cocked a know-it-all eyebrow at her. "You know that right?"

Scotland pouted and looked at her quizzically. "Well..." She acted a little hurt. "I can turn myself off from you too."

Carter snorted a laugh. She purred deliciously at her because she knew the truth, "You're so cute when you lie." She let her robe slide off her svelte frame and let it fall across the chair. Her nakedness was a sight to behold, and she had that silky sheen of after-sex that drove Scotland wild. She looked good and she always tasted good. "I'm going to have a dip in your pool before we go."

She sauntered toward the infinity pool and made sure to accentuate her hips as she did.

Scotland felt herself drip from the look of her incredible squat-induced, ass-bubbles bahdonk-a-donking as she strutted. She had one of those Olympic-pole-vaulter bodies that she never got tired of looking at. She licked her lips because she made her mouth water, and she drooled a little.

Carter stopped and turned to her with one of her trademark Lauren Bacall come-hither looks like she wanted something. She narrowed her eyes seductively and blew her a kiss. She sexily growled at her, "Are you coming, Scotty?"

Scotland did not have to be asked twice and was up and disrobed before Carter even dipped her toe in the water. She attacked her and pushed her into the gorgeous pool, and they frolicked like a couple of gorgeous Lipsticks just because they should, they could, and they would.

Chapter 19

Hansen was busy putting some condiments on his Pink's hot dog when he saw Stafford's SUV pull into the parking lot. He sucked the corn relish off his finger and got himself ready as he slowly walked over to his partner who was leaning against the side of the building as he watched Stafford park. He headtossed to Marx and he watched him walk over to the black Mercedes Benz G-Wagon, as he followed with his hands full.

Hansen sidled up to the passenger side and tried the handle – as did Marx behind him. They saw the window slide down and he looked at the driver with a perplexed glare on his face, as he juggled his hot dogs and drink. "Unlock the door." His head tipped down just in case he did not understand the verbal instruction to begin with.

Stafford turned to him and shook his head slightly. He pointed at his food and wagged his finger at him critically. He bellowed at him and at Marx even though he did not bother rolling down the back window, "Umm, you're not eating that in my G-Wagon."

Hansen cleaned his teeth with his tongue and narrowed his eyes at the pain-in-the-ass. He snorted sarcastically at Stafford, "Hey..." He scanned the vehicle. "Is this one bullet-proof like the one that guy chased Jason Bourne around Russia in?"

Stafford looked at him like he had two heads. "What?" He scoffed at him. "Why the fuck would I want a bullet-proof one?" He shook his head derisively. "I'm not a Russian Oligarch."

Hansen nodded and looked at Marx and then turned his attention back to Stafford. "Oh, because I thought an asshole with your attitude would surely have a bullet-proof one just in case Marx and I decided to shoot it full of fucking holes..." He leaned his head through the hole and yelled, "Now unlock the fucking doors!"

Stafford shot him a surrendered stare and pressed the button to unlock the doors. "Jesus..." He looked at them both as they got inside and made themselves comfortable. "What kind of bug crawled up your ass?"

Hansen narrowed his eyes at him and simply took a bite and enjoyed the snap of the dog or was that the hot – anyway it was delicious. He tilted his head at the door and murmured with his mouth full, "You may want to close the windows because what we have to say will get loud."

Stafford had little trepidation to the idle threat as he closed the window and locked the doors. They may seem intimidating to the perps they regularly roll for information, but they did not scare him. "So, why the sudden urgency to meet?" He had a dull quizzical look on his face like they were bothering him for nothing. "Huh?"

Hansen took another bite and sipped his beverage. He was impressed with the car and had to comment to Stafford. "How come it's so cool in here even with the engine off?"

Stafford nodded and smiled that it impressed the detective who, given what he paid him, could afford one too if he decided to take the plunge. "It's a plug-in hybrid and can run the air conditioner even with the engine off for thirty minutes."

Hansen smiled and nodded in approval. He looked back at Marx who was sipping his coffee and had an unerring and blank look on his face as he glared at Stafford. "That's impressive wouldn't you say, Marx?"

Marx nodded. "Technology nowadays. Mind blowing." He pursed his lips and nodded in agreement and still did not take his interrogative eyes off Stafford.

Hansen turned back to Stafford. "Anyway, the reason why we called you was…" He swallowed and washed the hot dog remnants down with another sip of his drink. "Why the fuck did you have someone try to kill Scotland Yarde and Carter Deklava?" His eyes were wide-open in an interrogative manner now. "Oh yeah, and kill Richard Moranis in County Lock-up?" He saw Stafford's quizzical look that he wanted to say something and but could not because he genuinely did not know what the fuck he was talking about. "Oh…it gets better…" He took another sip and forced a grin. "Then Scotland Yarde takes one of LAPD's police officers, who I'm sure loves the taste and touch of the ladies, to Spago and then someone tries to blow them both the fuck up with a dessert." His eyes had that deranged look just before he was going to take the boots to someone for being impertinent.

Stafford looked at Marx and then at Hansen like they had two-heads each and cleared his throat. "Just what the fuck are you talking about?" He shook his head because he did not know.

Marx chimed in from the back, "Don't you watch the news?"

Stafford smiled and shook his head. "I find I have a much more productive day if I stay away from all of the bad news."

Hansen looked at him like he was touched. "How the fuck do you stay up-to-date with current events?"

Stafford shrugged politely. "I just don't worry about those things. I pay people like you to worry about stuff like that."

Marx growled at the back. "Hansen…" He huffed and he puffed. "I swear to god I'm going to fucking murder this asshole and make it look like he came at me first."

Hansen looked at him and waved him off. He looked at Stafford. "So, you didn't hear about the attempt on the two lesbians, Moranis getting blown the fuck up and then the bomb at Spago?"

Stafford smirked and shook his head. "Nope. Didn't hear about it…" He held his hands up in surrender. "Didn't sanction it either."

Hansen chewed his thoughts and expressed his displeasure at his incorrect Occam's Razor deduction. He reached into his blazer pocket and pulled out the newspaper. "Then, did you see this?"

Stafford eyed him suspiciously and took the newspaper and unfolded it. "What am I looking for? Huh?"

Hansen took another big bite and chewed. He mumbled with his mouth full, "Just look. It's as clear as day."

All the blood in Stafford's face drained somewhere into his lower regions. He was aghast as he read through the story.

Marx snorted a giggle. "Looks like he saw it." He almost laughed out loud for the predicament Stafford was now in.

Hansen took another generous bite, chewed, and sipped his way through the remains of hot dog one, and two before Stafford finished the story. He cleaned his teeth with his tongue and washed it all down with the remnants of his soda. He slurped loudly as there was nothing but air and ice left and he was now done.

Stafford sweated as his eyes gleaned over the story, and he was having trouble breathing – now that things went pear-shaped between those pages. All the things he had done were now in the open for the public to scrutinize and the board of the California Public Employees Fund to call him on. This did not even scratch the surface of the police and surely the FBI. He shook with the paper in his hands and saw his livelihood and his career as a captain of industry and a mover and shaker erode in the time it took him to digest the story. He growled out and wondered what the fuck just happened and was it all a dream? "How the fuck did this reporter get all of this information?" He looked at Hansen and did not even bother with Marx. "Why wasn't I told that this guy had all of this information?"

Hansen looked at him coolly. "Well, we didn't know he had all of that information so there was no way we could have told you…" He shook the cup and noted there was no more damage he could do to that drink, so he stuck it in the G-Wagon's more than generous cup holder. "And you should really check up on current events more, so you know what the fuck is going on in the world."

Marx mumbled from the back, "How did he get shit on the operation so far back? There's like fifteen years of information there. That's when we first started this all."

Hansen nodded and returned his attention to Stafford. "I think you have a leak in your company."

Stafford looked at him. "It's not like I leave this information in a folder on my server that says, 'Look Here – Murder Conspiracy'."

Hansen looked at him intently. "Well, someone has fifteen years' worth of information on the murders we committed so your company could reap the rewards without paying out the cash. It won't take long for a state prosecutor to connect all of the dots and then it's lethal injection time for all of us..." He looked at them both. "And I know they halted them way back but considering the shit we've done and the number of people we've killed and had killed, the Governor is going to bring it back special just for us."

Stafford gulped, and his mind raced. He felt his phone vibrate and the call went straight to his center console head unit. His blood ran cold when he saw it was the office calling him. He let out a grunt, "Fffuughk." He pressed the 'decline' button.

Hansen looked at it and then turned to him. "Looks like the wheels are in motion, Dirk. It's closing time and there isn't time for one last drink."

Stafford looked at him with a terrified expression. "What do we do?"

Hansen marvelled at him and chuckled. "We?" He snorted a laugh and looked at Marx who smiled, and he turned back to a frightened Dirk Stafford. "There is no we in Federal Indictment, Dirk." He snorted a laugh. "It's your brainchild, your baby and your problem. You created the monster, you kill it."

Stafford looked at Hansen. "Now wait..." He started to sweat even as the air conditioner gently cooled the interior. "Your and Marx's fingerprints are all over this too. You can't let me take the blame for everything. You have to help me..." He started to shake with fear. He had never experienced something quite like this before in his life. He was swaddled and nursed from the teat all his life, and his parents always bailed him out, made excuses for him, or made things simply go away whenever he was caught between a rock and a hard place. "You can't just leave me dangling like this."

Hansen chuckled and looked at him. He knew he had the goods on them too but unlike him they kept a lower profile and could leave at a moment's notice, and still live like kings in some non-extraditable country. The wheels in his head turned and Marx and he had the advantage over Stafford and could exploit that for more money. "Well..." He smiled and he knew Marx would support him. "Getting you to safety is going to cost you, Dirk…" He smiled handsomely at the payday that they would receive for ferreting the weasel to safety, now that the jig was up. "It's going to cost you plenty."

Stafford knew he was fucked, and he needed their help. "Fine…" He let out an exasperated sigh. "What do you want me to do?"

Hansen rubbed his chin. "Where can you hide out?"

Stafford had a safe house, but it was more of a hide out where he would take his many conquests for a lot of unadulterated, extracurricular sex without his wife knowing. "I've got a place in the Valley."

Hansen smirked. "Of course, you do." He shook his head. "You need to lie low there and we'll contact you on your burner phone." He looked at him. "You also need to get rid of your current phone. We can't have anyone tracking you."

Stafford nodded. "So, how much is this all going to cost me?"

Hansen looked at Marx and saw a smirk and then his attention went back to Stafford. "No more than a million…" He snorted a giggle. "Each."

Stafford narrowed his derisive eyes at them both. "That's a little steep."

Hansen shook his head and narrowed his tell-tale eyes at the man. "Not as steep as that needle that's going to go into your arm." He leaned into his space. "Understand?"

Stafford looked at him and nodded. He now knew who he was finally dealing with. Before they were acquaintances who looked at things the same way when it came to what they wanted – money. Now they were adversaries who worked with one another not for convenience but because they had so much on one another that it would be precarious for them not to cooperate. He screwed his mouth to the side and nodded his head. "Fine."

Hansen nodded. "Also, who else is in this inner circle that you happened to include but didn't tell us about?"

Stafford thought about it and his eyes scanned the faces of both men. "He couldn't have ordered those hits. He's just a yes man following orders and getting paid for his contributions."

Hansen shook his head pointedly at him and pursed his lips derisively. He did not like to know after-the-fact that there was indeed another player in their sandbox. "Marx and I should've known."

Stafford shook his head. "It was better you and Marx didn't know about them."

Hansen looked at him quizzically. "Really? You're playing the plausible deniability card? Now?" He shook his head in disgust. "Why don't you tell us who they are, and Marx and I'll decide, okay?" He poked him in the chest, so he understood where he was coming from. "Marx and I've put our lives and careers on the line for this operation and due to you not being able to contain the information or keep it in your pants; it's blown out of control. We had a good thing going until someone grew a conscience, so let us tie up those loose ends. Got it?" His eyes burned into him.

Stafford nodded his head in approval. "It's the ME orderly, Cliff Manzell. I needed to pay him off on some of the cases that crossed his boss' desk."

Hansen shook his head. "Why don't I believe he's the only one?"

Stafford took a breath and pursed his lips. "One of the guards at the San Pedro Penitentiary, John Gates."

Hansen widened his eyes and pulled his mouth to the side. "Why the guard at San Pedro Corrections?"

Stafford looked at him. "You don't think those killers just happened to drop into your laps, did you?" He shook his head. "I needed cold-blooded killers to do the work you used to do before you and Marx moved to senior management."

Marx poked him in the shoulder. His voice dripped with interrogative derision, "Is that supposed to be funny, Dirk?"

Hansen looked astonished. "I didn't know you were pulling those strings for us."

Stafford shook his head and smiled at the detectives. "Not at all..." He held his hand up to calm him down. "You and Marx needed to distance yourselves from the killing so we needed a reliable crew to carry out those murders..." He smirked and murmured, "Without a lot questions, and who were capable..." He smirked knowingly. "Unlike your man that botched that unfortunate Vasquez incident. I liked what you and Marx did..." He nodded approvingly. "An accidental overdose for fucking up an accidental overdose. Nice." He grinned with approval.

Marx chimed in. "I suppose your ME buddy told you that."

Stafford nodded. "Yes..." He giggled at the two of them and tilted his head to the side. "It's nice to have people in low places."

Hansen shook his head. "Is that all?" He saw Stafford nod his head. "Question is, where did Moranis get all of that information from?" He looked directly at Stafford. "Were you keeping records?"

Stafford shrugged and held his hands up. "Now why would I keep incriminating evidence like that somewhere?"

Marx looked at him. "You tell us..." He let out an exasperated sigh. He loved LA and now he would have to call some other place home for the rest of his life. "Why would you keep that sort of information?" He poked him again in the shoulder. "Huh?"

Stafford turned to Marx and glared at him. "You better stop poking me, Marx." He narrowed his passive aggressive eyes which were now all aggressive.

"Or you'll what?" Marx leaned forward to poke him a lot harder this time and could not imagine how quick Stafford's reflexes would be as he caught his finger.

He at first felt the pause, then he reacted to the pressure, then he screamed out in agony – in the time it took to blink. He gasped and inhaled, and his face registered the pain that coursed from his broken finger to his brain. He screamed blue murder, "Argh!"

Stafford immediately let it go before Hansen could even ward him off, and he held his hand up to show that he was no longer causing the detective any more misery. He looked at Hansen blankly, and they turned to Marx as he held his hand and writhed in agony in the backseat. A smile curled over his mouth and he was satisfied with the pain he just caused the asshole-detective. He had wanted to do that for a long time – and it was a long time coming.

Marx clenched his jaw in agony and the pain was excruciating in the way Stafford bent his finger. He did not know how he did it, only that it hurt like a son-of-a-bitch. "Argh!" He would have pulled his gun and shot him, but he broke his trigger finger. "You fucking asshole!"

Hansen pursed his lips and narrowed his angry eyes. He growled at him, "Why the fuck did you do that?"

Stafford smacked his lips and looked at him matter-of-factly. "I warned him, and he didn't heed." He shook his head as the detective continued to writhe in pain. "So, I took action…" He popped-up his eyebrows and pursed his lips. "He's going to have to pick his nose and wipe his ass with his other hand for quite a while I'm afraid."

Hansen checked on his partner's condition. "Gene…" He winced as he saw the condition of his finger. "Are you okay?"

Marx shook his head and did not want to touch his finger. He spit as he spoke through the pain. "I think he fucking broke it, Jake!"

Stafford shook his head, and volleyed it between the two detectives. "I broke it in two places." The confession elicited a satisfied smile.

Marx looked at him. His face was red with pain and anger and he recklessly lunged at Stafford with his free hand. "Argh…"

Hansen could not stop him in time and his eyes were wide with fear for his partner. He could only gasp in terror for what might happen next.

Stafford leaned behind his headrest casually because he could see the trajectory of his assailant and he watched as his arm missed its target. This gave him ample time to ready his fist into a blunt instrument – much like a sledgehammer – and drive it square into the foolish detective's face – very, very hard.

Marx stopped in mid-air and felt the crunch of his nose being smashed; his eyes crossed, and he only saw the fist. He let out a muffled groan, "Argh!" He felt his entire body being forced back into the seat from where he started this foolhardy enterprise of trying to physically intimidate Stafford. His eyes rolled and he was knocked senseless, and he did not know if he should cry or scream in pain. He felt a warmth cascade down from his nose to his mouth and tasted blood.

Hansen's eyes were open wide, and he grabbed the handkerchief Stafford pulled from his suit pocket because Marx was going to need it more than him. "Fuck!" He reached over and pushed it against Marx's face and saw him torque back and howl in pain. "Hold it, Gene!"

Hansen ran out and pulled on the door handle, but it was locked. He glared at Stafford. "Unlock the door for fucksake!" He heard a click and he pulled open the back door and dragged Marx out. He stabilized him and needed to take him to the hospital due to the error in his ways.

Stafford looked at the condition of the backseat and pursed his lips and shook his head. It was going to be a problem getting all that blood off the leather. He watched Hansen get Marx into the passenger seat of their squad car and then swing around to the driver's side door. He dropped the passenger window and yelled out, "You've got my number so call me when you're ready to meet." He forced a grin as he saw Hansen simply snarl at him and get into the driver's seat.

The unmarked police cruiser backed-up fast and then the siren and lights went on and it peeled out of the parking lot.

Stafford took a deep breath and pursed his lips. Many scenarios ran through his head and he made his mind up that he needed to act – and fast. First, he needed to get rid of his SUV. It was good while it lasted and now this chapter had come to an end. He would have to get to his back-up car but first he needed to tie up some loose ends – and quick.

He knew just the man for the job for a few more accidents, but this time there was no need for theatrics. These accidents were going to be what they really were – hits.

He also thought he should bring in his back-ups, the ones that Hansen and Marx do not know about – because he neglected to share that information with them because that was just the way he was. He needed muscle and they were just the right people for the job. They have been valuable assets to him and have been feeding him valuable information for the last couple of years. He would need them now. He reached into his glove box and pulled out one of his burner phones and dialled the number.

Chapter 20

It was late afternoon and they finally got a hold of Hansen. He seemed more tense than usual and was probably having a bad day as always. He said he would meet them at Cedars-Sinai hospital.

"I wonder why he wanted us to meet him there?" Carter had a quizzical look on her face as she sat comfortably in the passenger seat. She looked casually at Scotland as she parked the Bentayga, and only saw her shrug.

Scotland looked over at her. "Maybe there something he wants us to see or they're doing an ultrasound to see if he has a brain." She snorted a giggle and saw Carter return the favor and chuckled at her. "Or if he's an asshole." She cackled giddily.

Carter snorted a giggle and narrowed her eyes as she scanned her surroundings. She murmured softly, "He and his partner don't need an ultra-sound for that."

Scotland licked her lips as she too scanned her surroundings. "Mm-hm."

"Did he say where he wanted to meet us?" Carter looked around and wondered if they should go inside or not. She scanned the buildings and noticed the Yarde Intensive Care Unit where Mrs. Vasquez was resting comfortably but still in her medically induced coma. "Or do you think Mrs. Vasquez is conscious?"

Scotland shook her head. "Emilio said he was going to text me if that happened so I'm not really sure why we're here, but he said to wait for him in the visitor's parking area."

Carter shook her head. "Yeah, that's not suspicious at all."

Scotland snorted a laugh. Meeting at a field in the middle of nowhere with a hole in the ground would be suspicious. Her eyes scanned the doors and she saw Hansen coincidentally walk out just at the right time. Marx was with him and he did not look like he was in good condition. She gasped and mumbled, "Jesus..." She winced as they drew closer, and she could see he was not in good shape at all. "What the fuck happened to him?"

Carter shook her head and wondered that too. "Maybe he cracked one too many jokes and..." She playfully unleashed a fists-of-fury one-two punch. "Wham-bam, someone punched him out."

Scotland looked at Carter inquisitively and pulled her mouth to the side in a sideways smirk. "Then why the hell hasn't someone kicked the shit out of you? Huh?"

Carter pursed her lips and narrowed her derisive eyes at her friend and lover, and growled matter-of-factly, "Because I've got a tight pussy and I'm fucking delightful..." She flicked her head back in protest just for effect. "That's why."

Scotland shook her head. "Hmm..." Her head tick-tocked from side-to-side. "Well, you're half right, babe." She smirked knowingly.

Carter adjusted her sunglasses up by middle-fingering it as she looked directly at Scotland and only saw her jaw drop playfully at her.

They both got out and met the detectives on their turf – closer to their squad car.

Hansen helped Marx into the squad car and looked at the two women as they drew closer. "Ladies..." He nodded to each of them and smiled generously which was a first. "Thanks for meeting us here."

Scotland looked at Marx and noticed he was not saying anything and he simply sat in the passenger seat and looked forward. "My god, Detective Marx..." She pulled off her sunglasses and her eyes were wide-open as she tried to get a good look but was blocked by Hansen. "Are you..." She looked at Hansen. "Is he okay? What happened?"

Hansen pursed his lips and shook his head a little. "He's pretty banged up..." He looked at Marx and turned back to the two women. "Junkie surprised him as we gave chase and knocked him down."

Carter looked at Marx and his injuries, and then turned her suspicious eyes to Hansen. "A junkie?" She shook her disagreeable head. "Did this junkie know Krav Maga?"

Hansen looked at her and any smile or smirk was now gone from his face. "Look ladies, you called us. Why?"

Scotland looked up at him a little shocked at his sudden change in temperament. "I don't like your tone, detective." Her hands went to her hips as she drilled her eyes into him. "We're here to help and I find it puzzling how the story leaked to the Times so soon after Richard Moranis' death."

Hansen looked at her and screwed his mouth to the side. To him, it did not matter now so he decided to tell her. In less than twenty-four hours they would be somewhere that was not here and living like kings. "We interviewed Joanne Middleton and Moranis gave her his access to all of his files and asked her to send it to the editor of the LA Times, and that's what she did."

Scotland tilted her head back to acknowledge the source of the material. "How did Richard get all of that old information on SoCal? There's over fifteen years worth of material. Who'd have so much on SoCal and Dirk Stafford?"

Hansen shook his head and gave a little shrug. "I'm not sure. Maybe Moranis had been digging up that information all this time or there's a whistle-blower no one knows about."

Carter shook her head pensively. "But there has to be a reason for it to come out now. Why the sudden urgency to bring SoCal and Stafford down?"

Again, Hansen shrugged. "Not sure. Only that this conspiracy runs deep, and they have been doing it for years."

Scotland pursed her lips and thought about all the information and the names, and her brain was busy putting it all together. "Do you have any leads?"

Hansen nodded. "Yes. Seems there's a guard who works at San Pedro Corrections that may know something about these hitmen who SoCal has been hiring to make these accidents happen."

Scotland perked up and her eyebrow cocked up at him. "You wouldn't be going there now would you?"

Hansen nodded. "He lives in Hollywood. Name's John Gates." He eyed both women and wondered if their company was in order. "You're welcome to tag along if you like."

Carter looked at Scotland and nodded to her.

Scotland nodded to Hansen. "Carter and I would be happy to join you. This case has intrigued us, and we would like to see it through to the end."

Hansen nodded. "We also have a lead on another person associated with the case. He's one of the medical examiner's orderlies. His name is Cliff Manzell."

Scotland nodded and wondered out loud, "So Gates first, then?"

Hansen nodded. "Follow us."

Scotland and Carter nodded and made their way back to the Bentayga. They made eye contact with each other on the way back. It was the detective's change of heart in including them in the case that made them suspicious.

Hansen got into the car and fired it up. He pulled out into traffic and made sure the Bentley was in his rear-view mirror as he made his way to John Gates' West Hollywood apartment.

Marx got comfortable and was still in a considerable amount of pain as he sat in the passenger side. "Why'd you invite them along? Huh?"

Hansen smirked. "I wasn't going to but then I thought, we're going to be gone in a bit and things can sometimes go wrong at these interrogations. Guns could be drawn, and Gates and the women could get shot."

Marx nodded and it hurt when he smiled, but it was worth some consolation to see the two women die at their hands in a hail of bullets. "I'm sure we can find a reason for our guns to be pulled and shots fired." He giggled like a kid who enjoyed pulling the wings off flies.

Hansen smiled and checked the rear-view mirror. "That's the spirit, Gene." He chuckled as he drove – content with himself and his genius.

Hansen pulled his unmarked squad car up North Fuller Avenue just off Hollywood Boulevard. He scanned the addresses and noticed that the Gates' residence was closer to Fountain Avenue. He checked his rear-view mirror, and the Bentley was still right behind them. A smug smirk curled over his mouth and his thoughts raced. 'Like leading lambs to the slaughter.'

John Gates paused as he looked at the package left for him by the mailboxes at his apartment complex. He pursed his lips and wondered why the building manager did not secure it like he was supposed to. He shook his head in dismay and narrowed his eyes. He grumbled under his breath, "I'm going to have another word with that asshole."

It was the package he was expecting, and he felt the heft. He was a little perplexed and murmured, "That set of t-shirts shouldn't be this heavy."

He turned it over once more to confirm the address block and his information was detailed in black on white. He tried to remember just what the hell he ordered and could not.

He pursed his lips as he continued to make his way to his second-floor unit and stopped to look at the people sunbathing, cavorting, and frolicking by and in the pool. They paid no notice to him because he paid no notice to them. He was not well liked in that complex and it suited him just fine. He mumbled under his breath as he side-eyed them, "Heathens." He shook his head with contempt and continued to his apartment.

He shut the door firmly and took the time to deadbolt, latch, chain, and barricade his door for the pending apocalypse which his pastor promised was just around the corner. He grumbled as he was now on hallowed ground, "They'll be sorry. They'll all be sorry." He took a deep breath to calm his nerves and he dropped his things where they should go.

He went to the window that overlooked the pool and it turned his stomach that those women would cavort with those men in such a way. It was ungodly and it disgusted him. There was a putrefied scowl plastered on his face. He picked up the knife stuck in the dining table and managed to get the blade into the box's slot so he could slash it open. This always excited him when he did this because it satisfied his cravings. He firmly held the package and was just about to rip through it when his buzzer rang.

He put the package down and wondered who it would be so late in the afternoon.

He sauntered over to his intercom. His finger pushed the button and he murmured, "Who is it?"

The voice asked inquisitively, "Is this John Gates?"

His tone was rude, because why not? "Yeah. Who wants to know?" His eyes narrowed inquisitively, and his mind was always suspicious and paranoid.

"This is Detectives Hansen and Marx from the LAPD Homicide Division."

"Yeah, what of it?" He knew they had nothing on him, so he was as belligerent as he wanted to be. There was a smugness plastered across his face.

The voice continued to crackle and prattle on. "We'd like to have a word with you."

Gates pondered the request for a heartbeat and wondered if it had something to do with Stafford. His thoughts clouded and he pulled his mouth to the side. "Unit two-ten." He pressed the buzzer to let them in because there was no way of preventing them from coming in – one way or another.

Gates swished his mouth from side-to-side and went to the Ikea dining table and reached his hand underneath. He slid his unregistered Smith & Wesson .38 Special out and checked the cylinder and made sure it was fully loaded and ready to rumble. A smile curled over his lips and he cocked the hammer and slid the piece back into the holster – safe and sound. He murmured under his breath, "If they want trouble, they've come to the right place..." He giggled with a satisfied grin on his face. "I'll give them trouble."

He looked at his package and was going to put it away until later but was curious to find out just what he ordered. He picked it up and slashed the knife across it...

"KABOOM!"

The apartment unit exploded in a flurry of fire and smoke.

Everyone by the pool cried out in horror and hit the deck – literally.

Hansen, Marx and the two ladies ducked down as they saw the immense fireball and then saw a burnt husk cannonball into the pool. Detritus floated like flotsam and jetsam in the water with the husk, and debris rained down across the inner courtyard – burnt or was still burning.

Women cowered in and out of the pool. They screamed with horror and terror as they saw the charred body float lifelessly prostrate in the water. They scrambled out into the waiting arms of friends and lovers and started to whimper and cry.

Scotland got up and helped Carter to her feet. They both stared at the grisly scene and their eyes were wide with horror.

Hansen swallowed hard and he looked at Marx again. They were in a state of shock and denial. Something was in play already. He tilted his head to the front gate and he marched quickly and with purpose.

Scotland and Carter looked at the body and saw the two detectives sprint past them. It took a few heartbeats for them to process why they were running the other way. They looked at one another and were astounded but surprisingly not surprised.

Scotland yelped out as they were already halfway to the front gate, "Hey..." She pointed to the body which was obviously John Gates. "Aren't you going to call for back-up and wait?"

Hansen yelled back without stopping. "We're the back-up! You call 9-1-1 if you want to play hero!"

Carter watched them hustle out, and she turned to Scotland with a quizzical scowl plastered across her face. "What the fuck just happened?"

Scotland narrowed her eyes and grumbled to her, "I don't think the detectives are telling us everything they know about this case, Carter." She pursed her lips. She looked at the people poolside taking pictures with their camera phones. "Hey! Someone call 9-1-1!" She heard them all mumble something and she gave chase after the two detectives. "C'mon, Carter..." She hustled and knew Carter would follow her dutifully. "Let's see where they're going."

They hustled out to the front and saw the detectives jump into their squad car.

Scotland heard a buzzing sound and wondered where it was coming from. She held out her arm like a crossing guard to stop Carter from crossing the threshold and looked up from under the canopy. "Do you hear that?"

Carter sidled up behind and placed her hands on her shoulders. "Uh-huh..." Her eyes scanned the skies and she had a feeling she knew what it was. "It's a drone. "The black object that zipped down the street only confirmed it, but it was not just any drone – there was a cradle underneath.

Scotland's eyes narrowed and she murmured, "I've got a bad feeling about this, Carter." She felt her friend pull her back.

Carter breathed heavy and she had a bad feeling too, but a worse feeling for the detectives. She stressed her worse feeling to Scotland. "I think it's heading for them, Scotty." She squeezed her shoulder.

Scotland cried out to the detectives, but it was too late. They slammed their doors just as the drone passed overhead.

The women dashed towards the detectives and feared for their lives rather than their own. They both waved their arms and tried to get the detectives' attention as they fired up their car and pulled out posthaste. They saw the drone catch up with the car, and it hugged the middle line of the street as it came up from behind the squad car and followed overhead – and released something from the undercarriage.

"Jesus!" Scotland saw small, black orbs pepper down at the detectives' car and somehow attach and stick to the trunk, doors, roof, and hood. The drone then zipped up and gained altitude, but her eyes were on the squad car that beamed its brake lights and immediately lurched to a stop with a screech.

The doors flung open, and legs came out.

"KABOOM!"

Scotland saw the flash, but she was quickly pulled to the side by Carter, behind a strategically and opportunely parked moving van – which shook from the concussive blast.

The detectives' car exploded with them still inside into a million pieces – followed by flame, smoke, and debris. Cars parked innocently on either side shook from the blast and windows in nearby apartments shattered helplessly as the contained blast exacted its collateral damage aimlessly.

They both peered out from the side and assessed the condition of the squad car on fire.

Scotland turned and leaned back against the van. Her startled eyes met Carter and she shook her head. "Someone's tying up loose ends, Carter." She pursed her lips disapprovingly.

Carter nodded. She screwed her mouth to the side. "There's just the one guy left..." She sighed helplessly. "It looks like we're going to have to save him, Scotty..." She thumbed at the detectives' squad car. "Because they sure as fuck aren't going to." Her eyes were wide with notable concern.

Scotland rolled her eyes at her and she groaned at her for her bluntness. "Jesus, Carter. Too soon." She just watched her shrug innocently. "C'mon..." She led the way back to the Bentayga. "We need to get to the Medical Examiner's Office."

Chapter 21

Scotland and Carter entered the front lobby of the Medical Examiner's Office. Their eyes scanned the foyer and they saw the receptionist wave them over.

"Hi." Joanne smiled at them both. "You're…" She paused and looked a little solemn. "You were Richard's friends."

Scotland nodded and recognized her. "Hi, Joanne…" She seemed a little paler today and she may have been upset about Richard and seeing Carter and her may not have made it better. "How're you?"

Joanne shook her head. "Feeling a little under the weather and I'm still upset about Richard…" She forced a smile and her face lit up. "May I help you with anything?"

Scotland nodded. "Joanne, we're looking for Cliff Manzell…" She popped-up her eyebrows. "Do you know where we can find him?"

Joanne smiled and nodded. "Yes, you're in luck…" She licked her lips and cleared her throat. "He just came back…" She pointed down the stairs. "He went back to the labs downstairs, but…" She pursed her lips at them. "It's a high security area."

Carter flashed a smile at her. "Joanne, he may be in some danger. We need to see him."

Joanne trembled and looked a little startled. "Oh really?" She hesitated as she touched the phone. "Do you want me to call security?"

Scotland shook her head. "I don't think it's come to that, Joanne. We just want to have a word with him and warn him about some potential danger."

Joanne was surprised. "In here?" She chuckled a little. "There are always police around. It may be the most secure place after the LAPD headquarters."

Scotland pursed her lips and nodded. She understood her hesitation but that the building was also secure. "Do you mind coming with us to see if he's okay?"

Joanne hesitated once more. "Umm, sure." She looked over at her back-up as she sat there filling out some paperwork. "Louise. I'm just going to escort these ladies down to the labs."

Louise popped her head up and smiled – the nod was to say, 'go ahead'.

Joanne led them down the stairs to the secure door which she buzzed them through. They walked down the pristine long hallway and there was a strong chemical smell which she was used to. Through two more secure sets of doors and they were in the inner sanctum. "His office is just down here." She pointed the way.

Scotland scanned the other rooms and it was quiet and a little eerie. Nothing was happening in the autopsy labs so it must be a slow evening. Her thoughts wandered because there will be three bodies she knows of that will be coming in soon – a little crispy though. Cliff did right to eat early but he was probably used to seeing a dead body in various conditions so they should not be a surprise to him.

They came to his office and Joanne knocked pleasantly on the door. "Cliff?" She pursed her lips and waited for him to answer. "Cliff, are you in?" She listened intently at the door and there was a pause until they all heard his voice call out to them.

"Come in."

Joanne opened the door and she smiled at him as he sat at his desk in his windowless office. "Hi, Cliff. Sorry to bother you…" She opened the door wide and exposed her other two guests. "These ladies would like to have a word with you about something."

Cliff's eyes were distracted by what he was reading on the screen but then perked up when he saw how the women looked. In his mind he thought he had a chance with one of them or both – in reality it was never going to happen. "Hi." He stood up as he took a sip of his beverage from the very large takeaway cup. He grinned from ear-to-ear and could not recall the last time he had two gorgeous women who wanted to be in his office – voluntarily. He touched his stomach and knew he should not have had that large burrito plate with extra chilli sauce, but he was hungry damn it. He took another sip of soda to see if that helped. 'Nope.'

Scotland nodded and smiled at the average looking orderly, with a pot belly, thinning hair, and horn-rimmed glasses. His white lab coat was grey and definitely not white, rumpled with more food stains than patient stains. "Hi, Cliff, I'm Scotland and this is my friend Carter…" She pursed her lips and decided to get right down to business. "Do you know a John Gates?"

Cliff stopped sucking at his straw, and he swallowed uncomfortably. He started to sweat, and his eyes darted around. "Umm, who?" He did not feel well suddenly, and in hindsight knew that burrito was definitely not a good idea. He took a healthy sip of his drink and gulped it down and hoped it would alleviate the digestive distress he was experiencing right now. He rubbed his stomach and was feeling light-headed and hot.

Carter narrowed her eyes at him. "John Gates, do you know him? What about detectives Hansen and Marx?" She watched him and he seemed more preoccupied with his stomach and his drink. She turned to Scotland and had a suspicious look on her face.

Joanne looked at him and she was nervous for the man. "Cliff…" She pursed her lips and worried he was not feeling well because he did not look well. "Are you feeling okay?"

Scotland saw the look and noticed his distress. "Cliff…" She decided to take her shot and asked him pointedly. "Do you and Dirk Stafford work together?" She saw him tense up and look her straight in the eyes.

Cliff swallowed and shook a little on hearing the name. "What about him?"

Scotland shook her head and could feel something was off about Cliff. "He's tying up loose ends, Cliff…" She pursed her lips. "And he's killed Detectives Hansen and Marx."

Joanne gasped in horror. "What?" She looked at her with wide-eyes. "They're dead? How?"

Carter looked at her and held her arm to steady her. "Someone blew them up in their car. Someone also blew up John Gates in his apartment."

Cliff turned white as a sheet. He croaked out in terror. "Hansen and Marx were killed?"

Scotland nodded her head and saw him lean over and he grabbed the table. He looked at his beverage cup and shook his head – perplexed at the possibility. "Cliff…" She wanted to move toward him but felt Carter hold her back. "Are you okay?"

Cliff looked at her with wild-eyes and shook his head. "I think they did something to me." He started to breathe heavy and fell back into his chair.

Joanne made a move to go to him but felt the firm grips of both women. She saw them shake their heads at her, and they turned and looked over at Cliff who convulsed and arched his back wildly as he slouched in his chair and screamed out in agony. "I have to help him!"

Scotland shook her head and looked at the beverage container. She saw his face turn beet red and steam came out of his nose and mouth. He torqued and cried out in agony and she knew it was over for him. "Outside!"

They all ran out, and Scotland pulled the door shut – hard.

Scotland pushed Carter and Joanne to the side and took cover.

They heard Cliff scream out in agony and then they heard a muffled explosion and felt the hallway shake. Then there was silence and an unpleasant odor. A red jelly like liquid started to ooze from under Cliff's door.

Scotland covered her mouth to stop her gag-reflex as she saw the ooze and she did not have to open the door to know what the scene looked like.

She looked at Carter and Joanne and both of them had horrified looks on their faces.

Carter gagged and swallowed. She had to hold whatever was in her stomach down. She too did not need to look inside to know it was not going to be good. "Jesus, Scotty..." She shook her head with contempt. "Which sick fucker would do something like this to another human being?"

A voice growled out down the hall. "Me..." He cackled at his madness and was impressed with his genius at the novel ways he managed to dispatch his assignments. No one ever got away except Scotland and his eyes twinkled at her. "That's who." He held a gun with a silencer up at them all and he smiled.

The women all put up their hands in surrender.

Scotland looked at him and recognized him immediately. "You were that dessert waiter at Spago..." She pursed her lips with contempt. "The guy that tried to blow us up."

He nodded and did a bit of a bow to take credit. "Guilty as charged. Call me Bomber-man. Everyone that knows me does." He pouted and looked her over. "You know..." He shook his head. "You're the only person who has managed to get away..." His head tick-tocked from side-to-side. "Not this time, though." He snorted a giggle.

Carter stood in his way to buffer him from Scotland and Joanne. Her eyes narrowed and she saw him smirk at her chutzpah.

Bomber-man dropped his arm with his gun and leaned into the woman and did not see her flinch one bit. His hand grabbed at her throat and he was surprised at her speed as she deflected his reach, and he felt his head snap violently back from the feral hit. He touched his tender nose and saw the blood, but she would have broken it if she hit him any harder. He smirked at her and pulled his gun up.

Joanne screamed at him. There was a terror in her eyes as she saw what he was about to do. "No!" She held her hands up to stop him. She only saw him smile with blood-tinged teeth and put his gun down.

Scotland pulled Carter back and wrapped her arm around her. She glared at Bomber-man. "What do you want with us?"

Bomber-man shook his head and smirked. He wiped his face clean of the blood and turned back to the hallway.

They all heard footsteps and looked over to see who was coming toward them.

Scotland recognized him immediately and her blood ran cold.

Bomber-man turned slightly and turned back to the women. "You can ask him." He thumbed back as Dirk Stafford came closer into view.

Dirk looked at Bomber-man and then at the three ladies. "What happened to you?"

He pointed at the woman who punched him. "Her. That's what happened to me." He scowled at her and promised he was going to make her scream for what she did to him.

Dirk shook his head and looked at the women. "Ladies…" He scanned the faces. "Scotland, nice to see you again."

Scotland interrupted and growled at him, "Wish I could say the same for you, Stafford."

Dirk snorted a laugh and continued down the line. "You must be Carter Deklava…" He felt enamored with the gorgeous woman. "Dirk Stafford from SoCal Fund Management." His eyes sparkled thinking he could get a shot at her. "I recognize you from your press secretary days and your press conferences…" He smiled and nodded. There was a salaciousness behind his eyes as he scanned her body from head to toe and made sure he checked out her best lady-bits. "I must say I enjoyed them so much I used to masturbate to them."

Carter rolled her eyes and shook her head. "Yeah…" She pursed her lips at him derisively. "You and everyone else, creep."

Dirk once again snorted a giggle, and then turned to Joanne Middleton. His eyes narrowed a bit as he studied her and her nametag. "You look so familiar…" There was a perplexed look on his face. "Have we met before?"

Joanne narrowed her eyes. "I used to work at your company as an assistant coordinator a few years ago."

Dirk shook his head, and then it tick-tocked from side-to-side. "That may have been it, but there's something familiar about you I can't put my finger on, Joanne." His eyes opened wide. "Wait…" He gasped at his discovery. "You're the one that released that reporter's story to the LA Times." He had a look of wonderment in his face at the discovery.

Joanne nodded. "Yes. At least Richard got his story out on you and what you did."

Dirk pursed his lips and tick-tocked his head from side-to-side. "Yes, but tomorrow I'll be in South America and no one will be able to touch me." He grinned helplessly at his good fortune and their predicament. "Whereas you'll all be…" He had a smug look on his face and looked up like a tormenting bully then turned back to them. "Dead."

Scotland narrowed her eyes at him. "Karma's a bitch, Dirk."

Dirk chuckled at her and could not believe her courage in the face of death. He leaned into the gorgeous woman and smiled. "Karma and I have a thing going on…" He thumbed his chest. "She leaves me be, and I fuck her in every one of her holes because she can't do a thing to me." He giggled at her and shook his head.

Scotland was trying to buy some time and hoped someone would come down to save them. "Why'd you kill Hansen and Marx and that prison guard? John Gates. Huh?" She narrowed her eyes at him interrogatively. "Were the detectives getting too close for comfort or were they trying to extort you?"

Dirk talked like he did not care what would happen in the time it took him to explain some of the information to them all. "You misunderstand, Scotland..." He smiled and relaxed. "Hansen, Marx and I were partners..." He leaned in comedically. "In crime, you could say." He was happy to regale them because most of the story was out in the LA Times already except for the backstory and some names. "I had pensioners that needed to be relieved of their lives and their remaining pension balances, and Hansen and Marx were the instruments of death. As we got bigger, they couldn't handle the killings, so we hired professional killers and murderers from the San Pedro prison. Hansen and Marx got too big, and I had to cut them loose. Same with John Gates..." He headtossed at Cliff Manzell's office. "And the same for Cliff." He smirked comically and held the back of his hand to his mouth to make sure he was only talking with them. "I'd recommend you not open the door because it's going to be messy in there." He giggled like a psychopath at the pain and suffering he caused.

Carter glared at him. "By blowing them up?"

Dirk shrugged his shoulders playfully and held his hands up. His lips pouted as he tilted his head at Bomber-man. "He's like a Subway sandwich artist. He takes pride in how he does his job." He popped-up his eyebrows at the gorgeous woman who he had to scan up-and-down every chance he got.

Scotland looked at him intently. "Why send the shooter after Carter and me?"

Dirk was perplexed at that. He shook his head and his face clouded quizzically. "Yeah..." He shrugged his shoulders. "I didn't send that one after you, although I have used him before." He tick-tocked his head and pursed his lips. "I can only guess Hansen and Marx sent him after you. But they swore that they didn't do it and blamed me – those fuckers, may they rest in pieces..." He playfully shrugged again. "They may have lied – they've done it before." He laughed. "Too bad they're dead and you and Carter took care of the shooter..." He looked at them with a satisfied stare. "Come to think of it, he did want to get cremated if anything happened to him and you managed to fulfill his wish. Mazel tov, Scotland."

Scotland shook her head. She looked up at Bomber-man and glared at him. "Why'd you try to blow us up at Spago?"

Bomber-man simply smiled and did not say anything. He did not have to spill his guts to the woman. He shrugged and had a smug look of satisfaction on his face.

Dirk looked at her. "Like I said. He's an artist and sometimes artists go off script like Tarantino or that Dutch director, what's his name?" He looked perplexed as his mind tried to recall the name that was on the tip of his tongue. "Lars something..." He kept snapping his fingers hoping that would help. "He makes those pornos for mainstream and calls them art..." He rolled his eyes at the movies. "What a fucking weirdo."

Scotland narrowed her eyes and scoffed at him. "He's Danish, you-knucklehead."

Dirk looked at her and he laughed out loud. "You got a sizable pair of balls, Scotland..." He giggled derisively at her. "I've got to hand it to you..." He looked at her and his eyes went dead like a shark's. "I'm going to kill you all. How slow or how quickly you want me to do it depends on you."

Carter got in his way. "Leave her alone, asshole."

Dirk glared at her salaciously. "You, Miss Deklava..." He smirked and could feel his cock get hard just thinking of the things he was going to do to her. "I'm going to leave you for last and take my time."

It was now Scotland who defended her. "Leave her alone, Dirk."

Joanne looked at him. "Why do I have to die? I did nothing to you." She teared up a bit and her eyes pleaded with him. "Leave me out of this."

Dirk smacked his lips, and he took a breath. "Because I like hurting women and..." He looked at the three of them and knew he was going to enjoy himself. He matter-of-factly growled, "You're women."

Scotland saw something behind them that caught her eyes, and she breathed a sigh of relief when she saw the uniforms come into view. She yelled out to them, "Nate! Kate! Help us!" She thought her eyes deceived her because Bomber-man and Stafford did not flinch as the police officers came up to them all.

Dirk did not even have to turn around. He smiled at her and could see the look of shock on all the women's faces. He thumbed back at Officers Hernandez and Murdock and smacked his lips with satisfaction. "They're with me."

Scotland looked at Kate and only saw an unerring and stone-cold killer look on her face and Nate's face. Their stares were not caring or loving but were almost robot-like and ready to take orders. She gasped out and hoped she could appeal to her lover's deeper instincts. "Kate, please..." She pleaded with her. "Help us."

Kate simply glared at her and stared right through her. Whatever they shared that evening did not mean anything to her – she was using them all this time. She was focused on her mission and that was to carry out Dirk Strafford's orders.

Carter looked at Nate and his look had changed toward her too.

While he may have acted submissive to her, Nate glared at her right there and right now and would kill her in a heartbeat if told by Stafford.

Carter thought it was almost as if Stafford hypnotized him and Kate. "Nate..." She shook her head at him with disgust and scoffed, "And to think I let you come inside me."

Scotland turned to look at her with disdain. "Jesus, Carter..." She pursed her lips derisively at her. "You really know how to roll the dice, don't you?"

Carter forced a grin and shrugged her shoulders.

Stafford smiled at the two women. He looked at his watch and he motioned to Hernandez and Murdock. "Are the cars nearby?"

Kate nodded. "Yes. They're around the back..." She headtossed down the hall. "We can head out that way."

Dirk nodded. He paused and sized the women up. He headtossed at them. "Zap-strap their hands behind their backs and let's go."

Hernandez and Murdock shoved the three women against the wall and tied their hands securely behind their backs.

"Ow." Scotland could feel the tightness constrict her hands behind her back. "There's no need to get rough, Kate."

Kate simply glared and shoved her. "Just shut up and move."

Nate did the same with Joanne and Carter and marched them to the back door.

Dirk took the lead and turned to see Joanne whimper as she was being led away with her assailants. "Don't worry Joanne. I'll make it quick for you. You won't feel a thing..." He heard Bomber-man snort a laugh, and he turned to her again. "I'm lying. It's going to be long and painful."

Joanne started to bawl uncontrollably.

Scotland glared at him. "Stafford..." She shook her head at him. "You don't need to be an asshole about it. Okay?"

Dirk shrugged his shoulders. "I say if the shoe fits." He smiled at them.

Chapter 22

"Where are we going, Dirk?" Scotland wanted answers because they were driving north.

Dirk turned from the front seat and looked at her. He separated them into the two cars but wanted Scotland in his along with Kate driving. "We're going for a jet ride..." He smiled yet again because he knew he was smarter than them all. "Only that you, Joanne and Carter won't be landing with us."

Scotland looked at him and shook her head. "You did all of this simply for money?"

Dirk nodded. "Uh, yeah..." He looked at her quizzically. "Why the hell else would I do it?"

Scotland shook her head derisively and narrowed her eyes at him. "You're like a Bond villain but without the class or charm."

Kate finally broke and snorted a laugh.

Dirk looked at her derisively and turned back to Scotland. "I'm the best kind of Bond villain, Scotland..." He raised his eyebrows for effect, and he smiled from ear-to-ear. "I'm going to get away with it, and you three ladies are going to get thrown out of the plane somewhere between here and Mexico."

Scotland chewed her thoughts and kept her mouth shut – for now.

The two squad cars pulled through the Whiteman Airport's automated gates and drove without interruption or hindrance to the private hanger owned by Dirk Stafford.

Kate clicked a remote and the door opened so they could transfer their cargo, sight unseen.

Scotland took another chance at reasoning with him. "Look, Dirk. You don't have to do this. Leave us tied up someplace and then fly away. It wouldn't matter if we say anything. You'd be long gone."

Dirk smiled and shook his head. "You ladies have each caused me grief in some way and I'm going to make an example out of all of you. If not for someone else's benefit so they can see what this cautionary tale held, then for my own pleasure because I really don't like you and your friends." He narrowed his eyes at her. His blank stare burned into her soul.

They pulled the ladies out and they all filed into the private G500 corporate jet.

Dirk moved to the cockpit and he looked at Kate and Nate. "Stick them in the seats and keep them there. I'll figure out where we drop them or decide if we want to have a little fun with them first." He smiled at Scotland

and Carter and only saw them gag at the prospect of being raped before being killed. He went inside the cockpit.

Kate and Nate shoved the ladies in the seats so they faced one another and put their seatbelts on and secured them tightly.

Scotland had a birds-eye view of the cockpit door and wondered what her next move should be.

Scotland and Carter looked at one another and their eyes darted around the cabin, and they were sending one another signals non-verbally.

Carter's legs stretched out and tapped Scotland's legs for comfort.

Nate came up to Carter and slapped her hard across the face.

Scotland yelled at him, "Don't touch her, asshole!"

Nate walked up to Scotland and wound up his hand to give her a fresh one, but Kate got in his way.

She growled at him, "Back off, Murdock." He backed up and held his hands up to surrender. Kate headtossed at the door. "Go secure the door."

Nate did as she said and watched Bomber-man secure Joanne in an adjacent seat and got comfortable in another.

Dirk fired up the engines, looked back into the cabin, and then secured the door. He started to taxi the jet.

It did not take long for them to start climbing and it seemed they were at a steeper angle than usual to gain altitude fast.

Bomber-man did not even wait for the seatbelt sign to go off and he unbuckled his belt and made his way to Joanne. He reached into his pocket and pulled out his butterfly blade and swicked it open. The blade was front and center and ready to do some damage.

Scotland eyed him without saying a word.

He simply smiled smugly at Scotland and turned his attention to Joanne and undid her seatbelt.

Joanne looked at Scotland and Carter and her once-upon-a-time innocent look turned sinister with a smile. She leaned forward and Bomber-man cut her restraints loose. She rubbed her wrists and smiled at him and then turned to the ladies and pulled her mouth to the side in a crooked smile.

Scotland and Carter looked up at Nate and Kate and they watched Joanne – and did nothing.

Scotland's eyes scanned them all and her mind started to race with the new information and the missing pieces of the puzzle started to appear and find their way into the gaps of the almost completed jigsaw puzzle.

Joanne got up and watched Bomber-man swick his blade back and he stuck it in his pocket. She walked up to the front with more confidence before and turned to look at Carter and then Scotland. She snorted a laugh. She murmured in an unerring way, "You don't seem surprised, Scotland."

Scotland shook her head and looked at Carter who was also not surprised. She turned back to Joanne and opened her eyes with the puzzle together. "Not at all, Joanne..." She smirked at her knowingly. "Or should I call you, Gwen?"

Joanne scoffed and chuckled at her and she shook her head. "Fuck..." She smiled, delighted at her intelligence. "How'd you know I was Gwen?" She turned to look at Kate, Nate, and Bomber-man. They were shocked to know that Scotland and most likely Carter were aware of their plans because they seemed calmer and more cognizant of their situation than expected. Her eyes zeroed back at Scotland and she clenched her jaw in a sinister way.

Scotland smirked. "I had a feeling you were playing everyone including Richard."

Gwen laughed heartily. "Oh, especially that guy. I was playing him like a fiddle. Even got him fired from his job just so he would be desperate enough to run with this story." She laughed. "He was all in when I fed him tidbits. You should've seen his eyes light up."

Scotland nodded. "I remember when the story was run, and I saw all of the names of the people SoCal killed for their pensions over the last fifteen years. There were hundreds of names."

Gwen smiled and leaned against the seat. "Go on. You're way too smart for your own good." She shook her head and pursed her lips.

Scotland continued. "Names of people Dirk, Hansen and Marx murdered or had murdered and made it look like natural causes."

Gwen nodded. "Murder by natural causes, yeah."

"Names like Hernandez, Murdock and Middleton..." Scotland looked at each of them. "Your parents were killed by them and you got nothing."

Gwen laughed and she looked up at the ceiling. She shook her head. "Fuck..." She licked her lips and smiled. "You're very smart."

"Then you probably met up with Kate and Nate at..." Scotland narrowed her eyes and this deduction was a stretch. "A support group?"

Gwen nodded and continued to smile. "Keep going."

"You probably became good friends and then lovers, but then you started to dig and dig and noticed that there was a pattern and then you really got suspicious and that's when you decided SoCal needed to pay. You were in it for the long game, so you got a job at the ME's office..." Scotland thought about it. "No. You got a job at SoCal first and became invaluable and worked your way up and put in long hours to get the records you needed." She saw her nod. "Then came the LAPD office, ME's office, then the San Pedro prison then the County Lock-up." She cocked an eyebrow.

Gwen looked at her with an unerring smile on her face because she was delighted someone figured out their grift. She wondered if Scotland was smart enough to discover all of the backstory and she decided she liked this girl and wanted her to live long enough to spill her guts. "Close enough, Scotland." She held up her hand and waited for Bomber-man to get up and hand his Glock to her. She gripped it expertly like she knew how to handle a gun and smiled at her as she unscrewed the silencer. "Keep going. You're doing really well." She popped-up her eyebrows because she really, really liked this girl – for now.

Scotland continued. "You surreptitiously fed information to Ron Little at the police station, and then he fed that to Richard. Then Ron retired and you probably got him a job at the ME's office when you found out his wife had died – most likely at the hands of SoCal." She saw her nod once more. "Then you fed him information or left it for him to find and he and Richard used to work together so you played those two patsies for all they were worth." She surreptitiously glanced at Carter and she saw her eyes scan every where and knew she was working on something. "Then you probably had Ron killed so you could get Richard's creative juices flowing and gave him enough information for him to start to connect the dots on the conspiracy."

They felt the plane level off and the engines backed off. It started to bank and turn but without a compass it was difficult to figure out which way it was heading.

Scotland continued. "You knew Richard had the listening device at Mrs. Vasquez's…" She saw Gwen purse her lips and shake her head.

Gwen smirked. "I didn't know he did that, but it seemed to work out for the best. I needed to know where he stored his information."

"But it was information you had been feeding him." Scotland paused and figured out another nugget. "But you needed it to look like it all came from him somehow and since he had it in the Cloud all you had to do was access his files and add all of the stuff you had built up over the years and he takes credit, and there's no way SoCal can contradict him because he's dead." Her eyes lit up. "So, the FBI and everyone else with an acronym will have no choice but to investigate the information the LA Times has, and they'll fill in the rest of the blanks."

"Mazel tov, Scotland…" She gave her a thumbs-up and tilted her head at Kate. "She said you were smart, and I wanted to find out just how smart…" She snorted a giggled. "That's why I sent that shooter after you, and when that failed, I had Bomber-man send you a little surprise at Spago."

Scotland narrowed her eyes. "That's when I started to get suspicious."

Gwen's eyes lit up. "Really? How so?"

"Well, it was first when Carter hooked up with Nate and he cried out your name when he came."

Gwen turned to Nate and saw him shirk his head down in shame. She turned back to Scotland and Carter. "Yeah…" She looked at their curves and her dirty thoughts wandered too. "When I was hot and fuckable like you two fine specimens, I could make Nate call my name for hours…" She smirked and tilted her head at Kate. "Kate, too." She smiled. "But you were saying you got suspicious?"

Scotland nodded. "I only told Kate where we were going for dinner, so how did Bomber-man know to drop off a bomb there?" She side-eyed Bomber-man. "Then I thought Kate had something to do with it, but I needed to be sure, so Carter and me tag-teamed her thinking she would slip up and say something." She shrugged a little even with her hands bound. "And she did."

Gwen looked at Kate and saw her just a little embarrassed but not much. She was trained killer. "Really? Kate told you?"

Carter smirked and thought she should chime in a little too. "She talks in her sleep."

Gwen looked at Kate and laughed. She did not see a single crack on her face. "Yes. Kate was quite upset with me the next day about sending that bomb to the table. I told her that I wanted to see just how smart you were…" She shrugged and held her hands up. "You passed with flying colors…" She leaned in and showed her sinister eyes. "But I'm also a very vain and jealous woman and they belong to me." She tapped the Glock against her chest. "Got it?"

The cockpit door flew open. "Okay, the auto-pilot is set…" Dirk was at first calm and then nervous when he saw Joanne loose and holding a gun. "What the fuck is going on here?"

Nate grabbed him and threw him into the closest seat, roughly. "Stay there." He pointed at him to obey.

Dirk's startled eyes wondered just what the fuck was going on. "Okay, okay. Easy." He got comfortable and held up his hands in surrender.

Carter looked at Scotland and mumbled, "Is it just me or is Nate so much hotter all of a sudden?"

Scotland did not look at her and growled at her through her clenched jaw impatiently, "Not-now-Carter."

Carter just sat back and pouted.

Gwen smiled at Dirk and tilted the Glock at Scotland. "Miss Yarde is just telling us the whole story of how things are and why they are what they are."

Dirk smiled and nodded, and then looked at her perplexed, "What?"

Gwen looked at him with a fiery glare. "Here. Let me explain it to you in a language you'll understand." She walked up to him, pointed the gun at his kneecap and pulled the trigger.

"Bang!"

Dirk's left kneecap exploded, and his hands went down to protect it, and he howled in agony.

Scotland and Carter were shocked that she would do that in the pressurized plane, but she had nothing to lose apparently.

Gwen smirked and watched Dirk writhe in pain and agony.

Scotland narrowed her eyes at her. "You're a psychotic bitch, Gwen..." She shook her head and pursed her lips with derision. "Just like your dad..." She headtossed her toward the front of the cabin. "Dirk Stafford."

Gwen's smile disappeared from her face. There was now an evil glare as she burned her eyes into the too-smart for-her-own-good bitch. She walked back to her. "What the fuck do you know about him? Huh?" She pointed the gun at her. "How about I kneecap you or better yet..." She narrowed her eyes and aimed at her head. "How about I just shoot you in the fucking face!"

Scotland leaned back in the seat and waited for the pain, but it did not come.

Bomber-man stepped up and held Scotland so Gwen would have an easier time to shoot her point blank in the face.

Kate yelled at her, "Gwen!" She grabbed her arm. "Settle down."

Dirk groaned and held his bleeding knee. He swallowed and he was in agony, but he needed to know. "Is that true, Joanne. You're my daughter?"

Gwen turned to him and had to come nearer. She placed her foot on his knee and pushed and loved how he screamed in pain. "Yeah. That's right, daddy. I'm your daughter."

Dirk clenched his jaw and howled in agony. Karma truly was a bitch. "Argh!"

Gwen looked at Kate and then turned back to Scotland. She took a deep breath and dropped her arm with the gun. "Carry on, Scotland..." She breathed heavy. "But tread lightly, bitch."

Scotland looked at her and wondered how she should play this with her armed and willing to shoot at body parts. Plead to her womanly instincts, or piss her off really good? She decided on option two. "Carter's contacts got us some information about Dirk when he was an up-and-comer mainly because he enjoyed having his sluts cowboy him, but some he forced himself onto and into, and others he drugged and had his way with them. He was a piece of work then, and he seems to be a piece of work still to this day. So, he got your mom pregnant, and his parents paid her off to disappear. She had you and never told you about him until..." Scotland thought about the turn of events as they played out in her head.

Gwen narrowed her eyes. While she entertained her sideshow with pleasure, the gorgeous woman was really starting to piss her off. "Keep going..." She pointed to Dirk. "Daddy needs to hear this."

Scotland looked at her and her body shape, her skin color, her yellowy eyes, and her stringy hair – which was obviously a wig. She gasped and now she knew everything. "Your mom worked for the California Government and then took early retirement when she got sick and then SoCal came knocking. They made it look like an accident. Overdosed on pain killers. You got nothing. No remaining pension trust and no insurance."

Gwen teared up. "She had at least two more years of fight left in her and they took her away from me." She took a deep breath and wiped her eyes.

Scotland looked at her. "So now you have cancer, and this is why the timetable for bringing SoCal down was accelerated. You needed to bring SoCal and your dad down before you died."

She turned and looked at Dirk and then turned to Scotland and thumbed at him. "I was only at SoCal for one month and do you know he tried to hit on me?" She shook her head. "He didn't even know I used my mom's name and I introduced myself to him and he didn't recognize the name..." She glared at him. "Or that he was hitting on his daughter!"

Carter looked at Scotland with a gag-face. There were things she did that would make Caligula frown upon, but incest was off the table – 'well, almost'. She simply saw Scotland roll her eyes at her and shake her head. 'Not now, I get it.'

Gwen leaned into him and placed the muzzle to his shoulder and pulled the trigger.

"Bang!"

Dirk screamed in agony as the bullet shattered bone and nerves and there was now more pain he had to deal with. "Argh! Jesus! Stop!"

Scotland looked at her. "Gwen. It doesn't have to end this way. Dirk destroyed lives everywhere not just Kate's, Nate's, and yours. If he goes on trial, it'll be more embarrassing."

Gwen shook her head and looked at Scotland. She reached up to her hairline and pulled her wig off and exposed her bald head. "I only have a couple of weeks left. It's a very aggressive form of pancreatic cancer. I want to see him suffer. Not let him drag it on for years. He needs to die." She stared at her with crazy eyes. "Now!"

Scotland side-eyed Carter and saw her nod slightly. She turned to Gwen who held the gun to Dirk's head, and she saw him cower. "Gwen…" She licked her lips and wondered if this was the best course of action but thought 'fuck it'. "So, I just need to know. When Dirk fucked your mom to conceive your sorry ass…" She looked at her with a puzzled smirk. "Did he do all of those things to her?" She saw the rage in her eyes grow as the gun arm dropped down and she tilted her head. "Because enquiring minds will also want to know if you mom liked it in the ass first or last."

Gwen clenched her jaw and she turned the gun toward Scotland, and she started to walk toward her.

Bomber-man held her.

Carter commanded in an instant, "Scotty!"

Scotland arched her back against the seat, and she saw Carter swing her kickboxing toe in a wide arc. It connected with the belt latch and clicked it free. In the blink of an eye, she found Bomber-man's soft-spots and her Krav Maga kicked in. She kneed him hard in the diaphragm.

The wind went out of Bomber-man and he could not even scream in pain. He folded over Scotland like a paper doll – and got in the way.

Gwen was going to shoot but Bomber-man was now in the way of her target.

To Scotland this was not the best position to be in, but she did not need her arms and hands free to fuck him up good. She re-cocked her leg once again and drove a punishing knee into Bomber-man's fragile face. While Carter may have bruised him earlier, this knee shattered his face with a blood-curdling crack.

Bomber-man instantly reeled back into the aisle with blood gushing from face.

Gwen aimed and pulled the trigger – too late.

Scotland spun out of the seat onto the floor.

"Bang! Bang!"

Bullets impacted the empty seat.

Scotland flexed her yoga-inspired shoulders down and crossed her legs in one motion to get her hands free in front of her. She saw an advantage and released her legs at Bomber-man's exposed chest. The double-legged, mule-kick threw him back with significant force towards Gwen, and like bowling pins she slammed into Kate and Nate.

Kate slammed headfirst into the wall and she toppled over, and Nate fell backward against the seat armrest and his back took the brunt of the fall.

He howled out in pain, "Argh!"

Being in closed quarters they all dogpiled onto one another haplessly.

Dirk saw his opportunity and reached for the gun Gwen dropped on the floor close to him. He howled in agony as he picked it up and pointed it at his daughter. His hand trembled and he was in two minds about whether to shoot her. All he saw was her smile.

Gwen did not skip a beat. She reached into her pocket and pulled out a grenade that she took from Kate's or was it from Nate's stuff. Never mind, she had been saving it for the right time – and this was the right time. She looked over at Dirk and she smiled. Her hand gripped the safety, and she pulled the pin. "Mom's waiting for us, dad." She forced a smile and threw the grenade backward toward the front of the cabin.

Carter saw what she did and knew it was going to be bad. She instinctively yelled out, "Scotty-on-me!"

Kate and Nate yelled out as they scrambled to do something with the grenade before it exploded.

Scotland got up and dove onto Carter and looped her tied arms around her head and shoulders.

"Boom!"

There were short screams of terror as the grenade ripped open the jet's door and loosened it completely from the fuselage. Anyone and anything that was not secured in some way was forced out into the atmosphere as the cabin depressurized instantly. Debris flew out the fuselage and some of it impacted the number-one-engine – sucked into the turbine. The engine did not like that and exploded. The jet shuddered violently and went into a steep dive.

Scotland held onto her friend as they were forced out of the seat for an instant but were held in place by the seatbelt that secured Carter. They yelled out at the release in air pressure and it only took a few seconds for it to stabilize.

Scotland and Carter looked up and they were all gone, and they were a little sad and dismayed that it had to end for them this way – but they had bigger problems to worry about. The cockpit door was ripped off in the explosion and they had a birds-eye view as the diving jet was accelerating towards the ground.

Scotland got off Carter and broke the zap-straps by holding her hands close and driving it toward her knees. Her hands were now free, and she unbuckled Carter.

Carter bent her yoga body and crossed her legs to get her hands to her front and broke the straps the same way.

They felt the steep dive and slid down the floor toward the cockpit like it was a slide. The air rushed past where there was now a gaping hole in the side of the jet.

Scotland got into the cockpit first and caught Carter as she slid inside too. Alarms and klaxons sounded in the cockpit because the jet was in trouble, and so were they.

They both got into the seats and buckled up and had to quickly assess their situation which looked grim.

Scotland looked at the state of the instruments and they were damaged but still registered information to her. She made sure the auto-pilot was off and she grabbed the yoke and pulled back on the throttle.

Carter looked at Scotland and she wanted to know what she needed from her. Scotland was the pilot not her, but she knew her way around the cockpit well enough to be a danger to herself when necessary.

Scotland's mouth was dry, and she thought furiously. She needed to save them – and fast. "Engine-one-on-fire! Pull the extinguisher! Put it out!"

Carter pulled the handle and checked that it was deployed. "Check!"

"Fuel, dump-it!" Scotland's eyes darted over the instrument panel.

Carter found the buttons and activated the fuel dump and checked that it was activated. "Check!"

Scotland pulled back on the throttle even more and tried desperately to hold the diving jet steady, but she was fighting with the controls. "Flaps-full!"

Carter's hand moved to the flaps and pulled the lever all the way back. "Flaps-full, check!"

Scotland looked out the windshield and the ground was coming up fast. There was a sweat beading on her brow because she was nervous. The hole was causing all sorts of turbulence, noise and the alarms did not help one bit. "Gear-down!"

Carter pulled the lever down and watched the lights indicate it was activated. "Gear-down, check!"

Scotland breathed heavy as she pulled the yoke back hard. She used all her cross-fit muscles to get the jet under control, but it was so badly damaged that she did not know if it was a losing battle. "Carter!" She bit her bottom lip. And her eyes were open wide. "I love you!"

Carter looked at her and had a look of desperation and wondered if it was all over for them. That was the only conceivable reason for Scotland's declaration of love for her. She paused for half-a-heartbeat and yelled out inquisitively, "Now?" Carter stared at her incredulously. "Why the fuck are you telling me this now?" There was a wild-eyed look of concern – or was it finality? She croaked out loud, "Huh?"

Scotland side-eyed her hesitantly and simply shrugged her shoulders.

Carter clenched her jaw and wondered if this was it for them both. She groaned out loud, "I love you too, Scotty!" She looked out the window as the ground grew nearer. "Fffuughk-me!"

Scotland's eyes were wild with terror and her body tensed up. "Hold the fuck on!"

She piloted it parallel with the highway leading into downtown Los Angeles. This late in the day the traffic would be light leading that way but heavy on the way out of the city. The jet shook violently as it started to stabilize and drop like a rock to the ground but at a much less steep angle – but still way too fast.

Carter protested out loud as the ground came into view a lot faster than she was used to. "Shit-shit-shit-shit…" There was still so much more for her to do and people she wanted to fuck. She did not want this to be the end. "This is going to be bad!"

Scotland eyeballed a large enough spot and maneuvered the jet lower and lower, and it was going to hit hard but not as hard as diving directly into the ground. She white-knuckled the yoke and pulled back hard so the nose came up.

The rear landing gears slammed down onto the highway tarmac hard and the impact torqued the already fragile fuselage. The wings flexed and slammed into the tarmac. The jet bounced back up several feet and slammed back down hard once again – bits and pieces broke off from the fuselage and crashed onto the highway. The nose gear came down less hard, but still hard enough that more parts of the jet broke off and littered the highway.

Scotland slammed the engines in reverse and heard them spool and whine in protest. The already damaged number-one-engine exploded as fan blades already loose become looser and gnashed and grinded metal-against-metal and destroyed the sophisticated machinery. She slammed on the brakes hard and felt the anti-lock pulse violently as it kept the jet as straight as possible. She was putting undue stress on the already badly damaged jet to get them to stop safely.

She saw the overpass ahead and knew they would not make it underneath and there was no way they could take off to go over it. Scotland only hoped the jet would stop soon and she was doing all she could. It was now up to the damaged systems to make them stop.

The jet groaned in protest as it slowed down to a more respectable speed, but the overpass would make it stop for sure – but badly.

"C'mon, c'mon stop damn you!" Scotland held the steering tight as she kept it straight and her foot firmly planted on the brake. The jet was just about to hit the overpass when she cranked the steering to the left and the jet skidded sideways– Fast-and-Furious-style. It tilted to its side and the wing banged against the highway. The jet slammed back onto its wheels and ground to a halt just a few feet shy of smashing into the concrete overpass.

Scotland let out a sigh of relief and turned off the systems quickly. She looked over at Carter and her fingers were dug into the soft parts of her seat armrest. "We're okay." She breathed normally and thanked her lucky stars.

Carter started to breathe again, and she looked over at Scotland. She had never been happier to see her best friend and lover than right now. "Fuck-me…" She looked down at her crotch, and was breathing heavy. "Scotty…" She pursed her lips. "I think I pissed myself…" She looked between her legs again just to confirm. "Shit. I picked the wrong day to wear a G-string."

Scotland shook her head and looked at her wild-eyed. "Fuck…" She caught her breath. "You're not the only one." She breathed heavy and closed her eyes and leaned back against the headrest and thanked every deity she could recall at that moment. She murmured over to Carter, "You may want to remain seated…" She pointed out at the instrument panel. "I haven't turned off the seatbelt sign, yet."

They saw flashing lights and heard voices from the motorists who had stopped to help.

Carter scoffed righteously and unbuckled her belt – got up and her head spun a little. She grabbed out and felt nothing and fell back into the seat. She moaned out, "I think I'm just going to wait right here." Her head turned to Scotland who did not even unbuckle her belt. She just sat there before even attempting to get up.

Scotland looked at her with a playful derision for not listening to her in the first place. "Told you."

Carter sighed and listened to the sirens and saw the flashing lights. She heard unintelligible voices yelling through the massive hole in the side of the jet, but her head was spinning to make out what they were saying to them both. She mumbled over to the captain with impertinence, "Shhuht-uuhp, Scotty."

Scotland shook her head and narrowed her eyes at her. She felt drowsy now that their adrenaline levels started to crash, and she needed sustenance. She murmured an enquiring and provoking question, "You wouldn't happen to have a Snickers, would you?"

The flashes were now visible inside the cabin and they heard commotion outside the jet.

Carter reached into her fanny pack and pulled out a full-sized bar and handed it over to Scotland.

Without even pulling open the Snickers with charm and grace she ripped it with her teeth and spat out a chunky section of the wrapper uncouthly on the floor. She took a healthy bite and handed the other half to Carter who gladly accepted it and shoved it in her pie-hole.

They chewed and felt their energy return just as emergency personnel entered the cockpit to tend to the shaken and stirred women.

Scotland and Carter sat at the back of the ambulance as the paramedics attended to them.

Scotland turned and looked at Carter. She rolled her eyes and darted to each attendant that were looking after them. She murmured to her in a polite low tone, "This is becoming a habit for us." She shook her head and pursed her lips.

Carter snorted and shrugged her shoulders. She saw the two suited men approach them with their badges clipped to their belts, their Glocks flashed in-and-out as their ill-fitted suit jackets swayed. They had their notebooks open like Star Trek communicators. She mumbled to Scotty, "Here come the cops."

Scotland nodded at each to them, and they smiled back at her.

"Miss Yarde, Miss Deklava..." The older and stouter of the two smiled and took a deep breath as he took in their gorgeous looks. "I'm Detective Hank Dempsey and this is Detective Devon Monroe..." They each just moved their jacket flaps to the side to show their badges. "May we ask you some questions?"

Scotland nodded. "Of course, detectives."

Dempsey nodded appreciatively. He thumbed back at the jet as the firefighters continued to spray foam around the area just to be on the safe side. "Quite a round of excellent flying there, Miss Yarde..." He pursed his lips. "I was just talking with the FAA guys over there and they mentioned that it would take a very seasoned pilot to land a jet in that condition on a highway like this..." He nodded in approval. "You did one helluva job."

Scotland nodded. "Thanks, detective..." She tilted her pensive head a bit. "The grenade didn't help." She headtossed at the massive hole in the side of the jet. She eyed him and wondered when all the questions would start. She felt exhausted even after the Snickers and it would take a while to explain everything to the two detectives – and she and Carter just wanted to sleep.

Dempsey smirked. "Yes, about that. This may take some time to get all of the facts down so we were wondering if you and Miss Deklava would accompany us back to headquarters."

Scotland looked at him. "Detective, would a video of the events and their confessions help you and you can call on Carter and me after we've had a shower and some sleep?"

Monroe nodded excitedly. "That would certainly make our jobs easier, Miss Yarde." He was kind of joking because he wondered where their body cams were. He scanned Carter and could not take his eyes off the gorgeous woman.

Carter looked at him, and although he was cute by her definition she was way too tired to flirt and fuck right now. She narrowed her eyes at him. "Umm, detective..." She pointed to each of her breasts. "These aren't body cams." Her mouth went to the side in a smirk.

Monroe gulped and blushed. "Umm..." He looked up at Dempsey and saw no help from him. He turned back to her and felt uncomfortable. "No, they're not." He then looked somewhere else.

Carter pursed her lips and looked at Scotland to continue the negotiation.

Scotland looked at Dempsey and then looked at Carter. She nodded and got up first and side-eyed Carter as she did the same.

Monroe and Dempsey thought they were getting ready to leave but they looked at the two paramedics who seemed to be taking much longer to assess the condition of the two women than they normally would.

They started to unbutton their blouses, and there were gasps and low guttural moans but zero protestations to make them stop. They ogled them as they unbuttoned the buttons one-by-one and saw them reach under their arms and retrieve something that they had taped to their bodies. They each undid the top buttons and pulled them out with the packages as a unit. Scotland and Carter then held the unit for the detectives to see – and the detectives and paramedics wished they had continued undressing.

Dempsey looked at the units and them quizzically. "Umm…" He took them and felt the warmth of the units but could not make head or tail of what the gorgeous women just handed to him. "What're these?"

Scotland looked at him and started to rebutton her blouse. "Those are body cams. Just plug the end into a USB."

He and Monroe looked at them and could not believe they were so small. It was the first time any of them had seen such a device.

Monroe looked at both women. "You recorded the entire exchange?"

Scotland nodded her head and smirked. "Right from when Carter and I met up with Hansen and Marx and…" She pointed at the torqued and unsalvageable jet and tilted her head and widened her eyes. "Right up until we crashed onto the highway, detective.

Carter looked at them both and her mouth dropped open. "Okay…" She pursed her lips innocently and a little guiltily. "You'll hear quite a bit of swearing and a few protestations of our love for one another but that's because we thought we were going to die."

Scotland looked at her. "You didn't mean any of it?"

Carter hemmed-and-hawed. "Well, some of it."

Scotland pulled her mouth to the side. "Thanks for nothing, Carter."

Carter shrugged her shoulders and looked at her innocently. "Hey, I say a lot of shit in the heat of the moment. Why should this be any different?"

Scotland smirked and shook her head. She let out an exasperated sigh and turned to the detectives. "You'll get Carter and my views and…" She pulled out a card from her wallet. "This is the web address for the Cloud storage of the back-up recording."

Monroe looked at her and the devices in Dempsey's hand. "That's some pretty cutting-edge stuff."

Carter looked at him. "Should be…" She smacked her lips and looked at him with wide eyes. "Only the CIA and Mossad use those." She tick-tocked her mouth from side to side. "I'm going to need those back after you've downloaded the footage, though."

Dempsey nodded. "Then…" He looked at Monroe. "We'll leave you ladies and we'll be in touch if necessary."

Monroe looked at them. "Do you need us to drop you off somewhere?"

Carter saw her Bentley as it pulled up on the other side of the highway and turned to the detective. She shook her head politely. "We're okay…" She headtossed to the car in waiting. "We've got a ride."

Chapter 23

Scotland piloted the Bentayga north on Riverside Drive and heard the customary ding as a message flashed across the main head unit. She smiled when she saw Emilio's message that his grandma would be released in a day or two.

Carter read it and she murmured happily, "Aww..." She looked over and smiled. "That's great that Mrs. Vasquez is feeling better."

Scotland nodded and pursed her lips. "Yes. It's also nice that the pension fund will be releasing all of the money from her husband's pension to her and Emilio and paying for her medical bills."

Carter scoffed. "I think it's the least they could do."

Scotland nodded approvingly. "Yeah..." She side-eyed Carter and was impressed. "And I'm sure in no small part thanks to Deklava Fund Management..." She turned back to the road ahead. "Now that they're managing the pension."

Carter shrugged and smiled pleasantly. "I'm sure the letter from Yarde and Yarde managed to persuade them too."

Scotland shrugged her shoulders knowingly. "I'm sure it helped."

Carter looked ahead and wondered what they were doing in this part of Los Angeles. "Umm, Scotty..." She saw the Bentayga veer off Riverside and head up Crystal Springs Drive. Her mind raced and it had been a while since she visited the area. "Are we heading to Griffith Park?"

Scotland nodded her head. "Mm-hm..." Her mind raced as she continued to concentrate on the road ahead. "We'll be there soon."

Carter pursed her lips and what she saw ahead piqued her interest now. There was a police line, and police and fire trucks that blocked the entrance. A grave foreshadowing clouded her thoughts and she wondered what had happened because if it was bad out here it was going to be considerably worse when they got to where they were going. She groaned out, "Why do I have a feeling I'm going to be seeing something bad?"

Scotland only told her that Dempsey and Monroe had reached out to her. She pursed her lips and nodded. "Thanks for coming with me." She side-eyed her lovingly.

Carter smiled at her in solidarity. "You know you can always count on me, Scotty." She touched her arm. "No matter what, I will support and protect you..." She lounged in her seat and looked at her. "Always."

Scotland smiled and gave her a salutary thumb-up, as she slowed the Bentayga down and dropped the window. She smiled at the officer.

"Scotland Yarde and Carter Deklava to see Detectives Dempsey and Monroe."

The officer nodded and waved to his colleagues who moved the blockade out of the way so they could continue along up the road to where the detectives were waiting for them.

Carter could not help but notice that the vegetation was nice and lush for this time of year especially after a decent rainfall. She turned to Scotland. "Do you know why they called us?"

Scotland shook her head. After Carter and she handed the detectives the video of what happened last week, and then a follow-up, the detectives went dark and then the State and FBI went to work on SoCal. "I have no idea. I thought we had seen the last of the detectives."

Carter did not seem impressed. She could not imagine what was so important for them to be reluctant participants in. "Hmm. Me too."

Scotland turned up Fire Road as directed by the officer at the end of the street and she saw the mass of police cars and vans set up alongside the road. "This does not look good, Carter." She moved toward the Merry-Go-Round and entered the usually busy parking lot but now filled with emergency vehicles and an Operations trailer purposefully parked so the police could command the crime scene from that location.

Carter shook her head and had to agree. "Did a jogger get lost, Scotty?"

Scotland snorted a giggle and pulled up to an empty spot and parked. "C'mon…" She shut the Bentayga down and opened the door. "Let's go see what the detectives want."

They started to walk up to the command trailer and Dempsey and Monroe came out to greet them warmly.

Dempsey smiled and waved at them both. "Miss Yarde…" He nodded. "Miss Deklava…" He acknowledged her warmly. "I'm so glad you could make it."

Scotland smiled at both detectives and looked at them. "Our pleasure…" There was an interested but perplexed looked on her face. "Has this something to do with the SoCal case?"

Dempsey chuckled. "Oh no…" He shook his head excitedly. "Thanks to you both, that case was pretty much a slam-dunk for the LAPD, and now the State and FBI can deal with the fallout…" He shook his head, and his look became grave. "The Commissioner recommended that we call upon you both to see what you can make of this." He thumbed to the Merry-Go-Round surreptitiously cordoned off with a white tent that covered the entire ride to block out the elements and any prying eyes.

Scotland was a little perplexed at why she and Carter would be called over to a crime scene, but she was willing to indulge the detectives a little while longer.

They walked up the walkway to the tent and were ushered inside and put on disposable haz-mat suits.

Dempsey smiled that them both as they put them on, and he murmured. "I'm sure you understand that we need to preserve the crime scene."

Scotland and Carter both nodded and threw on the haz-mat suit and the booties.

They all entered and saw what the trouble was all about. In the middle of the Merry-Go-Round that was where all the action was centered. Heads, eyes, and attention turned to the party that just entered. Lights were on and there was something in the middle of the carousel that crime scene investigators were working on.

Dempsey ushered both women closer and he wanted to see their reactions to the body that would surely take their breaths away. "It's right over here."

Scotland was the first to see it and the blood drained from her face. She could tell Dempsey and Monroe were watching her, observing her for some unknown reason.

Carter had a look of terror in her eyes as the horrific scene almost made her gag. She had seen a great many things but nothing like this. "What-the-fuck?"

Scotland shot a look at Dempsey and she yelled out at him, "Detective? Why the hell would you want to show Carter and me this?" She was incensed at the surprise.

Dempsey looked at the lead crime scene investigator. He tilted his head. "Tell her what we have here, Joe."

Joe Chan pursed his lips and looked at them all. "Seems we have a body that has had all of the skin pigment removed somehow and every follicle of hair has been removed and the body was dressed and laid out here for us to find."

Scotland paused, and forced a smiled at him and turned back to Dempsey. "Again, why the hell are we here detective?" Her lips pursed and if there were not so many witnesses around, she would have hit him.

Dempsey looked at her blankly and turned back to Joe. "Tell them the rest."

Joe raised his eyebrows and pursed his lips. His head volleyed between the two detectives and wondered if that was such a good idea but obviously, they knew what they were doing. "So, when we took a closer look, we determined that the body had been frozen and moved here. With the cellular degradation from the freezing, it is difficult to figure out when they were killed and placed here."

Scotland looked at Dempsey and little more pissed off than perturbed and she yelled out, "Detective, why the fu..." She stopped mid-sentence to berate the detective and her head snapped back to Joe. She swallowed as she processed the information. "What do you mean you don't know when they were killed and placed here?"

Carter narrowed her eyes and her head volleyed between everyone and she took a closer look at the body. Her head scanned the rest of the area and every available person was only concentrating in this area. "Yeah. What did you mean by they?"

Dempsey forced a smile and headtossed at Joe. "Show them."

Joe lifted the sheet that covered the body. He could tell none of the ladies had ever seen anything like it. "All of the legs, arms, head and torso are from different bodies and the joints look like they are fused, and there are fine scars on the skin where they were joined..." He shook his head. "Damnedest thing I've ever seen, and I've seen some pretty weird shit. Even the genitalia have been removed."

Dempsey cleared his throat and squirmed. "Yeah, thanks for that, Joe."

Scotland and Carter looked at Dempsey with an incredulous stare.

Scotland took a breath, and she pursed her lips a little less angrily at the detective but still enough to be disturbed and puzzled at what it had to do with them both. "So, that's very interesting and creepy as fuck at the same time, but I'd like to know why we're here, detective. What makes you think we'd be interested in this 'Silence of the Lambs' thing you've got going on here?"

Dempsey looked at them both, and he turned to Monroe and headtossed at him to bring the package. "Show them."

Monroe went to the table on the side and pulled out an evidence bag. He walked back and pulled out the sweater. He looked at both women and showed them the piece of clothing. "Seems that someone dressed up the body rather nicely to make sure it was warm, but this took us all by surprise."

Carter and Scotland looked at the sweater and it looked clean and luxurious.

Monroe eyed Dempsey and he almost smirked as he turned over the label on the inside and showed them the tag. He watched their reactions and got what he was expecting. "Seems this sweater belonged to you..." He held the tag out, so it was obvious to anyone. "Scotland Yarde."

Scotland's eyes were as wide as saucers as she saw the nametag clearly marked with her name in her handwriting. She gasped out loud and her mind thought furiously at the last time she saw it. Her mouth went dry, and she was speechless.

Carter looked at the nametag and the designer label. Her mind thought furiously at what Scotland's name would be doing on the tag and then on the body with the different appendages. She was shocked and she turned to Scotland and exclaimed with horror, "Oh-my-god..." She shook her head at her. "Scotty, how could you do it?"

Scotland was knocked out of her stupor, and she snapped her head at Carter. Her eyes narrowed and she pursed her lips angrily at her. She growled at her derisively, "Shhuht-uuhp, Carter."

The End.

Made in the USA
Las Vegas, NV
28 February 2022